ARKHAM HORROR

It is the height of the Roaring Twenties – a fresh enthusiasm for the arts, science, and exploration of the past have opened doors to a wider world, and beyond…

And yet, a dark shadow grows over the town of Arkham. Alien entities known as Ancient Ones lurk in the emptiness beyond space and time, writhing at the thresholds between worlds.

Occult rituals must be stopped and alien creatures destroyed before the Ancient Ones make our world their ruined dominion.

Only a handful of brave souls with inquisitive minds and the will to act stand against the horrors threatening to tear this world apart.

Will they prevail?

ARKHAM HORROR™

MASK
of SILVER

Rosemary Jones

First published by Aconyte Books in 2021

ISBN 978 1 83908 015 9

Ebook ISBN 978 1 83908 016 6

Cover art by Daniel Strange

Distributed in North America by Simon & Schuster Inc, New York, USA

Printed in the United States of America

9 8 7 6 5 4 3 2 1

ACONYTE BOOKS

An imprint of Asmodee Entertainment Ltd

Mercury House, Shipstones Business Centre

North Gate, Nottingham NG7 7FN, UK

aconytebooks.com // twitter.com/aconytebooks

PROLOGUE
Fitzmaurice House, 1823,
Arkham, Massachusetts

Smoke filled the air and confused the senses. He was raging somewhere in the rooms above her head, waving his silly sword about and shouting words that she didn't understand.

"Never mind," she whispered to the children clutching her skirts. "Never mind."

The corridor seemed to go on forever. It was the mirrors. She hated those mirrors, having to dust them daily and clean them with soap and water every two weeks. Useless things, mirrors, just showing reflections of a plain New England house and her own plain face. Except when they didn't. Sometimes, she saw things in the mirrors. Shadows of things that weren't there. But she never told anyone that. The women in her family had learned to hold their tongues a long time ago. Speaking of shadows brought them closer.

The children were coughing and crying, wanting their

mother. "Never mind," she said to them. "Never mind. Just follow me."

He had brought the long narrow mirrors and all the other fancy furniture to Arkham, wagonloads of the most silly stuff, chairs gilded and sitting on lion's feet, little useless tables topped with even more useless vases. Just things to dust and no more practical than those endless rows of mirrors.

The mistress was a sweet gentle lady, soft spoken and shy, often overshadowed by her big shouting husband. But she adored her children. She tried to keep them safe.

Not like him. Typical of the master of the house to thrust his enormous portrait in her arms and tell her to save it, along with the chest of papers that he shoved into the grasp of the bewildered little boy now clutching her skirts with one hand and his father's papers under his other arm. His sister toddled beside her, weeping openly now, frightened by all her blustering father's curses, the smell of fire, the smoke, and, if one dared to admit, the shadowed figure watching them from every mirror as they passed.

"Never mind," she said, as much to herself as to the children, "never mind."

They ran, burdened by fear as much as the items they carried, to the back of the house, to the kitchen where she had blessedly left the door propped open for a little breeze on a warm midsummer day.

Out the door they went, the strange trio of weeping children and grim maid, down the steps and into the vegetable garden. With a sigh or perhaps a sob of relief, she dropped the wicked portrait in the radish patch and pulled both the children close to her. The boy still carried his father's wooden chest of papers. The girl clutched a mirror, almost as large as herself, that her father had foisted on her. How the child had held onto it and still clutched her skirts, Rebecca Baker would never know.

She turned back to look at the house. The flames were sprouting through the roof now. Smoke poured from every window. Such heat, such fury. She listened for the shattering of glass, the destruction of the other mirrors, but heard nothing. Later when they shifted the ashes and found those six mirrors still intact, she would suggest burying the wicked things. But nobody listened to her. She was, after all, only the maid.

But she had gotten the children out. As she sat, suddenly exhausted, on the ruins of her radish plants, she gathered both children into her arms and gave them the same awkward comfort that her own mother gave for bruises and scrapes.

"Never mind," she said. "Never mind."

In the upstairs window, a silver cloaked coldness was outlined by the flames. The shape of a hooded man, a faceless man, who watched her nevertheless without eyes. She pretended that she did not see it. She was good at that. All Baker women were good at ignoring such shadows. It was looking straight at such silvery, shadowy figures that entrapped the soul.

The crows in the wood were cawing with dissatisfaction. Crows liked dead spirits. They knew that their job was to guide them. The dead that escaped to other starless places glimpsed in the depths of mirrors. Such an unnatural occurrence would confuse and alarm the crows. She knew that, but there wasn't a single thing that she could do about it. She had no bell, no book, no candle powerful enough to ward off such evil. Still, strange incidents were not uncommon in Arkham. There were others to come that could deal with such events. That much she knew from her dreams.

"Never mind," she said to the crows as much to the children. "Never mind."

The day was done, the sun was setting, red behind the flames flickering now in every window. Shouts and cries drowned out the fussing of the crows as the neighbors finally roused themselves to come up the long drive and begin the battle to save the house. They would fail. The place would be ash by dawn. Rebecca Baker knew that too from her dreams.

She waited there, both children now leaning against her, too stunned and exhausted to cry any more, as the flames ate the house and all left within it, all except that which could not burn. Rebecca Baker mourned the mistress, small and kind, who had thrust the children into her arms and told her to run.

As for the master, she cursed him a little, but under her breath so as not to disturb the children.

The house collapsed completely by midnight. Smoke and sparks swirled up in the air, obscuring the stars and the rare blue-tailed comet that streaked across the solstice night sky.

The neighbors carried away the children along with the bits and pieces that had been saved from the house. She tried to keep them from taking the mirrors, but failed. They even carried off the master's fire-blackened sword, after they detached the remains of his hand from the hilt. Why anyone would want that nasty blade, she could not imagine.

Rebecca Baker sat and waited for the ones who took charge to leave, one hand trailing in the cool green leaves of her garden, threading them back and forth through her fingers. Then the others came up the long drive. The widowed women of the town, the servant girls, the cooks, the laundry ladies, and all the others who worked behind the scenes to keep things orderly. All towns had them, all towns needed them, even a town like Arkham.

Someone thrust a cup of cool water into her hands. Another draped a shawl around her shoulders. The murmuring of women rose around her as they watched the final sparks of fire to fade and waited for the house to die.

When the dawn finally came, cool but with the promise of summer heat, she rose very stiffly and walked down to Arkham town proper with that huddle of women. She didn't look back. She had done what she could.

"Never mind," she told herself. "Never mind." But Rebecca Baker felt a deep sorrow for those who would come to Arkham later. She wished there was a warning that she could leave them.

CHAPTER ONE

The dreams still come at night. Not as many. Not as fierce. But the shadows are there, tinged with silver and fire. Dreams of a mask that I wish I had never made. I wake far too early in the morning, throw open the windows, and breath the salt air from the Pacific. But in my dreams I smell smoke and something else, something not altogether of this world. The scent of a shadow, a perfume of death, that clings to me even awake. Sometimes, out of the corner of my eye, I even see a shadow on the wall or glimpse a hooded face. But then I turn and face it directly, and there is nothing there.

Eleanor said that writing our story would make the dreams fade. But in her last letter she spoke of waking still to the visions of Lulu in the coffin. So I am not sure if writing this down will make it better. But I will try. I will always try, for the sake of those who could not escape the mask that I made.

It started at a party. Most of Sydney's worst ideas did. Perhaps because we were tired, and I must admit, a little drunk, it sounded like a good idea. Sydney's proposals often seemed like good ideas until they weren't. Until people got hurt. Until, in Arkham, people died.

But, in the beginning, that late May night in California, we were enjoying a "reviews are in" party, the type of party we always held in Renee's pretty garden apartment. The French doors stood wide open to the courtyard so couples could wander in and out. The open windows also kept the worst of the cigar smoke and whiskey fumes from overpowering the fresh flowers that filled the McCoy vases lining the mantle. For this particular Saturday night, we mingled late orange blossoms with jasmine. People always expected red roses, but Renee hated them. She said red roses were a cliché if you were a dark-haired beauty. She allowed white roses in the winter when we couldn't get anything else. Later, after Arkham, hothouse flowers smelled too much like funerals and the vases sat empty.

As usual, Sydney made us wait days before giving the party. He wanted all the reviews to read out loud, even those sent express from New York, Boston, and Chicago. Which meant Max, Sydney's assistant, had driven down to the train station and bribed a porter or two to turn over the studio's mail to him. Once Max had collected every possible clipping, and Sydney had read them in secret in his apartment, then the party was allowed to properly begin at Renee's.

As I recall, it was well past midnight when Sydney began talking about the next film. Max leaned against the oak bookcase behind me. Renee concealed his beloved imported whiskey there. She kept his bottles stashed inside the hollowed-out works of Walter Scott. I was in my leather chair in that corner, neatly tucked in with a sketchpad and an idea for dress that would resemble a shooting star.

Renee and Sydney had their usual place in the center of the room. Renee reclined across her chaise lounge, the one that we called Marie Antoinette's fainting couch. We'd found the frame in a sweet little secondhand shop in Pasadena. I'd covered it all in material left over from some French Revolution costumes. Renee hadn't played the queen, of course, but she received great reviews as the Parisian fortuneteller who cursed Marie and all her court after a royal carriage ran down her only child. Sydney adored Renee in that role. It led to her starring in his first nightmare picture. Renee liked to say that the Queen died for her career. We certainly sacrificed a dress or two for the upholstery.

While Renee reclined with one shoulder slipping out of the simple little silk dress that I made for her flapper girl appearance in an earlier comedy, Sydney sat straight upright on the other end of the chaise lounge. He had his usual unlit cigarette in an ivory holder clenched in the corner of his mouth. His hair was perfectly pomaded and the shine made the lamplight seem to shimmer around his head. There was always a sense that all lights shone directly on Sydney, even when he was outside of the spotlight and yelling at all of us to "get that scene right."

The rest of the actors were busy drinking everything we had, and a few stray bottles that somebody had brought from another party, while the crew wandered in and out of the dining room in search of something substantial to eat.

But everyone kept an ear tilted toward Sydney to catch his every remark.

"Listen to this," he roared, pulling the cigarette holder out of his mouth and gesturing at the page spread flat on Renee's coffee table. "'The Showman's latest nightmare picture is simply wonderful and probably unfit for public exhibition.'"

"Is that the *Times*?" asked Max.

"No, *Variety*." Sydney was obviously pleased. He adored his nickname, "The Showman to Know", and added to the legend by always wearing his top hat, tails, and crimson-lined cape to openings. Renee often teased him that it made him look like a ringmaster from a seedy circus. To which Sydney retorted, "I wore a red coat in the circus, never black, so they'd follow my every move."

Sydney grabbed another newspaper and spread it open. "This is even better," he said. "Quite the most terrifying thing to be seen on screen so far in 1923."

"Isn't that the one when they mention Chaney's new picture?" said Max, which earned him a terrible frown from Sydney.

"There might be something at the end. Nobody reads to the end," Sydney said.

Max bent over to me and said softly, "It says that Chaney will deliver his most spectacular film yet. Universal is spending nearly a million dollars on the sets, costumes, and hundreds of extras."

Sydney, who had the hearing of a bat when someone was talking about the movies, chimed in: "Anyone can make a movie for a million dollars. It's making quality with far less that shows talent. Why, give me a thousand dollars and I can outshine Wallace Worsley any day."

Max smiled a bit and asked: "Should I tell the studio that you're cutting your fees?"

"Never!" cried Sydney with an exaggerated shudder. "After all, I need to pay all of you." He waved his hand at the actors and crew laughing at the exchange. Sydney's spending on sets, costumes, and extras could be, and often was, far more extravagant than the studio liked. Max was sent to us by the studio a couple of years ago "to keep an eye on Sydney." He did his best to hold the expenses in check, but in the end Sydney nearly always won. The studio paid because, whether they liked his terror pictures or not, his films certainly sold tickets. By 1923, Max was clearly one of us, rather than a studio flunky, and had even taken to dressing and talking a bit like Sydney. He certainly shared his more expensive tastes for good whiskey, among other things.

Fred wandered in from the garden, smelling faintly of pipe smoke and engine oil. He dropped onto the floor, leaning back against the arm of my chair to peer at my sketch. "Nice dress," he said. "Which role?"

"Sydney is talking about casting Renee as a mesmerist who lures men to their doom. The dream maker, he calls it," I said. I rolled my knees out of the way so Fred could get a better look. For comfort, I wore my black pajama pants, made out of silk, and an embroidered tunic top to all of Renee's parties. I hated fussing with garters and stockings. And rolling your stockings down and rouging your knees was even worse. Besides everyone knew I was half Chinese and figured that the outfit was inherited. It wasn't.

I got the tunic from Anna Wong, who had it from some director or other who was trying to impress her. She wasn't impressed. Rather like being told that you had to like chop suey just because you had black hair and dark eyes. I never did like chop suey. Mostly because it tasted all wrong, a mix of American ingredients trying to look like Chinese food. But I loved the tunic. Not for where the tunic came from or what it represented. But for the gorgeous flower embroidery that started at the shoulder and spiraled down my back. When I wore it, I felt glamorous but not Hollywood. Someone both inside and outside the crowd of flappers in their beaded dresses and the men in their suits. Fred teased me about wearing the same outfit to every party to avoid having to think about clothes. Except I thought about clothes all the time.

Anna traded the tunic in return for my making her a tailored velvet coat with a fur collar. She wanted to impress a director and prove that she could look like a flapper, and didn't have to play a girl named Lotus Blossom. Didn't work. They cast her as Lotus Flower in her next film. That's the trouble with being Chinese-American in Hollywood. They only see you as one type of character if you're in front of the camera. It's a bit better behind the camera, even if you do have to work twice as hard to prove yourself. So I worked hard, sketching ideas constantly for movies that we made and movies that we might make.

"What material will you use?" said Fred as he looked at my sketchbook that night. As our cameraman, he always wanted to know ahead how something might translate to black-and-white film.

"I've got a few bolts of a silver lamé. It will shine in the lights."

"As long as it doesn't reflect Sydney waving his arms."

"No more mirrors. I promise you."

Our last picture dealt with a cursed circus, which Sydney knew something about, having once been a ringmaster. He read out his own quotes from the newspapers with glee. "'My time in the circus taught me how spellbinding and terrifying these acts could be. And how an audience can be trained to look where you need them to look. It is a combination of wicked magic and temple ritual, all triggered by the smell of greasepaint and the whistle of the calliope!'" he said. "You know that's what we should have done for the opening. Had someone blow in the smells of a circus ring. Sawdust, peanuts…"

"Horse manure," muttered Fred. "To say nothing of elephants." He filmed several small circuses as additional footage for the picture. I often went with him for costume and makeup ideas. We'd both been horrified by the poor battered creatures in cages and tiny traveling stalls.

In our circus picture, which had only one lovely horse on set, Renee played the charming, mysterious performer who rode that white horse round and round the ring, mesmerizing the hapless males in the audience. Mesmerizing was a label that Renee began to despise that year, but it was the way that Sydney wrote her characters, mystery women who lured men to their doom. And, as she often said to me, that was better than being the screaming ingénue victim.

The doomed circus performer role turned out to be

more difficult than usual. Renee hated horses and was furious with me when we found that the mirrors on her costume reflected Sydney directing off camera. That ruined nearly a day's filming and meant she needed to mount the beautiful but bouncy horse for a second day's shooting. I smeared all the mirrors with grease before we reshot the entire scene. And then we all suffered through another day of Sydney yelling about Renee's posture on a horse as the silly creature trotted instead of cantered in all of its scenes, despite being able to do a lovely canter the day before. Which meant even more bouncing about by Renee. And more yelling by Sydney. Perhaps even a little weeping by the trainer who swore that Rex was a wonder horse and should be in pictures. Fred, as always, stayed calm and kept the camera rolling. He even salvaged some of the earlier footage. But afterward, I swore to Renee to never ever let Sydney put her on a horse again.

The whole crew was glad to be done with horses and circuses. I hoped our next picture would be full of sophisticated party scenes. We'd been talking about another hypnotist picture, with elaborately staged sets.

Fred rested his head against my chair and traced the lines of the dress in my sketchbook with one stubby scarred finger. The man fiddled with engines and anything else that whizzed or whirred, and his hands bore the traces of his work in a network of tiny scars and freshly healed cuts. If I turned my hands over, I could see every callus, every prick, every mark that costuming left there. People always said that we didn't work, that we just played, when we were making movies. Our hands told a different story.

"If I adjust the lights, she'll look like a silver ghost emerging from the shadows. And that head dress!" Fred said, tapping the page. I had drawn a close-fitting cap set with long silver spikes that formed a star-shaped frame for Renee's head. "That's finer than a 5th Avenue getup. Good work, China girl."

I slapped his hand away before he smudged my drawing. "Not China girl, just plain Oakland, that's me."

Fred grinned up at me. "Hello, Oakland. I'm Brooklyn. Want to dance?"

"You just like me because I'm the only woman in the room shorter than you."

"Nah," said Fred. "Adore you for that. And your mean game of croquet. The way you'll play gin rummy when we get a rainy day. Oh, and your costumes. That one is something. Sydney will love it."

"I'll love what?" said Sydney from across the room. Mention his name and he always heard you.

"Jeany's new costume for the mesmerist."

"Oh, that tired old idea, I'm not making that. It's too close to *Caligari*. Even with Renee as the hypnotist."

"Well I'm delighted not to play a hypnotist, but I do love Jeany's idea for the silver dress. Can we use it in the *Mask*?" Renee said.

"Oh course. I'm sure it's exactly what Camilla should wear on the night that she calls for the stranger. Along with a silver mask," Sydney put his cigarette holder back in his mouth and waited for everyone to catch up with him. The crowd grew quieter and moved a little closer. This was the boss talking about the next job, the one that we all hoped to be part of. "This is my best idea ever."

"You want a mask with this dress?" I said. I liked making masks and had built a couple for past pictures. I thought about how the material could be applied to the form. "How much of the face should it hide?"

Sydney thought for a moment and then slid into his storytelling voice. "I see a woman emerging from the shadows. Her face is covered in a silver mask, so highly polished that she appears to be wearing a mirror or liquid mercury, a mask that reflects our world and distorts it. She pauses on the threshold of light and shadow. The audience grows uncertain. Is she a beauty or a grotesque hiding behind the mask? The audience will be both attracted and repelled. Slowly the mask of silver reflections becomes transparent, revealing the face of a lovely woman, our gorgeous Renee, but then her face in turn changes. She becomes a creature of glamorous horror, a siren both alien and familiar. And the audience will know that is the face of truth."

I was scribbling as fast as I could on the corners of my sketchbook page. A full mask, with the barest slits for eyes, to give Sydney the blank form that he wanted? Polished silver to make it reflective? But that would create the same problem that any mirrors on a set created. Perhaps a metallic paint that mimicked metal but would not create reflections? With the right lighting, it would give off a luminous shimmer like the dress itself. Fred could film that, stop the filming, Renee would remove the mask, and then Fred could resume filming. We had done a similar dissolve two pictures back, when Sydney turned Renee from a withered ancient corpse to an enchantress who lured the hero to his final doom.

Fred, like me, was obviously working through the sequence in his head. "So will the siren be a second mask or something else? Makeup like Chaney is doing for his hunchback?"

"Oh something else entirely," smirked Sydney. "Something that hasn't been seen before."

Fred and I both sighed. That line normally meant that Sydney hadn't decided what he wanted and we'd be doing trial after trial of possible combinations of costume and makeup. When we had to make the witch woman turn into a werewolf to avenge her dead husband, Sydney had ranted for days on the combination of furs, wigs, and makeup because everything made Renee look too hideous. We ended up creating the shadow of a wolf on the wall with one of the crew manipulating a puppet head that I built. Then Fred filmed Renee stepping out of the doorway and wiping the blood from her lips with the white cravat of her husband's supposed killer.

"So we're not filming the hypnotist story? But, Sydney, the studio has started on the sets," said Max. Three lines appeared on his forehead. You can take the guy out of accounting, but you can never quite erase the bookkeeper from the guy. Fred called him "Brooks Brothers down to his second pair of pants." I told Fred he was just jealous that Max owned a suit that fit him. Also, the girls liked the Harold Lloyd tall and skinny type. Fred tended toward tweed jackets and canvas pants, stuff that was constantly being pulled out of shape by the gadgets stuffed in his pockets. Fred was a Brooklyn tough, who powdered out of Brooklyn as soon as he could talk the army into taking him. He drifted to California after he was invalided home for losing a toe in France. At least, that was Fred's story. We all had stories that were a little bit true and much more what we wanted people to believe.

"Call them in the morning. Tell the studio that I don't want their tacky interpretation of a historic haunted house. I'm taking you all to Arkham, Massachusetts. We'll film where Puritans mixed with witches and Colonial ghosts still ride the lanes."

That set up a storm of comments and questions. Sydney sat grinning like the Cheshire Cat in the middle of it all until we stopped. Then, having gained everyone's attention, he started to tell us his latest, greatest idea. He would make a movie, a wonderful, terrible, frightening movie set in an ordinary little New England town that none of us had ever heard of.

"But what's the story?" said Max.

"Later, Max, just arrange all the necessary bits and bobs for travel," said Sydney, who could be maddeningly Continental when he felt it made him sound important. "Jeany can start by designing the mask now. That's key. The rest we can do when we get to Arkham."

I nodded, not really listening, because I had an idea. I drew a nearly perfect oval over the face I sketched. Shading it lightly with the pencil, I then extended the shadow behind the woman on the page so another, stranger being stood behind her. The spikes on the crowned headdress took on a more fluid, twisted shape in this shadow image.

The points of the shadow's sleeves also flowed down, like the strangely delicate tentacles of jellyfish, dwindling away. Then, further behind both figures, I drew the hooded man. The last was Sydney's signature creature, a man dressed in a hooded cape. The character never appeared more than once in a film and never in the same type of scene twice, played by whoever wasn't already in the scene. Also, oddly, the hooded man never did anything. Never spoke or interacted with any character. He was just there. Watching. Often it was so subtle that many people missed it, but the critics had taken to looking for those appearances and speculating what Sydney meant by it. None of us knew. Sydney liked to say to the reporters that it would all be revealed later. But that movie had not been made yet, despite the topic being raised frequently by Max since he joined our company. Apparently the studio felt a hooded man picture would be the biggest seller yet. Sydney tended to go sly during those discussions, telling Max to mollify the studio for a little while longer. Poor Max, he was stuck between two difficult and very different bosses: the unseen and, for the rest of us, unknown studio heads and Sydney, the driving force in our daily lives.

"That's clever," said Fred as I sketched out the two figures behind the woman in the mask. "We could create the second shape behind her by backlighting a screen. Does it need to move?"

I looked at my drawing. "I think so," I said slowly, the idea sparked by Sydney's words growing inside of me. A terrible, wonderful idea, quite unlike anything we'd done before. "Can we make the shadow reach out from the wall and engulf her? Like ink, or blood, running dark over the mask and revealing the woman beneath for just a second or two. Then they both disappear."

Fred nodded. "Good idea, Oakland. I predict half the audience faints and the other half leaps out of their seats with a yell."

This was why we worked with Sydney. Because with just a few words, he could set a mood that inspired all of us. I knew Fred was right, that we would weave the shadows and reflections into something just as terrifying as anything Chaney could create with a hump and a limp. But Chaney's specialty was grotesque makeup. Our terrible monster was beautiful, always chillingly beautiful, that glamorous horror that Sydney talked about.

I added a few more lines to my sketch and then stopped. Too much and it would disappear into a mess of charcoal on the page. Restraint was the most important lesson that I'd learned from Sydney, the most flamboyant showman. The suggestion of a shadow cast by a man in a hood, the merest glimpse of the monster in the mirror, a pallid mask of silvery shadows, those were the things that would terrify the audience. Why we should we want to evoke terror, that was the question that I failed to ask myself that night as Fred and I sat up long after the rest had left.

Finally Renee came over to our corner. "Go home," she said to Fred. He rented a tiny house all the way out in Santa Monica and had borrowed a friend's car to avoid being stranded by the Los Angeles streetcars shutting down in the early hours. With a friendly grumble, he unfolded himself from the floor and wandered out the garden doors into the predawn pallid gloom. I wondered if he'd sleep in the car or drive himself home. Either was possible with Fred.

"Are you done?" Renee asked me. "Can you get home all right?"

"I only have an elevator ride of one floor," I said, as if my only sister didn't know that. Of course she did, but everyone else only knew that I lived in the building. Our relationship was a closely guarded secret, from the press, from our friends, and, most especially, from the studio where we had been working for the last five years. Because while everyone knew that I was a Chinese-American from Oakland, nobody knew Renee's true heritage. If the studio knew, she would not be a leading lady. And if Renee was not a star, the rest of us might not work. So while we knew exactly what lies we were telling, the rest didn't have much reason to ask uncomfortable questions. Everyone understood Renee and I had always worked together in Hollywood, and left it at that.

I eyed Sydney stretched out on Renee's chaise, still leafing through the magazines and newspapers that Max had brought. At this point in the night, he was past the reviews and reading about others' triumphs and failures. He knew how to turn such knowledge to his advantage. He could, and often did, stay up for hours after the rest of us had collapsed. One disgruntled extra conjectured that Sydney didn't sleep, just rested lightly in a coffin like some creature from one of his films. It wasn't true. Sydney slept very soundly when he did sleep and not, as some speculated, at Renee's apartment. He had his own a floor above. She always threw him out before she went to bed herself. Sometimes she used as an excuse the need to put up someone at the party who had too long a journey or had too much to drink. Then that unfortunate soul, quite often me if she had no other sacrifice to avoid Sydney's snores, slept on her wildly uncomfortable chaise lounge.

"I'd rather sleep in my own bed tonight," I said, uncurling from the leather seat that I had claimed earlier.

"Come to lunch," Renee answered. "I'd like to talk about this costume." She pointed to my sketch, set aside on the table as Fred and I had gone over possible ways to trick the audience's eyes into seeing what did not, could not, exist. She glanced at Sydney. "He'll be gone in a few hours and I want some sleep too. But we'll order something splendid for lunch, just the two of us."

I nodded. When a picture was done, Renee tended to withdraw into luxurious comfort. She tipped generously and had a dozen restaurants nearby ready to deliver whatever she felt like eating. Renee adored her slender candlestick phone and welded it like a fairy godmother's magic wand to deliver the bounties of the Los Angeles shops and restaurants to us. She called it her "cocoon before the butterfly time."

Sydney called it "hiding," but he was the exact opposite. After a picture was done, he would drive all over town, even up the coast to San Francisco, to talk to people about everything and anything that interested him. With Sydney that could mean visiting the latest airplane demonstration or a strange occult shop hidden down a back alley. The occult was a particular obsession that we all knew about. We even joked that his forays were Sydney researching terrors for his next picture. Séances weren't quite as popular as they had been a few years before but there were still plenty held around Hollywood. Sydney knew all the tricks and liked to reveal frauds to his friends. Sydney was never fooled by slate writing, spirit pictures, table tipping, or rapping. But he collected odd "safekeeps," as he called the items that he picked up from people who did not like to tell where their treasures came from. Renee called these artworks ghastly and refused to have any in her apartment.

"Thank you very much," Renee said when she clapped the lid on some box or other that Sydney had handed her as a gift. "But it still looks like a bunch of bird bones and feathers to me. Put it in your apartment, please."

"But, dearest muse," Sydney would reply. "What if the spirits take you from me too soon?" For Sydney, spirits were less ghosts of dead ancestors than emissaries from a world that we could not see except out of the corner of our eyes or in the reflections of a mirror. In his best scripts, the ones that he wrote for Renee's villainesses, Sydney turned hauntings into an "invasion from beyond," where spirits or supernatural creatures lured humans, usually males, out of the world as we know it and into a twisted landscape besides and beyond our world. The "safekeeps" acted as locks, according to Sydney, to keep shut doors that should not be open. Anything could be a door, even a mirror upon the wall or the reflection in a silver mask.

"It's casting the right reflection, at the right moment," Sydney said that night as he discussed the script with Renee and me, while we struggled to stay awake. "The right reflection allows us to control the door and the spirits beyond. The right reflection, at the right time, in the right place. While the mask protects the priestess or the Muse."

"But it has to be a silver mask, a reflective mask," I said, thinking once again about the problems with the mirrors in the last picture.

"Oh, yes," said Sydney, "a mask to cast its own reflection back into the mirror." I shuddered considering all the issues that would cause for Fred in filming such a scene.

Renee yawned and punched Sydney's shoulder lightly. "Go work on your script and let us sleep. If we're going to someplace on the East Coast, we'll have days of travel to work this all out."

That night, when I reached my bedroom, Sydney's idea of the silver mask consumed me. Even after I climbed into my bed, I continued to sketch variations on my first idea, often surrounded by a circle of mirrors casting reflections back and forth until endless repetitions appeared. In the glow of the electric lamp, the images on the page turned into a chorus of featureless faces, watching me with the empty eye sockets of a drama mask. These fanciful thoughts slid into nightmares, and I woke with an aching head atop the crumpled pages of my notebook.

At lunch, as I consumed cup after cup of black coffee, Renee described her own nightmares to me.

"It began after Sydney left," she said. "I must have been asleep for less than half an hour, but the nightmare felt like it lasted forever."

"We all ate and drank too much last night," I said. "And then Sydney started telling us about his latest horrid idea."

"I'm quite sure that you're right," said Renee with a sip of her own black coffee. Both of us usually preferred our coffee sweet, with plenty of sugar stirred in, but this morning nothing would do but the bitterest of brews. "I dreamt that the film went in reverse. Rather than the mask dissolving to reveal my face, I was watching my face become the mask, just a silver mask that reflected everything but me. It was as if I was being erased."

My nightmares of a lost Renee reflected in a mirror showed me a tangle of hallways, all leading into shadows. Behind the shadows, someone watched us. Sydney? It felt like something older, something more terrible. But I shook off my memory of the dream, and convinced Renee of the source of her fears. "Sydney's ideas for the mask. I'm sure that prompted your dream."

"Sydney called me this morning, just to talk more about Arkham," Renee said.

I felt relief that he had just telephoned and not come downstairs to share our breakfast. An excited Sydney, planning a new picture, was the worst companion for a headachy morning. "He kept talking about how long it had been since he had been in Arkham but how he was sure that it hadn't changed. How much he was looking forward to going home."

"It's hard to imagine," I said. "Sydney as a boy in an idyllic little New England town."

Renee smiled. "Yes. I never think of him as anything other than the Sydney Fitzmaurice striding through the world in his silk cravats and stylish hats. Do you suppose he wore short pants and had skinned knees from falling off his bicycle?"

For some reason that thought doubled us up with laughter. Wiping those cheerful tears from her eyes with some choice words about the impact on her mascara, Renee swore that this would be her last nasty nightmare picture for a while.

"Sydney's brilliant," she said. "But I need to find a lighter script, a romance or a comedy, or I'll end up playing nothing but murderous women in impossible hats. Remember what Sennett said to me? That I had a flair for comedy."

"That's just because he wanted to stick you in one of his silly bathing suits," I said. "And those caps are far less fetching than any hat that I designed for you."

She shrugged. "Better that than another terror role with a costume that weighs two tons."

"My costumes never weigh more than one ton," I countered and we both giggled again.

I left Renee's apartment feeling much more cheerful. She was right. Sydney's nightmare stories were starting to turn into real nightmares. What we needed was a picture that wouldn't stay with us in our dreams.

One trip to Arkham, and a summer trip at that. By the time we returned in July, at worst August, if filming went long, we could look around for the perfect project for the fall. Renee's contract was with the studio, not Sydney, and they always wanted her to work with other directors. Fairbanks had approached her about an *Arabian Nights* fantasy that summer, but she disliked the script and especially the character of the girl who betrayed the hero to his enemies. "Not another scheming spy," she said. "I don't want to be known only as the beautiful but murderous woman." But I loved the idea of working on such a picture, with palace scenes and fairytale characters. I discussed it with Fred, who had heard about the flying carpet being built, and he suggested that I go to United Artists with my costume designs and see what was available. It would be easier for me to work outside our studio too. Our studio was less possessive of costumers than they were of their few proven stars like Renee and Sydney.

Chatting with Renee that morning, I asked, "Would you mind if I talked to other studios? Just when you're not working on a picture."

Renee looked a little startled. We'd been together our entire careers in Hollywood, but now it seemed like we might have reached a time to grow more apart.

"Jeany," she said, reaching across the table to squeeze my hand, "you should do what you want. As long as you promise to design all my hats when they cast me as the romantic lead!"

"All your hats and your party dresses," I promised.

So I packed for Arkham with far too light a heart. While my sketches of shadows and masks, still scattered across my unmade bed, made my hand tremble a little as I gathered them up, I stuffed the pages with great determination into my portfolio and knotted the ribbon around it twice. Thus I thought that I could contain the nightmares spawned by Sydney's description of the silver mask.

CHAPTER TWO

The first problem with Arkham was that it was in Massachusetts. "Could have been worse," said Fred. "Could have been Maine."

I looked at the map spread across the table in the train's dining car. Then I checked my timetable. "I think we have to go through Maine to get there," I said. "Isn't Boston in Maine? Don't we change trains there?"

"Well, ma'am," said Joseph, the porter, coming to fill our water glasses, "you'll transfer in Boston but that's in Massachusetts. And your company paid for all your cars to be switched. So you folks don't have to do more than sit tight and wait for a little bump."

I found the right spot on the map. It still seemed a terrible long distance from California, the only state that I'd ever known. Unlike Joseph, who had worked as a Pullman porter all across the country, I'd never been farther north than Oakland or farther south than Los Angeles.

"How did Max talk the studio into paying for our own cars all the way to Arkham?" said Fred.

"Because it was cheaper than the private train that Sydney wanted them to commission. As is, we have four cars, including baggage, on this one," said Max, shifting a cup so Joseph could see that there was no coffee in it. The porter smiled and took the water carafe away to exchange it for a silver coffee pot. Four private cars, including baggage, meant the studio had bought out first class. The first class dining car was ours throughout the day and night, although we probably didn't tip as well as the regulars would. The porters were nice about it, and nice about me riding up front with the rest. We were taking a northern route, and Joseph didn't anticipate any objections, although he warned me to stay away from compartments further down the train. "There's some folks with no manners at all sitting in second class," he said. I looked into his warm brown face and wondered what he'd heard over the years.

"Just tell them that we're in pictures," said Fred on the first day, when some conductor or other fussed about the sleeping arrangements and, possibly, a Chinese-American woman riding with the others. Even after nearly five years at the studio, I ran into stupid prejudices despite others like me in Hollywood. There were successful actresses like Anna May Wong, cameramen like James Wong Howe, who started with DeMille in 1917, and more. I wanted to make my own career, my own way, but it was a battle. I owed my early assignments to Renee and later Sydney insisting on my designs. It probably helped that I worked behind the camera and not in front of it. Still, I appreciated that Sydney kept the executives and other busybodies off his sets, insisting on working with his favorite artists in picture after picture. In return, he made the studio a lot of money and they gave him funding for his next picture. And, for the last couple of years, that studio funding came with a Max tied to it. Luckily we liked him.

And, for this trip, Max had persuaded the studio to pay the extra expense of leaving California in style.

Renee and Sydney each had a private compartment and a sitting room in between in their car. The rest of us, the men and women, were bunking in two open-section sleepers but it was only us, no other passengers allowed. All the bunks had privacy curtains and converted to seats during the day. A furiously contested poker game raged there when people were not sleeping, which is why Fred, Max, and I preferred to work in the dining car.

Joseph, with his knowledge of train gossip and ready hand with the coffee pot, was another reason to stay there.

"Oh, everyone working on the train knows you work in the movies, sir," said Joseph. "Couldn't miss you all getting aboard at La Grande." Our parade of luggage and chattering actors had been followed to the steps of the train by an equally large crowd of reporters and fans. Also, Fred made the biggest fuss as we boarded the train in Los Angeles, because they wouldn't let him sleep with his nearly new Bell and Howell camera. They insisted on stowing all the gear in the baggage car. Fred wanted to move his bed to the baggage car, just to keep close to his equipment. A couple of porters and the stationmaster finally convinced him that the camera was safe enough where it was.

Now we were east of Chicago, passing by cornfields, and trying to get as much work done as possible in the nearly four-day trip. The dining car turned into our workshop. Joseph kept us well supplied in coffee and ignored the times that Max or Fred tipped a little extra into their cups from their hip flasks. He even brought me a pot of tea on the first morning, but I told him that I preferred coffee with sugar.

"I still don't see what Sydney wants in our opening scene," said Fred. He looked at some notes scrawled in Sydney's atrocious handwriting. "They enter a house, it is not clearly their house," he read. "How do we show that?"

"They carry luggage but nothing too large," I suggested. "As if they were gone for just a few days. Or it could be that they are new to the house and moving in. The audience decides."

Max scribbled something in his notebook. Because this was the start of production, his tiny pocket notebook had neat crisp corners and a blank cover. By the end of the shoot, it would be dog-eared, dripping with receipts, and numbers would be scribbled on every corner of the cover. The notebooks were legendary. Rumor stated that each one was specially done for him in a stationer's shop. Max did have his name stamped in gold inside the front cover of every notebook that I saw, which argued for the truth of the custom-made rumor.

Max never lost a notebook, no matter how many times he pulled it out and was interrupted by some request by Sydney. His ability to hang onto it, and to turn all the many jotted notes into coherent reports to the studio, was truly magical. What happened to the notebooks after a film was done and the final report filed, I never learned. Fred was of the opinion that they deserved a ceremonial burning, like a Viking funeral, and more than once offered to build a little ship so Max could launch them flaming on the Pacific. As far as I knew, Max never agreed to that.

"Do you need to buy bags or can you just use ours?" Max said with a pencil poised to jot down that potential expense. "It would make the studio happy if we could keep away from too many purchases on this trip." Max liked to keep the studio bosses happy, and apparently endless reports on expenses made them very happy indeed. We all suspected that the studio paid Max a bonus whenever he whittled down Sydney's budget. Which was good, because Max liked buying costly clothes and accessories for himself.

"Renee can carry her hat box," I said. "The one with black crocodile trim. She has that white ensemble with the small round hat that would look good with it." I flipped open my sketchbook, quickly turning past page after page of masks sketched with shadows dripping across them. The nightmares continued on the train. I often found myself awake and drawing to relieve my terror. Joseph had become used to me arriving in the dining car well ahead of everyone else and juggling my breakfast around my propped-open sketchbook.

"That settles Renee's costume. What about the other girl?" Max asked.

"Is she supposed to be the maid or the best friend?" We hadn't seen a full script from Sydney. Not unusual. He often hid details until he was filming, just to shock the actors and create a stronger reaction from them. At least that's what Sydney said. Often we felt it was because he didn't know the end of the story until he was halfway through it. "Is Betsy playing her?" Our usual ingénue, Betsy Baxter, was back in a sleeping car, betting next month's salary on poker. Betsy most often portrayed girlish servants, the kind who flirted madly in the corner and caught the audience's eye with her smile and dimples. Betsy always cleaned up in card games, as she looked so sweet and spoke with a bubbly squeak that made the men go mushy and miss that she was counting the cards. Fred refused to play with her after she took twenty dollars off him in one night of gin rummy.

Max checked his cast notes. "Betsy is the maid. Renee is the older sister and Lulu plays the younger."

"Renee has a sister?" I drew a belt to add to Renee's traveling coat so it wouldn't look so much like what she wore in the last picture. I could borrow a belt from another dress that we probably wouldn't use. I wondered how we could dress the other actress to make her relationship clear with Renee. It would be a new challenge. Renee usually played the lone temptress. The hero often had family, a kid brother or kid sister, that helped him out. Or mourned him after he died. Sydney could go either way with his stories. "Who is playing her? Maggie stayed behind for that role with Chaplin." Maggie often played the hero's kid sister or an innocent friend of the heroine.

"Maggie is never going to get cast with Chaplin," said Fred, fiddling with a bit of wire. He had spent the morning checking his hand-cranked Bell and Howell model 2709 (serial number 242, as Fred would tell anyone foolish to ask about the camera) and the rest of the gear still stored in the baggage car. Though he visited his beloved camera regularly to make sure nothing was joggled loose, there wasn't much else that he could do until we arrived in Arkham. Except drive the engineers crazy by pestering them to let him ride up front and see how all the engine's levers and switches worked. Actually the engineers liked Fred. He disappeared for several hours each day to return coal-dusted and grinning, his ragged old checked cap further scarred by smuts and stray sparks.

"Sydney isn't planning to bring Maggie later, is he? We don't need two fainters," asked Max.

"No, Sydney hated that Maggie stayed behind for that *Hollywood* film," I told Max. "Where everyone in the cast is a star playing themselves except the girl who comes to town to become a star. There's a bit with Chaplin. Maggie wants the role of the flapper who goes off with the tramp." The film itself was a stunt, a gimmick more than a script with famous actors in dozens of parts. Sydney sneered when he heard about it, and frowned even more when nobody from our company was invited to take part. His nightmare movies might sell well at the box office but we definitely weren't as famous as some. Even if Maggie got a bit in *Hollywood*, she wouldn't be playing herself like Chaplin and the rest. She'd just be a "Flapper" in the credits.

"Maggie never hits her mark and has two left feet," said Fred. "Can't see her making the final cut with Chaplin. So, Max, who is our fainter for this picture?"

Once Maggie got into place – and Fred was right, she never remembered where she was supposed to walk – she was a champion fainter. Sydney often had her hit the floor just as a shadow crept up the wall or a hand reached around the door. It never failed to make the audience jump. It was hard to imagine a terror picture without a fainter.

"Yes," I said, "who is going to be terrified by Sydney's tricks so the audience knows when to gasp? Is he planning to use Renee? She hasn't played the innocent for a while, but it worked in *The Vampire's Doom*."

"Lulu McIntyre," said Max. He flipped a page in his notebook and looked over some information there with the suggestion of a sigh. "She's driving from New York and meeting us in Arkham. She asked for quite a lot to do this picture."

The name sounded familiar but not too familiar. "She's not in the movies," I said, and it wasn't a question.

Max nodded. "She's been on Broadway the last few years in those plays by Eleanor Nash. That's part of the contract. She's coming with Nash, who will be working on the script with Sydney."

"Sydney hates sharing a writing credit," I said. He generally got first billing as "Written and Directed by Sydney Fitzmaurice," in letters that filled the screen. Renee had been arguing for the last few pictures that her contributions to the scripts be acknowledged, but so far Sydney had slithered out of that.

"Oh, he wanted the writer as much as the actress," said Max. "But it was the headlines about Lulu's performances that caught his eye."

"The Screamer?" said Fred and then I remembered. There was an actress famous for her "haunting wail" starred in something very like *The Bat*. Except it wasn't *The Bat*. Sydney had been obsessed with the reviews for that show, especially about the technical tricks played on the stage to terrify the audience. He kept reading Lulu's reviews out loud almost as often as his own. Something about her voice driving men mad.

"What does it matter if she can scream?" I asked. "Nobody will hear her except us."

"She can open her mouth," said Fred, "and the organist can let out the train whistle or something like that. Will there be a score for these films?"

"There will be a score. You know Sydney. But he doesn't want the organ tricks," Max said. "Sydney wants you to try recording her. Something about sending a cylinder with each film for playing."

Fred shook his head. "Won't work. Better to just mark the score and have the organist or piano player make a shrieking noise."

Max objected to that. Fred started a long explanation on why recording sound to sync with film was a fascinating idea but not practical for large distribution. Something about microphones, and speakers, and why nobody would bother to convert a movie theater because it would just be too much money. Also everybody was making more money with silents than live theater, so why bother going backwards and adding spoken dialogue to a story. Then he talked about the work being done by DeForest that had been inspired by a Finnish scientist. For a kid from Brooklyn who never quite finished high school, Fred liked to read, only he read the type of articles in magazines that sent the rest of us to sleep. He also went to demonstrations, as many as he could find. Inventors flocked to Hollywood, all convinced that they could make a fortune in pictures. Fred loved to listen to them and discuss their new ideas. He'd been terrifically excited with some radio magazine that had reported a director using a radio to signal directions to large groups of extras in an outdoor scene. He thought it would be much more efficient than Sydney's megaphone.

"But can we record her scream?" Max finally said. "That's important according to Sydney's notes."

Fred shrugged. "I can rig up a microphone. If that's what he wants. Waste of time. Waste of money. We would have to record the scream and then film her screaming."

"He wants everyone to hear her scream in the movie."

"They'll hear the clatter of the camera if I record while we are filming," Fred explained. "Old 242 is the darling of my heart, but noisy as hell. We'll have to match the sound and picture later. It's an effect that any big organ can do better."

"But can you make it work?" said Max.

"One theater, one time, might be able to do that." Fred looked a little more intrigued and asked to borrow some paper from my sketchbook. He started doodling notes with a stub of a pencil that he pulled out of a pocket along with a couple of screws, a toffee wrapped in wax paper, and a ball of string.

Max looked satisfied with Fred's promise. Myself, I didn't like the sound of how this was developing. As if Lulu's scream was more important than anything else. As if she was taking top billing over Renee. I needed to talk to Renee about this, find out if she knew. We watched each other's backs, that's what we always did, because everyone knew that success only lasted until the next picture, the next darling embraced by an increasingly fickle public. If Sydney thought someone else could sell tickets better than Renee, then the studio might think that. And if the studio thought that, so much for roles that needed fantastic hats and fabulous dresses. I excused myself and went forward through the smoky sleeping cars. Betsy waved from her seat where she was holding court with a deck of cards, a pile of matchsticks standing in for chips. Paul and Jim, two other actors who worked in almost all of Sydney's movies, were about to be parted from their money.

"Want me to deal you in?" Betsy giggled. "The boys need someone easier to bluff."

I shook my head. Walking through the cars, I could still hear Betsy's usual chatter about the next stop, and whether there would be time to get off and pick up something from the station. An older actress, Pola, was catching a catnap wrapped in her coat, head bobbing a bit with the swaying of the train. Watching cornfields made everyone sleepy after a while. Hal, one of my favorites, was reading a magazine that he'd picked up during an earlier stop.

"Hey, Jeany," said Hal, whose rotund shape and balding head made him the perfect judge or doctor in Sydney's films. "Seen the script yet?"

"Not yet," I said, steadying myself against the back of his seat as the train creaked and rattled round a curve. "Just some notes on characters and how they are supposed to look."

Hal chuckled. "That's Sydney. Has to be the most mysterious man in Hollywood. Don't know why we bother working with him."

"The reviews?" I said. It was an old joke, shared among the crew and cast.

"Nope, the cash. Max always makes sure we are paid on time," said Hal. "Got my eye on a chicken farm in Salinas. That's the life for me."

"What do you know about chickens?"

"Absolutely nothing! That's the allure. I know too much about other things to try them." He waved his farming magazine at me. "There's always a need for chicken farmers. I'll just buy some eggs, wait for them to hatch, and then have lots of more eggs."

"I am not sure that it works that way," I said.

"Everybody needs eggs. Chickens produce eggs. Seems like a sure bet."

I wished Hal well with his dream, knowing that by the next picture he would be talking about buying an orange grove in Anaheim. It changed with every picture, but one thing stayed constant. Hal loved acting, and dreaming about not acting, more than anything else.

After the chatter of our cars, the private salon shared by Sydney and Renee seemed deathly quiet. Neither were in the parlor area but that wasn't unusual. Sydney had barricaded himself in his room with loud orders that nobody but Max was to disturb him while he wrote.

I went to Renee's door and knocked quietly. She called out and I entered. The bed had been converted into a long seat with a small table unfolded beneath the window. Another seat was opposite that. I slid into it.

Renee was playing solitaire, the red and black cards in a fan pattern taking up the small table.

"How much longer?" she asked me. She asked the same question every time I visited her, but she rarely came forward to the dining room or mixed with the others in the sleeper car. It was, she once said, part of her mystique. It was easier to maintain in Hollywood, where she could go straight from the apartment to the studio and home again. Nobody ever wondered there why she was always in full makeup or hidden under a hat and veil during daylight trips. On the train it was harder to stay out of the direct light and away from too many close looks. Still I never felt she had to hide. With this crowd, she had established her persona. Sydney's beautiful muse. But Renee was firm. She kept her distance from everyone except Sydney and me, the two people that she trusted not to betray her secrets. But I was the only one who knew all her secrets. As far as I know, she never told Sydney her real name or where she came from. And, to be fair, he never seemed to care about that. As long as she was willing to be his inspiration, he was happy to accept whatever story she told to the press as her true biography.

"Less than two days until we are in Arkham," I said. "We switch trains in Boston, and it is just a few hours beyond that."

She sighed and flipped another card into a growing pile on the side. "Why did I agree to this? Mile after mile of boredom."

"For the reviews?" I said again.

One eyebrow flew up. I always envied Renee's ability to do that. She achieved that perfect lift from practicing with her reflection. She used to do it over and over when night turned the windows over the kitchen sink into murky mirrors. We spent a lot of time staring into those windows while washing dishes in the orphanage. From the time she was fifteen, Renee knew exactly what she wanted. She wanted to be famous. She wanted to be rich. She wanted to arch her eyebrow at anyone and everyone who ever called us a dirty name. She wanted to make them feel small. My sister wanted us to be safe from them all.

I was jealous of her certainty then. Her ambition and her single-minded pursuit of her goals. At twenty-one, I still wasn't sure exactly what I wanted. Not the way that Renee knew.

"Has Sydney given you the script yet?" If anyone had seen it, it would be Renee. He generally turned to her first, to sound out his ideas. She said it was because he loved her. I knew it was because she had a flair for adding the details that gave strength to a scene. Renee remembered small gestures that people made, the ways that they picked up and fidgeted with objects when they were angry or sad. Playing a lovely poisoner, she once rearranged a set of combs and brushes on a dressing table in a way that gave her "a chilling authority," according to one review.

"I haven't seen a scenario yet. Why?"

I picked up the discarded cards, running them through my hands, flipping them over to finish off Renee's fan.

"Jeany, what is it?"

"You have a sister."

Renee stopped dealing her own hand of cards. "Are we having this discussion again? You know I cannot tell anyone…"

"No," I said. "Not that. In the script. A sister. It's in Max's notes about costumes needed."

Renee cocked her head, a little intrigued. Sydney never gave her any family in his recent stories. She was always alone. "Is it Betsy?"

"No, he's bringing someone from New York. The actress who can scream. Lulu something."

Renee placed the ace of spades over the king of hearts. She looked up at me. "Lulu McIntyre. Sydney keeps talking about her. Some review or other caught his eye. And then there's the divorce stories in the newspapers."

"Whose divorce?"

"Hers. She married a banker and he decided that he didn't want an actress wife. And he named Eleanor Nash as co-respondent."

"A woman?" Such affairs were known around town but rarely mentioned in the press. The studios knew that it didn't sound good in Peoria and worked hard to keep that type of story out of the newspapers. I wondered at Sydney daring to cast Lulu if she was that big of a scandal. With Taylor's murder last year and Reid's drug-related death in January all the Hollywood and New York studios and theater chains felt strongly about the morality of their players. At least the public perception of their morality.

"Sydney thinks the scandal will attract attention. He said that the first director to cast her after the divorce would see even more people flocking into the theaters."

That sounded like Sydney. If there was any person more single-minded about becoming famous than Renee, it was Sydney. I thought it was the thing that they truly had in common. Perhaps terror pictures could be a bit more scandalous than love stories or domestic dramas. Certainly our studio wanted to sell tickets more than anything else, if Max's account of meetings was accurate.

I finished up the tail of the fan; three of clubs and then two of hearts and then ace of clubs. Six, it added up to six, and that was a lucky number. Maybe this would all work out.

Renee also counted and sighed. "I was hoping for seven. That's lucky."

"Not for us. Mama always said people got that backwards. That six was luckier."

"Maybe for you, little sister," said Renee, naming the private relationship that we never shared in public. "Maybe six is your lucky number. But I'm not Mama's daughter any more. Seven is my number now. And this is my seventh movie with Sydney. This is the one that will be lucky for me."

"Perhaps. But I feel better with six," I said. Something about Sydney's secrecy bothered me. Renee was certain of his loyalty to her, but I had never felt so sure about him. Maybe this was the movie where he would replace Renee with another actress. That was our greatest fear, that someone would find out about Renee and me, that we were sisters, the daughters of a Chinese mother who could never marry our big Swedish immigrant father under the laws of California. All of which would make Renee a less desirable star with the studio's new drive for toeing the line and conforming to how they thought the world should look.

"So I have six and you have seven. Maybe Arkham will be lucky for both of us," I said, trying to quiet my own fears.

"Or at least not as bad as that circus pony," Renee said. "I made Sydney swear that the only thing I will ride in this movie will be a motor car. Driven by someone else."

"Oh, I'd like to learn to drive," I said.

"Wasn't Fred teaching you?" Renee asked.

"I only drove about ten feet before he decided to do something to the engine. After an hour of waiting for him to come out from under the hood, I left. But it was fun. Next time, he promises to have it tuned up before the lesson."

"After we get back, I could buy you a car," Renee said. "And some driving lessons."

"Renee, you can't. You know you can't. People would ask questions if you gave me a gift like that."

Renee shrugged. Pretending that we were just friends and occasionally admitting that we grew up in the same orphanage when pressed about how we became friends – that had all been Renee's idea. I looked too obviously like our mother's daughter for anyone to believe that I was white. But Renee was taller, thinner in the face, and her eyes were almost hazel in certain lights. With wigs, makeup, and later a good hairdresser to bob her hair and give her auburn highlights, she passed. Especially after we made up stories for the press about her descending from the family of a Hungarian princess. After all, Hollywood was all about the make-believe. Nobody really wanted to know that Theda Bara was the daughter of a Jewish tailor named Goodman. They preferred to believe that Bara was the half-French daughter of an Arab sheik or an Italian sculptor. Backgrounds and family histories were fluid in Hollywood, shifting with an actor's current roles and needs.

"I may not tell people about who we were," said Renee. "But I will never forget my responsibilities. I'll always take care of you, Jeany. You know that."

"I know," I started to shrug too and then stopped. We tried very hard not to have the same gestures. She did take care of me. From her very first picture, she found work for me. Work that I loved, making her costumes and now the costumes for the entire cast. People came to me to tailor clothes or design outfits even when they weren't connected to one of Renee's movies. Whatever she had, Renee shared with me. Everything except her name. And why that would bother me now, after so many years in Hollywood, I didn't know. It wasn't smart, wanting to tell people, tell someone, anyone, that we were sisters.

"So, according to Max, what type of person am I? Sydney is being more mysterious than usual about this script." Renee continued shuffling cards, trying a little too hard to sound calm. Sydney rarely kept secrets from her these days. But he had secrets, we all knew that, and sometimes Max was a more reliable source of information.

"Max doesn't seem to know much as usual since Sydney abandoned the mesmerist idea," I said.

"I'm glad he dropped that. There's too many films about hypnotists. I don't think we could make that truly frightening," Renee said. "This picture sounds different."

"So did Sydney say anything about your role?"

"Only that I am the catalyst of all terror."

"He said that about your last two roles. What about the plot?" I asked.

"That it was terrible in its simplicity and irresistible in its truth."

"What does that mean?"

"Absolutely nothing. At least to me. He probably stole the line. The man is a magpie when it comes to stories. He collects them from everywhere and never remembers where they came from."

"Well, as long he remembers that you are the star of the picture."

"Oh, I won't let him forget that. I'm sure Lulu is just a casting stunt and a small part," said Renee. "After all, what good is a screamer when you can't hear a thing she says?"

We both laughed at that. Then, after a long chat about how Renee could show up Lulu in the first scene by carrying her white travel bag with the crocodile trim, we both felt better about what was to come in Arkham.

We were both wrong.

CHAPTER THREE

For those who wonder, our deception began when we ran away from the orphanage in Oakland. Well, I ran away. Renee was eighteen and old enough to leave. I was barely fifteen and the nuns wanted me to stay in school. Since Renee wouldn't leave without me and they wouldn't let her take me with her, I climbed over the wall. We walked nearly a mile to the train station with Renee's cardboard suitcase banging the backs of our legs as we switched off carrying it. The War was just starting for our boys in 1917. Soldiers and sailors filled the train to Los Angeles. Some were on leave, heading home and chatty about what they would do when they got there. Some were heading back to their camp and quick to tell tales of what they'd seen in San Francisco. Only the brand-new recruits were silent, too nervous in shiny crisp uniforms to talk much. We stood up part of the way until two older ladies got off. Then one soldier shoved another soldier in the aisle so Renee and I could sit together.

Several flirted with Renee. She flirted right back as if

she'd been flirting with boys all her life. Watching her, I bet none of the sailors guessed that she spent the last five years of her life in a Catholic girls' orphanage. Our landlady in Oakland, Mrs Ryan, sent us there after our mother died during an influenza outbreak. Our father had been dead for three years by then. "Better you have an education with the nuns than try to support yourselves," the apologetic but firm Mrs Ryan said. "When you're older, you'll thank me."

I'd been sick, same as Mama, and remained frail for weeks afterward. If I hadn't been so ill, I think Renee would have run off then and there. But she agreed to the orphanage in 1912 and there we were for five bitter years. Bitter for Renee, at least. I never minded the nuns, but Renee disliked all their rules. She hated missing high school and high school dances, and snuck out whenever she could to visit dance halls and practice all the latest steps. That was how we knew about the window that didn't latch properly and the best tree to climb to get over the wall when it came time for me to run away with her.

We never wrote to Mrs Ryan. Even after Renee did become famous in the pictures. We probably should have thanked her. Because we learned a lot from the nuns. At least I did. I used my education, especially art with Sister Theodora and sewing with Sister Dorothy Anne. I think Renee actually learned something too. After all, Renee developed her patience, her persistence, and her ability to raise one eyebrow. Without those years of doing dishes after being caught climbing back in the orphanage windows, she would never have gone so far, so fast, in Hollywood.

Of course, Renee's tenacity started long before the

orphanage. Mama always said that mountains should bend out of the way when Renee came marching toward them. If she couldn't go over, she'd go straight through. But the orphanage sharpened her skills, especially when it came to winning fights with the other girls who tried to bully me.

I was, from the first, the odd one out. The only one obviously Chinese-American amid a group of girls abandoned by fate to the care of the nuns. Because I was frail due to a bout of influenza, small for my age, and, later proved to be good at school, the nuns made something of a pet of me. Which didn't help in the dormitory where daughters of Italian, Mexican, and Irish immigrants, tired of being called dirty names outside the convent walls, decided to knock down someone even more obviously *other*. Many didn't realize that Renee was my sister until she punched them on the nose or knocked their legs out from under them. Then Renee was disciplined for fighting. I would stay beside her in the kitchen, drying the dishes that she washed, and talking about what we could do when we finally left Oakland.

"For we are not staying here," she said. "There's nothing here for us."

"Where will we go? San Francisco?"

"There's nothing there either," said Renee with decision.

"Tye Leung," I said, very bravely disagreeing for once with my big sister. "She lives in San Francisco." My heroine was the first Chinese-American woman to cast a vote in 1912. I carefully cut out all the newspaper stories and pictures of her and pasted them in a scrapbook for us both.

"New York or Los Angeles, that's where we should go,"

said Renee, whose interest in politics was then and forever minimal compared to her interest in the movies. "Some city where we can be in pictures. That's what we will do. Become famous. Look at the Gish sisters."

"There's sisters in the movies?" I said.

"Of course. Dorothy Gish and her sister Lillian. They are renowned beauties of the cinema." That last sentence I recognized as a quote from one of Renee's magazines. She had a fearsome memory and could repeat a line days after she read it or remember a dance step after only one try.

Renee snuck out to the nickelodeon once and loved Dorothy Gish in *Little Meena's Romance*. After that she'd bartered and begged for newspapers and magazines about movie stars. She slipped scraps and smiles to the garbageman's son. He saved things up for her. She never minded if a story was weeks old, as long as she could read it out loud to me and the other girls in the kitchen or in the back of the choir loft. Anywhere that the nuns didn't hear us. There was as much debate then as now on whether the pictures destroyed a young girl's morals or improved her knowledge of the world. The nuns, except for Sister Theodora, fell firmly into the camp that cinema was a fearful source of sin. Sister Theodora was known to catch a picture at one of the many nickelodeons in the neighborhood.

"I rather think it does no harm," she once said to us, quietly after hours when we had finished putting all the dishes away and she was inspecting our handiwork. She ignored the stained movie magazines spread on the clean kitchen table. "To have some place where a body can go, and see something that makes them laugh or makes them cry, and know that everyone around them, no matter where they came from, is feeling just the same. That might be a powerful force for good. For not since the Tower of Babel fell have we all been able to understand each other. It may be that the pictures will be our common language given back to us."

Many years later, Sydney expressed the same view but from a quite different motivation than Sister Theodora.

As soon as she turned eighteen, Renee decided that Hollywood was closer than New York, and easier to reach on the small sum that the nuns had given her upon graduation to purchase clothing for an office job, also arranged by the diocese. Renee spent her money on the two cheapest train tickets possible to carry us out of Oakland. Then she packed what clothes we both had into the cardboard suitcase, walked down the stairs, and said a very cheerful goodbye to the nuns. Many regarded her docility with suspicion. Sister Theodora just shook her hand and winked at me.

That night I dutifully followed Renee's directions, climbed the correct tree, and ran off to the train station with everything I cared about, namely my sketchbook and pens, stuffed in a satchel that I had won for good deportment. Years later, when I told Fred some but not all about running away from the orphanage, he asked "But weren't you scared?" Of course I wasn't scared. I was with my big sister, who had protected me all my life, even though I just called her my friend when discussing this with Fred. Being without Renee would have frightened me, would have broken my heart, for she was all the family that I had. As for our destination, the whole world was moving to California in pursuit of a fortune in pictures. Hadn't Fred done just the same once his war was over and the army let him go?

"But it is different for men," said Fred, who joined the army the same year that we boarded our train for Hollywood.

I swatted him with a fabric swatch for that comment. "It wasn't different for me," I said. "Hollywood was the place where I could do what I wanted to do. Isn't that why we all ended up in Sydney's little troupe? Because he let us be us."

Fred had to agree.

In 1917, while being jostled by soldiers of all types in a slow-moving train down the center of California, we made the discovery that made all the rest even easier. Outside the orphanage, much as inside, people did not take us for sisters. "Who's your shy little friend?" one sailor asked Renee. "Where did she come from? Shanghai or Singapore?"

I started to say "Oakland", but Renee pressed down on my foot. I resented the "shy" comment, something so many assumed just because I wore an orphanage dress and walked behind the nuns to church. I was about to tell the sailor that I was as bold as brass, brave as Tye Leung, because I climbed a tree to freedom that very night. I wasn't shy, but it was hard to get a word out before Renee started talking. Over the years, I developed the habit of letting her speak first. Otherwise she'd kick my ankle in that way that didn't bruise but definitely smarted. As much as I loved my sister, I knew from age three that it was best to let her do most of the talking.

"Where do you think that I'm from?" Renee asked, opening her hazel eyes wide and staring straight at the sailor.

"San Francisco," chorused several returning soldiers. "All the beauties are from there!"

"New York," said another.

"St Paul," said a third. "You've got cheekbones like a Swede. And you're tall like the girls I knew there."

Renee smiled and then picked a city straight out of our geography lessons. "Providence, Rhode Island," she said. Then she added the plot of *Little Meena*, mixed with stories that we had read in the *Saturday Evening Post*. "But my family was Dutch. I was educated in Paris and all over the world. That is how I met my friend, Miss Jeany Lin. She kindly agreed to accompany me to Hollywood."

The soldiers may have hollered and hooted a little at that, but nobody out and out called her a liar. As Renee said later, nobody ever says they come from Providence, Rhode Island, and it did sound pretty grand.

"But's what your name, lovely?" asked the first sailor who had forgotten all about me when Renee started talking. That was something else that I was used to having happen and one of the things I noticed first about Fred, when we met him. Fred was friendly with everyone, but he never lost track of me when Renee was in the room. Now he did tend to lose track of everyone when he had a new invention going, but that's just Fred being Fred. I'm the same when I'm drawing or sewing, said Renee, more than once.

With a gleam in her eye, my not shy older sister told the entire train car, "Why, I am Renee Love."

So my sister acquired her new name. Later that night I swore to her that I would never tell what her name was before Renee Love. And I never have.

It was during that train ride that I took on the role that Renee had cast me in: best friend. After we arrived in Los Angeles and started making the rounds of the studios looking for work, she never told anyone that we were sisters. We shared a room in a boarding house, one run by a Japanese landlord who wasn't going to make trouble for me but wasn't too sure about Renee living in the neighborhood.

Renee started by playing the same parts that every newcomer was cast in: the partygoer, the maid, the hatcheck girl, and so on. But she quickly caught the attention of directors at the studio with her penchant for adding just a little extra to a role. A turn of the head, a way of walking, that wasn't quite like the other girls. Because she was an extra, she had to supply her own costumes, and that's where I came in. After her first picture, the other girls started asking me to help fit their dresses or add some trim to make them as noticeable. I did help, but I saved my best ideas for Renee's characters. Then Renee played the fortune teller who cursed a queen, and Sydney snapped her up to star in his movies. By their third picture in 1919, the movie magazines dubbed them the king and queen of terror. Eventually the studio bowed to both Sydney's and Renee's demands for a piece of the box office profits. One night, pooling our money on the worn little table in our shared room, Renee announced, "I'm moving into Alhambra Luxury Apartments and so are you."

"Together?" I said. We rarely admitted we lived in the same building, let alone the same apartment. We took different streetcars at different times from the studio to get home and practiced other small deceptions.

"You'll have an apartment upstairs. I'll have a garden apartment downstairs. It's all arranged."

"And what about Sydney?" By then they were tangled in a romance. How deeply, I did not know, and tried hard not to think about it. She was my older sister. I didn't want to know, mostly because of the one fact that I was certain of. She could not marry Sydney. Not without lies or leaving the state. He was white. She had a Chinese mother. The state of California had laws against such marriages.

"Sydney's divorce is final and he's deeding the house to his wife. He's taking an apartment at the Alhambra as well," Renee said. Sydney married an heiress from Pittsburgh at the end of 1918, just before he arrived in Hollywood and met Renee. The heiress financed his first films and built a mansion with a great seashell-shaped saltwater swimming pool. Sydney held exactly one party there for all the cast and crew, but we never met her. As we were leaving, stumbling a little in the early morning light after hours of dancing, swimming, and an impromptu tennis match in the empty ballroom, I'd looked back at the mansion and seen the silhouette of a woman in a lighted room on the second floor. I wondered at the time if that was Sydney's wife and what she thought of us. What she thought of Sydney became the stuff of legend in the newspaper articles that came out after Arkham. It all added to his reputation. But at the time of the divorce, she remained quiet and faded from view. At least, from our view. I don't think we ever knew her full name.

"Well, she paid for the house," I said, a little spitefully. "It is only right that Sydney gives it to her."

"He says that no man needs two mansions, and he'd rather keep the one that his family built," Renee said, ignoring my tone and answering in a way that told me that she understood my unvoiced objections to Sydney all too well. I had my own romances, mostly sweet boy-and-girl stuff like drinking a soda or going to the movies. But after Renee started working with Sydney, and insisted on me making all the costumes for her pictures, I found myself wanting to do even more. I worked with Sydney's chauffeur turned cameraman, Fred, on how to create ghosts or werewolves for Sydney's terror pictures. Designing props as well as costumes consumed more of my time, and romances with silly actors seemed a waste of it.

"Sydney has a family mansion?" I asked that night as we discussed moving out of our boarding house and into separate apartments.

"Yes, he comes from some town called Arkham."

"Well, why doesn't he live there?" I said, and was instantly a little ashamed of how petty that sounded. I tried hard not to be jealous of Renee's relationship with Sydney. But I didn't like the deceit that had to go with it, with Sydney's marriage and Renee's heritage. And, of course, I never quite trusted Sydney's charm. He switched it on so easily, and there was always something rather cold about the way that he'd watch people in a movie theater. Of course, all directors did that. Went to their own pictures to watch not what was on the screen but how the audience reacted. But with Sydney, it seemed more calculating, more considering, as if he was waiting for something other than a scream or a sigh from the collected people in the theater.

CHAPTER FOUR

Sydney's family home was not what we expected. Although in Arkham proper, it gave off an air of isolation, hidden behind a high hedge and iron gates. But once past those gates, a short drive led to a pleasant country house, weather grayed to a dull silver on the outside. The back of the house revealed an altogether different aspect, with a steep lawn leading down to a tangle of woods.

The other houses of French Hill were hidden behind the trees or the high hedges that bordered the back lawn as well. There was something about the entire neighborhood that made me feel strangers were not welcome in this part of Arkham. Once we drove up the drive, the high hedges around the Fitzmaurice house effectively cut off all views of the neighbors. It was as if we were alone on an empty island. Empty except for a flock of crows that cawed and wheeled overhead, streaming like a black cloud past the crooked chimneys and sagging roofline of the Fitzmaurice house to destinations unknown.

"There's a gate to the woods, and a path leading to a pond," said Sydney as we climbed out of the cars that brought us and the luggage from the train station. Max paid the drivers, who seemed eager to be away after they dumped our trunks in the drive and on the porch. Sydney ignored this activity, describing instead his ancestral grounds. "We will need to investigate the woods. I have an idea for a scene out there."

"But, Sydney, we are not staying here, are we?" asked Renee, looking a bit forlorn surrounded by all her luggage on the front veranda. "Isn't there a hotel?"

"We have twenty-two rooms and five baths here," said Sydney. "And my idea is to film at all hours of the day and night. It will be much easier if we are together in the house."

"But what about meals?" said Fred, who would have slept in the barn as long as he knew he would be fed.

"I telegraphed my old housekeeper, Mrs Mayhew. She's already arranged all the rooms as well as a cook for the days. There's Humbert, too, he lives down the road, to handle the outdoor work."

Inside, the house continued to reveal its divided nature between Colonial antique and country summer house. Obviously some attempts had been made to update it, probably when it was electrified, so the lower floor rooms had been joined together with arches and columns, each room flowing into the next. The electric lights snapped on without any fuss. Fred expressed his satisfaction with the fuse box positioned in the kitchen and even wandered down to the basement to check on the furnace arrangements. With summer heat already making its sticky impact, we were unlikely to need the furnace. Fred just wanted to see what was there and how it worked.

But the house was odd. A row of long, thin mirrors

hung in the downstairs hallway. Although all the same size, each mirror's narrow frame bore distinctly different hieroglyphics around the edge. With the opening of King Tutankhamen's tomb the year before and the popularity of Bara's Cleopatra movie last decade, Egyptian motifs were common in Hollywood. But these mirrors appeared much older than even Bara's 1917 smash hit. Standing in the center of the hallway, I realized that the mirrors captured the reflections in strange and crooked ways. Walking into the dining room, I had the clearest view of the front door, and the shadows of people moving around on the veranda, even though I had turned a corner from the entry to get to where I was. It felt like I was spying on everyone. Or something else was spying on all of us.

Beyond that, I felt warned off as I wandered through each downstairs room. Although warm enough inside, shivers coursed through me as I looked at the interiors where we were supposed to film. I sensed that strangers were never welcomed here.

"Ghost catchers," said Betsy, looking down the hall lined with mirrors.

"What?" I said.

"My mother used to talk about it. How ghosts can be caught in a mirror. How you should cover a mirror during a funeral to keep the ghosts out."

"I never heard that."

Betsy laughed. "I used to have a Halloween card, one that proclaimed that I could see my fate in a mirror. How did it go? *On Halloween look into the glass and your future husband's face will pass.*"

We both glanced at the mirror. Max's reflection could be seen as he moved across the veranda to talk to Sydney. For a moment he paused. In the narrow mirror, it appeared as if he stood shoulder to shoulder with Betsy.

Betsy winked at me. "Do you think it counts if it isn't Halloween?"

I laughed, shaking off my depressed reaction to the strange mirrors. My uneasy feelings stemmed from the difficulties of filming in such a location and nothing more, I told myself. Discussing Betsy's interest in mirrors and marriages was a far more cheerful subject. "Who knows. Maybe your rhyme counts double. We are here for a month or more. Isn't June the month for weddings? You could honeymoon on the trip back to California."

Betsy's pursuit of Max waxed and waned. Sometimes she seemed set on attracting his attention. Other times she talked solely of her career and plans. Betsy was smart and she had an amazing confidence, something that Max, who was often overset by Sydney, didn't seem to share. "I don't think he sees himself quite as wonderful as I do," she told me once. "And some days, I'm not sure if I should wait for him to find out how truly magnificent I am."

Upstairs revealed a much more old-fashioned and cheerful warren of tiny bedrooms spread across two floors as well as the five promised bathrooms. Renee immediately claimed a room with double windows that looked out over the front veranda. A four-poster bed, not old enough to be Colonial but trying very hard to look important, dominated the center of the room. It had been made up with a satin quilt and several pillows. All the pillowcases were lushly trimmed with lace.

My sister eyed with disfavor the oil lamp sitting on the table closest to the bed. "Why is that there?" she said to Sydney, who poked his head into the room to see how she was settling.

"What where?" he said.

"That oil lamp. Don't you have electric lights upstairs?" Renee said.

"Oh, they turn off the electricity at midnight unless someone has paid to keep it on longer. I'll have Fred or Max call the plant manager. We'll want power on the nights that we are filming."

"Every night," said Renee. "I don't want to be stumbling about in the dark after sunset. Neither do you. You're usually up until midnight or later working on your papers."

"Yes, yes. But for tonight, you might need to use the candles or the lantern. Mrs Mayhew always puts a fresh box of matches in the nightstand," said Sydney. "It is so wonderful to be back. I can feel my family history inspiring so many ideas, so much that's never been seen before."

Renee sighed and muttered something about a modern hotel, never mind family history.

I continued to explore, looking for a room to sleep in. Toward the back, I found a place where somebody had added more rooms, building out over the kitchen and the old back porch. The hallway had an odd half-step as I went past the bedrooms to a tiny screened-in sleeping porch. The cot there was made up, just like the four-poster bed in the room that Renee claimed, with a bright crazy quilt and well-worn sheets. Under one window, an old bookcase was filled with battered favorites. I pulled out *The Emerald City of Oz*, *The Window at the White Cat*, and *The Lightning Conductor* to pile on the bed. I'd read all three several times at the orphanage. It felt like discovering old friends at Sydney's house.

Renee stepped down onto the sleeping porch while I was re-reading the endings of all three books and trying to decide which one to start from the beginning again. "You always choose the funniest corners," she said. "It's like that apartment of yours."

I loved my efficiency unit on the second floor of Renee's building, with my east corner windows at the end of the kitchenette. The building super cleared out the table that was there and moved my drafting table into that corner. Since I usually ate downstairs with Renee or at the studio, I kept the kitchen drawers and cupboards filled with my sewing and art supplies. With a Murphy bed that folded up into the wall when I needed more room for pinning costumes together on fidgeting actresses, the apartment suited me. But Renee felt it lacked dignity and, over the last year, kept trying to talk me into a larger apartment on the ground floor near her. She pointed out more than once that she could afford it on the salary that she negotiated with the studio. I reminded her that there was no reason for her to be paying my rent. My apartment looked right for my position at the studio.

"I like it," I said to Renee about the screened-in room, stating the obvious as I slid my suitcase beneath the cot. I set my handbag and sketchbook on the table next to the bed. "It will be airy, and I can hear the birds singing in the woods." At the moment, all we heard was the cawing of crows, but I refused to give up my ideal image of a country house stay, with birds singing at dawn.

Renee gave an exaggerated shudder. "Birds. Just another reason to regret this idea. Do you remember those seagulls when we filmed *The Siren's Net*?"

One of Sydney's earliest nightmare films cast Renee as a strange creature who either was the daughter of a mad lighthouse keeper or came from another world beneath the waves. I made Renee a long wig, one that cascaded nearly to her knees. I knotted shells and large fake pearls into her braids. Sydney wanted to suggest that her hair was the net that dragged men under. The press raved about the "blonde siren" who lured men to their watery deaths. One reviewer said, "At first it appeared that the only persons who looked likely to escape drowning by the end of the picture were the director and his cameraman." And my favorite part of the review: "Miss Love wears such remarkable gowns as she walks along the seaside that all the women patrons in the audience may wish to shop wherever the siren does."

What the reviewer didn't record was that the seagulls, perhaps attracted by the shells in Renee's wig, or perhaps by Fred's famously greasy bacon sandwiches, harried us for one memorable afternoon at the beach until even Sydney lost his glossy look and fled wild-eyed back to the cars.

We didn't make another picture outdoors for nearly a year. Renee also turned down Mack Sennett's proposition to be a bathing beauty on the grounds it meant filming near the shore and those malevolent gulls. That didn't discourage Sennett. He kept sending her flowers and reminding her that he always had room for another beauty in his casts.

Betsy popped her head in the door. "Are you taking this room? It's darling."

I nodded. "Where are you?"

"One floor up. I'm sharing with Pola. We decided those were the best mattresses. And it's right next to a bathroom. You know I never mind sharing with her. She's always so calm and never takes any time at the mirror." Pola Vasily had worked for years in vaudeville before films. She took every "matron" role that Sydney dreamed up, usually the mother or the housekeeper of the hero. Her favorite parts required her to be murdered early in the plot, so she could spend the rest of her time on the set knitting stockings. She also made endless scarves. We all had a few pieces given to us from Pola's generous work bag.

"Max is on this floor, in the room next to Sydney. Jim, Paul, and Hal took a bedroom with an attached sitting room next to us and are going to rotate who sleeps alone on the couch by the strength of who snores the loudest. Fred's down the hall from them, converting what looks like a broom closet into a workshop with a cot. He liked the shelves," Betsy crooked a finger at both of us. "I was sent to tell you that Sydney is having a talk downstairs. Before the New Yorkers arrive."

Sounded like everyone was settled, although I wondered if there would really be enough bathrooms. We weren't a large crew but we'd filled the house quickly. Luckily everyone could double up on roles in front or behind the camera. Our films often seemed like we had large casts but we weren't DeMille or even Sennett. Sydney liked to work with a small hand-picked company and fill in with locals when available. In Los Angeles, with an extra on every corner, it wasn't so big a deal if we needed additional players. But in Arkham, we might have to do everything ourselves.

Pola and Betsy, of course, could transform themselves into a range of ladies, from the matron to the flapper. Hal played the wise father or the malevolent uncle, and loved being a butler too. Jim could be made up into young crooks, servants, and men about town. Paul played the older versions of those roles. He helped Fred with the lights and could even double as a cameraman. Paul had been an electrician before the War, according to Fred. I never knew much about Paul. He was one of those men who tended to grunt when you asked him a question.

"So are you ready to meet the New Yorkers?" Betsy asked us as we made our way down the hall

"Ah, the New Yorkers," said Renee. "The screaming Lulu and her partner. I suppose Sydney wants to tell us about them."

Betsy giggled. "I think we're about to be lectured on being professional and all that. Or maybe Sydney just wants to boast some more about this house. Oh, Fred said that he found sandwiches in the kitchen and might be persuaded to share."

"For sandwiches," said Renee, "I'll come down."

I hurried after the pair, realizing that I was also hungry. My morning cup of coffee and bread roll on the train seemed such a long time ago. As I followed Renee, I noticed a small alcove that I'd missed on my earlier exploration. Hidden behind a half-drawn chintz curtain was the landing for a small staircase. It twisted up to the second floor and also went down. I took the downward twist only to find myself in a sizable pantry, well stocked, with one door leading to a side terrace and another, upon opening, into the kitchen. In the kitchen was Fred, balancing a large tray of sandwiches and trying to hook a coffee pot under his arm.

A sour-faced woman, who introduced herself as Mrs Mayhew, and another tiny little lady, who said "Call me Ethel," were clustered by the stove.

"It's a beast, Mrs Mayhew, that stove. Should have been pulled out years ago," said Ethel.

"It is indeed, Mrs Roxbury, a beast of a stove," said Mrs Mayhew. "But I trust you'll be able to keep it under control. Three meals a day for five dollars a week, I think we agreed. I will be bringing the supplies each morning from the farm and twice a week will come with my girls Maggie and Hilda to sweep out the place."

I wondered what Max would make of the cost of the cook, to say nothing of Mrs Mayhew's supplies and girls, but decided that was the studio's problem.

"I'll take that," I said to Fred, grabbing the coffee pot

"Thanks," replied Fred. "Max took the cups in already."

I followed Fred and the sandwiches into the spacious main room. A deep fireplace occupied one whole end. Sydney arranged himself in front of the fireplace, one arm along the mantel in a pose that I recognized from a past photo essay entitled "The Great Showman at Home." Over the mantel hung an oil painting, very dark, showing a man with Sydney's features but in a fine uniform tunic with a fur-edged jacket slung over his shoulder like a cape. Both tunic and jacket were adorned with silver braiding and several rows of buttons. Below the portrait hung a curved sword, oddly blackened and burned about the tip.

"My friends," said Sydney. "My fellow artists. My most brave adventurers into the wilderness of Arkham."

I settled into a cozy chintz chair and took a large bite of chicken sandwich. From the introduction, I expected Sydney to tell us the plot of the movie and exhort us to reach new heights of creativity. The coffee was black and bitter, and strong enough that I guessed Fred had made it or that Ethel had Fred's attitude towards the liberal use of coffee beans.

"It is fitting that we gather here, under the gaze of my most revered ancestor, that daring French hussar who brought his little family to Arkham following his own grand adventures with the Emperor Napoleon in Egypt."

"I was in a film about Napoleon," Betsy whispered to me as she settled in the chair next to mine. "Maid to Josephine."

Sydney glared at her. Betsy mimed "sorry" to him and the great man continued his speech.

"It was Saturnin Fitzmaurice who battled in the shadow of the mighty pyramids, and later served as part of his emperor's envoy to the young American Congress. It is his stories that my grandfather so lovingly preserved within our library. It was Saturnin's discoveries and the descriptions in his journal that inflamed my youthful imagination. From his writings, translated from the tablets unearthed by this very sword," he flung up a hand to point at the fire-blackened blade, "we will draw our latest script and create a story in silver and shadows to enthrall and terrify audiences around the world."

Sydney paused. From long habit, nobody said anything. The pauses were for dramatic effect only. We knew he disliked being interrupted in full flow. Besides, we all wanted to know the plot.

Gravel crunched beneath tire wheels. A long melodious horn blast sounded outside the windows. The New Yorkers had arrived. Sydney swung around with a wide smile to stride from the room and greet them on the veranda.

Fred swallowed the last quarter of his sandwich in one enormous bite. "So," he said to me, "how do you unearth something with a sword?"

"It looks like somebody used it as a poker," I said, eyeing the soot stains along the blade. It was thoroughly blackened, and I wondered if the chimney smoked. But I liked the look of the uniform still vaguely visible in the painting over the fireplace. I considered taking such braid and trim, and adding it to the hero's coat for a continental dash. "Fred," I said, "who is playing the hero?"

Fred shook his head. "Max never said."

I thought about the actors who had accompanied us. Sydney liked to switch the actors playing his heroes from film to film. Sometimes, instead of a romantic hero, he wrote in a charming but hidden male villain manipulating events until caught.

Hal wouldn't do for such roles. He was too short, too round, too bald, and too old to fit the studio's idea of a romantic lead, good or bad, which was a pity because he had more charm than most.

Skinny Jim Janson played everything from jewel thieves to rustlers, but again looked too juvenile for a lead. If a villain, Jim was the second villain, the one that was easy to spot in Sydney's scripts.

Same for Paul Kopp, who either played an obvious heavy or a detective. He often showed up just for the denouncement in the final act, which was good as he worked best as Fred's back up for the camera and lights. Fred, after one unbelievably bad scene in *Siren*, never acted in any picture. He was a genius at capturing emotion on film and a complete bomb at portraying it on film. Besides, he hated having anyone crank the Bell and Howell except himself. Said it took days to get 242 feeling right if Paul or someone else turned the handle. He had an older Pathé that he preferred to give to Paul.

I never even tried to act. That was Renee's talent. Mine was to make everyone look good in their clothes and makeup.

My theory, never expressed to Renee, was that Sydney's constant rotation of leading men was to prevent her from becoming part of a couple for one of the studio's publicity pitches to the press. She was Sydney's muse and his alone. Although his marriage and her own reasons for concealment kept them from being an obvious couple around town, much to the distress of more than one publicity agent.

The men who consistently worked from film to film with Sydney never posed a romantic threat, at least in Sydney's eyes. As for the women, I suspected he kept with the same ones because they understood his tricks. It wasn't unusual. All directors had their "regulars" for supporting characters.

Working with Betsy, Maggie, and Pola was comfortable for Sydney. He never liked change and insisted on loyalty and even some secrecy on set, to better surprise the public when our terror pictures opened. Maggie leaving us for the *Hollywood* picture had been a blow to Sydney. I heard him tell Max earlier in the trip that he wouldn't work with her again. Sydney could, and did, carry grudges.

Still Renee was his only leading lady once he started directing his own pictures. He always wrote her into the leading role as either *femme fatale* or ingénue. Although, by 1923, Sydney liked her best as a mystical and deadly otherworldly creature. The press and the public loved her in those roles too. When she played the wolf woman, the studio staged a photo with Renee standing over the bones of her devoured victims. It was a clear copy of a Theda Bara publicity photo. Later we heard that Bara's studio wasn't happy that our studio was pushing Renee as a new breed of vamp. Although Bara's career was nearly over by then.

Bringing in an outside actress, and a New York stage actress, like Lulu McIntyre, marked something new. I wondered if Sydney was assigning her the hero or villain role that normally went to a male actor. Or, as I feared, Lulu might be meant as a replacement for Renee in the supernatural category. A hidden villainess, perhaps.

"Maybe our male hero would be another New Yorker?" I said to Fred. "Or would Sydney cast a local as the hero?"

"Could be." He turned in his chair and yelled at Max. "Didn't you say something about a theater in Arkham? Any actors coming from there?"

Max wandered over, distracted by trying to watch Sydney and the New York ladies through the window. "Yes. Sydney directed something locally, several years ago, before he came to California. But we may not need more actors. Sydney says this script is very focused on just a few characters, the sisters in particular."

"Will we need more costumes?" I asked, thinking about what we had shipped from Los Angeles. Most were general items that we used on our regular troupe and fitted for them. Hal's butler outfit and his dining out suit, Pola's matron dress and another longer dress for being the wife of a distinguished gentleman, usually Hal, at a party. Various ensembles for Betsy, from the parlor maid to the flapper on the sidewalk. Same for Paul and Jim, outfits that turned them into anything from servants to menacing toughs. And, of course the cape.

"Will we be using the man in the hood?" I said.

"Can't have a Sydney Fitzmaurice film without him," said Fred, and he wasn't joking.

The hooded man scene was our signature scene and made a horror film a Fitzmaurice terror picture.

Sydney loved that cape, which could cover a large man from foot to head, and had a deep hood that hid the wearer's face. I made it for the very first picture that we ever filmed with him. It was yellow material, lined with gray, and we could turn it inside out, depending on how Fred wanted it to film. Over the years, I draped that one costume over multiple actors to make them look far more mysterious and menacing than they were. Luckily the camera didn't show how many times I'd hemmed it up or down, depending on who had to wear it. That cowled and caped figure always stood somewhat out of focus in each of Sydney's pictures. Also the hooded man just watched the scene for a moment or two, and then disappeared. A few enterprising reporters asked Sydney when he was going to reveal all about this recurring character, but he just laughed and told them to come to the next picture.

My speculations with Fred on leading men and plots were interrupted by the return of Sydney with a lovely blonde clinging to his arm. Her other arm was clutching a pug of particularly unpleasant expression. Ropes of glistening glass beads were entangled with embroidered scarves that floated all around her. Sliding off her bare shoulders was a gorgeous coat trimmed with feathers and fur. The effect was, as intended, quite startling. An elegant brunette followed them into the room. She wore the most beautifully tailored checked suit and dangling earrings that emphasized her long neck and narrow features.

"My dears," said Sydney, "my company. Here's the famed Lulu McIntyre and her writer friend Eleanor Nash." The blonde Lulu waved at all of us with a great fluttering of scarves and a slight growl from the pug.

The brunette Eleanor bared her teeth in a smile that radiated even less good humor than Lulu's dog. "Sydney, it's been in the headlines for weeks. For goodness sake, call us lovers. That's what we are. And if any of you gossip to the press about us, just know that I am descended from Salem witches and will curse you from here to California."

"Oh, Nell," said Lulu, "you don't mean it. We're just so very, very excited to be in pictures."

Renee rose out of her chair and crossed the room to shake hands with Lulu and Eleanor. "We are delighted that you could join us. I hear that you are quite the screamer."

Lulu blinked at her. "Oh yes, you're the one who plays my sister. So fun to have a film actress to work with. I've only worked with real actors before. In a legitimate theater."

At that fatal statement, silence filled the room. Renee ignored it. With a smile just as broad as Eleanor's and just as deadly, she said, "Yes, Sydney cast you as the younger, sillier sister. So lucky that the camera doesn't reveal true ages. Mary Pickford is able to carry off young girls even though she's past thirty now. I'm sure as a real actress that your age won't set you back at all."

Eleanor gave a snort that might have been a laugh. Lulu let out a howl for Sydney, still standing close at her side, that argued for the veracity of the claim that she was the greatest screamer in showbusiness. Renee continued to smile.

And thus that particular battle began. Later it would seem trivial.

CHAPTER FIVE

By Friday, Fred and I decided to leave the house, and the warfare within, to find a diner. While the meals served up by Ethel were large, filling, and often even delicious, the ongoing battle between Renee and Lulu over the importance of Camilla, Renee's role, versus Cassilda, Lulu's character, continued to engulf the whole company.

Lulu's inexperience with movies didn't help. Her first attempt at makeup proved to be a disaster and delayed filming for a couple of days. She was used to preparing for the stage but almost everything she did was wrong for film. Fred explained, patiently, that red would photograph black, so she couldn't use her normal lip rouge. She didn't believe him until he carefully photographed her with a still camera he used for such tests and processed the pictures in the darkroom that he'd created in the basement.

"We sometimes rouge the cheeks," I explained as Lulu moaned about how hideous she looked in the photos. "That creates dark shadows and makes your face look hollow. You can put it on your eyelids for the same effect.

But light carmen looks best on the lips."

Betsy chimed in. "Yes, don't worry. We all looked terrible at first. Once you've got the grease paint and powder on, it's just finding the right shade for your eyes. Jeany and Fred are a whiz at it."

Many older actresses and actors still preferred to do their own makeup, figuring that they knew best how to make themselves look right for their parts. After all, many made their own costumes until just recently. Chaney famously insisted on creating all his creature makeup himself. But as I started to design costumes and props for each of Sydney's pictures, I'd also taken over the initial design of the makeup for the characters. The greatest emphasis, of course, was on how Renee would appear as the mysterious temptress, but Pola and Betsy were used to my laying out their basic makeup, even though both were quite capable of doing themselves up without my help. Fred added a few more tricks that he learned from cameramen around town, like Howe's technique of placing black velvet in a large frame around the camera to make somebody's eyes appear larger and darker.

Of course, the studio, and their proxy Max, loved that I could double up as both costumer and makeup person. Probably if I hadn't done it, they would have insisted on all the actors continuing to do their own. They definitely didn't like it when I started buying Factor's shades, deeming them more expensive than other brands, but his blends were meant for movie work. I had nearly thirty colors by then in my kit and kept them locked up when we weren't filming. Not that Pola or Renee would ever steal my makeup. But

Betsy and Maggie both "borrowed" some when going out on dates. Hence the locked case by the time we went to Arkham.

"Listen to Jeany," advised Pola. "The stage is not the same as film. We all must learn this."

"I am known for my beauty on stage," said Lulu. "That's why all my husbands married me." Turned out that Lulu's divorce was her third and, according to Lulu, the only one that gave her any trouble. The others, again according to Lulu, were sweethearts who had been most generous and understanding when she decided that the time had come to part. As she probably was still in her early thirties, it was an impressive history. Later, Eleanor would tell me not to be deceived by the feathers and beads. Like Betsy, Lulu was far sharper than she pretended to be. Although married at a very early age, in part to escape a managing stage mama, she had left her first husband before she turned eighteen. She quickly went from being in the chorus in Chicago to headlining Broadway shows in New York.

"The important thing was," said Eleanor, "Lulu really married men for love and the fun of it. The first two were creative but very poor. One was a painter and one was a trumpet player. She still sends them gifts every now and then to help them out. She always sends money to her mother and even lets her visit. Lulu's biggest mistake, and probably her only one, was marrying a rich man the third time. He was used to owning things. Lulu will never be owned."

"And her affair with you?" I said in those days after Arkham when I tried to understand all the motives of the people who Sydney gathered under his roof for his horrific film. "How did that come about?"

"She rather swept me off my feet," said Eleanor with an uncharacteristic blush. "I just was looking for the perfect woman to place in peril in my horrid little plays. And there she was, all feathers and pug dog, and as perfect for me as she was for my plays. You saw her at her worst, at the start. She was terrified about going into moving pictures and didn't want to show it."

Finally during that first week of filming, to mollify Lulu's anguish about how different it all was, Eleanor intervened. With her help, we got Lulu to listen to our advice as we changed her look into something that would work in the movies.

"We can shadow the corners of your eyes with brown," I told Lulu. "And then outline them. You will look lovely." Lulu had very light blue eyes. Renee and I had learned various tricks to make Renee's eyes look rounder and lighter. Looking at the photographs rather than Lulu herself, I could see a different style was called for. Perhaps even a little red near the ears to make Lulu's face longer and less full.

"Lulu's character is supposed to be the frailer of the two sisters," said Eleanor, looking at notes that Sydney had given her. "Perhaps recovering from an illness. So her older sister has brought her to this house for her convalescence. Can you convey that and not make her look like a walking corpse?"

I nodded as I showed Lulu how to powder her face properly, a tricky technique until an actor got used to layering the grease paint and film powder for the right effect of flawless skin. "You'll look very lovely and frail," I promised her.

And she did. After a few more experiments, and photographs quickly processed by Fred, we settled on a look for Lulu that made her appear very young and innocent. So much so that Eleanor laughed and asked if she could send a few copies of the photographs to the press that had bothered them so much in New York. "Not that those hounds would care," she said. "But given all the stories that her husband spread about us, it might make a few of the readers doubt his claims of Sodom and Gomorrah on West 57th Street."

Lulu professed herself equally charmed and ready to start her film work. Which led to the next disaster, a simple scene in which Sydney wanted Renee and Lulu to enter the house with "bewilderment and trepidation."

Lulu had taken one look at Renee's ensemble, which I had created by retrimming her traveling coat and hat, and insisted on an entire new costume for herself. Which had to be sent from her apartment in New York, another delay but one that gave us a couple of days to settle the question of her makeup

After Lulu's desired coat and hat arrived, and were approved by Sydney, with Max muttering about telegrams and express charges, Lulu then upstaged Renee's entrance twice. The first time she dropped her bag as they descended from the car. The second time she stepped in front of Renee in an awkward cross that left them both teetering slightly on the stairs.

Fred sighed and stopped the camera. With the clatter stilled, we all stood in awkward silence.

"Twelve cents a foot for film," muttered Max beside me. "And this is only the first scene." He took the slate in his hand and changed the chalked take number to a three. Max excelled at numbers, was a disaster at acting like Fred, and never could be trusted with anything too mechanical. But from the beginning, when we all wondered what to do with the upright accountant that the studio had sent to keep an eye on Sydney, Max had fallen in love with the slate. Keeping track of the take numbers was an important task. We all knew of productions where somebody forgot to do it, which led to disasters in editing. Max never made a mistake. He always had the right numbers written on the slate and waved it with quiet dignity before the camera lens at the start of every take.

The second time that Lulu ruined Renee's entrance, Sydney removed his cigarette holder from his mouth and used it to gesture Lulu up the stairs. Renee, recognizing what he was about to do, stood with great tranquility by the open car door. Jim, costumed as their chauffeur and disguised with a large pepper-and-salt mustache so he could play other roles later in the picture, leaned against the hood and napped in an upright position.

"Lulu, my dear, I fear you may have misunderstood my directions," Sydney said with the purr that indicated that his voice could grow much louder. "You are not to rush into the house in girlish glee, knocking over your sister on the way."

Lulu laughed. The rest of the cast, knowing Sydney, kept quiet. I watched Paul and Hal, neither of whom had any part in this scene, head around a corner of the house with their pipes. We'd put a couple of decrepit willow cane chairs on the back lawn. The gentlemen had turned those seats into their favorite smoking spot.

"While some directors prefer to film the scenarios willy-nilly, I follow the course of a script as closely as possible," Sydney continued. "The emotions seen on the face of my actors must remain as true to nature as can be contrived. This is your first encounter with the house, your first trip to Arkham. In this scene we should see a vague fear, the trepidation that some great shadow is about to descend upon you. That is what must show in this scene. Not your petty desire to be first through the door!"

The latter came out as a roar. Lulu, neither foolish or reticent, stood her ground and stared Sydney straight in the eye. "I have been acting since I was three and my mother placed me in a lion's cage," she said. "If there is one thing I know is how to walk into a room so the entire audience notices and cares about my character."

Renee now added her bit. "Sydney, be patient. Circuses and vaudeville shows call for exaggerated motions. You can't expect Lulu to know about your technique of absolute realism. That movie actors must act as naturally as possible. What did you tell me? That our expressions must be no more pronounced than they would be in real life. That the slightest deviation leads to mortifying results on the screen. Petty physical tricks cannot be a crutch for the performance. Unless we are thinking about what we are trying to portray on the screen, the audience will become instantly aware that the emotion is false."

Sydney thrust the cigarette holder between his teeth and rushed down the stairs to grasp Renee's hands. "You are always my bright muse," he said. "My wise Camilla. That is it exactly. Now, Lulu," he turned and faced her. "Do you think that you can contain your natural enthusiasm and portray a delicate young lady beset by illness and fear?"

With a huff, Lulu turned on her heel and marched back to the car. "Of course," she said. "Shall we begin again? Lead, dear Renee, and I will follow, properly fearful of shadows."

After that, Lulu behaved, but Sydney struggled to find the angle that he wanted, making Fred circle about and film them from various positions, through a half-open door, looking up the steps, and once halfway down the drive looking back at the house. All of that took time as Fred shifted the black metal camera and its solid wood tripod from place to place. Then he would begin to crank again, smooth and even, and the clatter of 242 would drown out the crows cawing from the trees.

"Twelve cents a foot," Max groaned with every change of Fred's position as he jotted notes in the notebook he carried in his breast pocket. The take number on his slate was erased and rewritten and rewritten again.

Betsy discovered a croquet set stashed under the veranda and dragged it out. Half the balls were missing. But the iron wickets still bore white chipped paint and very little rust. We set it up on the lawn and played round after round while the filming dragged on. Pola proved particularly wicked at knocking away her opponents' balls. Even Hal and Paul abandoned their pipes to join the game.

When the sun finally dipped below the hills and real shadows swamped the veranda, Sydney called a halt for the day. Renee and Lulu trod up the stairs a final time. Both disappeared into the house with strained smiles. Eleanor had pleaded a need to work on the film scenario for the next day's shooting and had left much earlier.

Fred stowed his camera and then collapsed on the lawn next to Betsy. He watched me ricochet a ball through two wickets and smack the final stake. "How about dinner in town tonight?" he asked.

I glanced at the house. If they came to dinner, there was sure to be tension between Lulu and Renee. And Eleanor dropping her own barbed comments to Sydney about the scenario that they were supposed to be scripting together. Although Sydney had hired her to script out the entire film, and seemed to want her talent for creating terrifying scenes as much as he wanted Lulu's scream, he had decided that he wanted her to write only "the next twenty-four hours of filming" rather than a complete scenario for the movie. It was an unusual choice. His vagueness about what was to happen next had reached new highs with this film and was not to Eleanor's liking. The rest of the cast and crew tended to tuck their heads down and swallow their dinner without comment. Even voluble Betsy grew uncommonly quiet at the table these days. None of us wanted to be drawn into the warfare raging between Renee and Lulu, and, in a slightly different but equally poisonous manner, Eleanor and Sydney. I would, of course, support my sister, but I found that I quite liked Eleanor and even the vainer Lulu. I think the rest of our small company felt the same. Eleanor and Lulu made us all laugh, when we weren't wincing at the barbs flying around the table.

"I think a dinner in town would be splendid," I said. I hadn't been past the hedges since we arrived. Max had taken various trips down to the train station and into town to fetch items for Sydney. Fred had gone with him as he waited for filming to begin. I'd been spending most of my time sketching out ideas for Sydney's silver mask as well as various possible designs for costumes and props. Like Eleanor, I was frustrated by Sydney's vagueness. I felt more than ready for a night away from the house. "Where do you want to go?"

"Max and I found a diner not far from here. They aren't fussy. The food's good and cheap," said Fred. "We can take the big car."

Max had hired an ancient but stately touring car for the arrival of the sisters in the first scene. Sydney loved the double row of leather seats and yellow painted wheels. As soon as he saw it, he told Max to keep the car for future excursions. Max had sighed, made another note in his notebook, and arranged that we would have the car for the rest of our stay in Arkham. "Do you want to ask Max and Betsy to come along?" I said.

"Still trying to promote that romance?" said Fred with a chuckle.

"I have no idea what you mean," I said. "But she's sweet and better at math than he is. He'd be lucky to have her."

"I'm sure you're right," Fred said. He turned his cap right way round. It had been pushed backwards so he could peer into the lens without interference. "Let's grab them and go."

I was still wearing my working slacks. "Do I need to change?"

"It's just a diner. They'll think you're an amazing Oakland doll when they see you."

"So none of the other women in this town wear pants?"

Fred shrugged. "Not that I've seen. But they have a university. There's women students and professors. Bound to have been a few pants wearers among them."

In the three years since women got the vote nationally, hemlines had crept up. But pants were still considered fairly scandalous outside of certain cities. I glanced down at my working pants, a pair that I'd styled for myself off the linen trousers favored by many men for the summer. Side-fastened, wide-legged, and with deep pockets, I had more than one actress approach me after a shoot and ask where they could purchase a pair. I'd run up several for the more daring women of Hollywood. But I wasn't sure that New England was ready for ladies in trousers.

I said. "I'll change. Meet you by the car."

Fred nodded and ambled over to Betsy to explain our plans. She squealed a little and lit out for the house. No question that Betsy would change into a prettier dress for a dinner with Max. So it appeared her interest in him was on the rise again.

Neither of us took much time. We both beat Max to the car. Fred finally had to go back to the house to pull him away from changing into a new silk tie for a dinner out. Max and Betsy took the back seat. I rode up front next to Fred so I could get a better look at the gears and pedals. I reminded him that he still owed me a driving lesson.

"The steering's stiff," he commented. "But I knew gals who handled worse, driving ambulances in France. Tell you what, let's take this car and a picnic basket down some farm lane when we get our next break. You can practice then."

"You mean when Lulu decides to halt filming for another dress order from New York?" I said with a laugh.

Max groaned in the back and Betsy giggled.

Fred just clashed through the change of gears and grinned. "You can drive back and forth while I eat all the sandwiches."

As we rolled into the Easttown neighborhood, the houses started to look friendlier and more ordinary. The high hedges, walls, and locked gates that separated the mansions of French Hill were left behind. We all started to laugh and talk about Lulu's mishaps. It felt like an ordinary day again, with Max complaining about the waste of money to pamper a New York theater actress, Betsy wondering if Sydney would give her a scene dressing Renee and Lulu for a party, and Fred complaining that they didn't even know if there would be a party scene.

"Oh, there's sure to be a party," said Betsy. "Sydney knows the audience wants to see a crowd all dressed up and looking lovely. Especially for a story set in a big fancy house."

"We'll need to get more extras from town if we do that," I said. "I wonder what the society types would wear in a town like this."

"Perhaps some girls and boys that we can recruit from the university?" said Betsy. "They'd be thrilled to be in a film."

Max brightened at that thought. "You're right. I suspect we could cast students for little or no wages."

"Max!" we all cried.

"Well, we'll pay something," he grudgingly said.

We parked the car right in front of Velma's Diner and tumbled through the doors a very merry crew, debating the ethics of making extras work for experience and little else. We'd all had that happen to us. It was a common trick.

"When I think of all the dollars that I've spent on my munitions," said Betsy, "I used to think that it would be cheaper for me to pay the studio to work. I always hated how the studio kept saying we should invest in our look." Her moan about the money that any actor had to put out for good makeup or clothes was common. Sydney and many bigger directors were starting to want more control over the look of a film. Some were starting to costume their entire casts and outfit makeup artists. But, as Renee also complained, our studio often operated like it was 1913, not 1923, and we were making serials for the nickelodeon crowd.

We plopped down into the seats nearest the window. A young woman was adding up her tips behind the till. She headed toward us with menus and stopped when she got a clear look at me. Then she said, "We don't serve chop suey."

Max and Betsy looked puzzled. Fred, who had been out with me before, started to scowl but switched to his biggest grin. "Well, then, that's too bad. I love chop suey. But can you cook a steak? Or should we try La Bella Luna instead?" said Fred.

The girl stood there with her mouth hanging open. It was

a common reaction to Fred. A second waitress came up behind her and smacked her shoulder. "Suzie, go on back to the kitchen and help Ted with the dishes."

"But I don't wash dishes, Florie," said Suzie with an edge of whine in her voice.

"Now you do," said the older woman. "I'll finish up your tables and maybe split the tips with you if you don't break anything. Go on. Scoot. Or do you want me to tell Velma that you tried to chase away the famous stars of the only movie ever filmed in Arkham."

Suzie gulped a little and fled to the kitchen.

"Not the brightest thing," said the waitress. "But she's Velma's niece. We have to keep her or Velma's sister raises a ruckus. Now coffee's on the house, here's some menus. I recommend the fried chicken myself, but Joe does a nice steak too."

I buried my head in the menu. Once Suzie was gone, I thought of several things to say in response to such a cheap and common insult. And a couple more things to say to Fred about how he did not have to play knight errant. I could fight my own battles. But everyone was looking at me and it was easier to read through the whole menu twice. I agreed with Florie that the fried chicken sounded like the best choice.

"Joe makes the best fluffy mashed potatoes to go with the chicken," she said. "Now, do tell me that you are from the Fitzmaurice place and are making a movie in Arkham."

"Yes, ma'am," said Fred with a twinkle. "But we are not the stars. Just working stiffs."

"Oh, call me Florie, Florie Wilson is my name," she said.

"You're something new and that makes you newsworthy in this town. The *Arkham Advertiser* has been writing up stories about Sydney Fitzmaurice coming back to town and making a movie here for months."

"Months?" I said. "But Sydney only made this decision weeks ago. Max, didn't you say that the studio was furious that he changed plans after they'd agreed to the budget for his mesmerist idea."

"The studio is always upset," said Betsy. "That's why Max is going gray around the edges." She looked at him expectantly, waiting for Max to respond about how the studio always knew best.

Max, funnily enough, didn't trot out his favorite phrase. Instead he just shrugged and asked about the steak, the most expensive item listed. Betsy and Fred picked the chicken.

"Well," said Florie, tucking her notepad into her apron pocket after getting all our orders. "Mrs Mayhew got a telegram more than three months ago asking her to open up the house and get it ready. Can't keep a secret in Arkham, that's for sure. Now, you leave room for pie. We've got both apple and cherry tonight."

"Sydney might have said something about Arkham earlier," Max told us after Florie walked away. "He wanted to do a different approach. The studio said that if he filmed here, he had to deliver on all his promises."

"His promises?" I said, wondering what that meant.

Max pursed his lips. "The hooded man."

Fred looked up at that. "What about that gimmick?"

Max fiddled with his napkin and silverware. Betsy

glanced at me, but I shrugged. The hooded man got people talking about Sydney's pictures, but the appearances never seemed to mean much.

"You know how the fans have been," Max said. "A big reveal. The power of the hooded man. Sydney said that the mesmerist picture would do that. But then he said that he had to film here. All the right occult signs and so on. It's been hard to pin Sydney down. You know what he's like."

Betsy patted his hand. "I'm sure that nobody blames you, Max. Everyone knows how hard you work to stop Sydney spending money."

Max shook his head. "It's not the expenses. It's the other promises Sydney made to the studio. That this picture will be the one. He had better be right this time. The studio knows that I can keep the money under control."

Fred and I both laughed at that. Nobody could ever stop Sydney from spending, certainly not gentle Max with his perpetual lines of worry carving his forehead. Most people thought Max had been with us forever, but he was actually the third attempt by the studio to organize Sydney. The first one lasted through two pictures but fainted nearly as much as Maggie at the sight of blood. Real faints too, unlike Maggie, even though the blood had been fake. The second kept trying to get Sydney to sign invoices, usually right when Sydney was in the middle of reading reviews out loud or doing other activities he enjoyed more. Sydney banned him from all sets for all time. Max had been a relief. He never argued with Sydney, and he was even mildly useful during filming with the managing of the slate and his perpetual note taking.

"Enjoy your dinner," Fred said to all of us, "and don't worry about Sydney's plans. He'll tell us when he feels like telling us."

"Excuse me," said a woman seated at the next table, "but did you say that you are staying at the Fitzmaurice house?" Dark-haired and closer to Florie's age than mine, she had a careworn face, with noticeable circles under the eyes, and the slight squint of a woman who spent a lot of time with her nose in a book. But there was something compelling about her gaze as well.

Since I was sitting closest to her, I answered, "Yes, we're staying there. We're making a movie with Sydney Fitzmaurice."

"Oh, yes," she said. "I knew Sydney. I was teaching a course at Miskatonic University when he directed a play with an amateur theater troupe. A very odd play. It killed one of my students."

I blinked, certain that I had misheard her. The woman swiveled away from me to pour cream in her coffee. She stared into the cup and refused to meet my eyes. I had the distinct feeling that she deliberately ignored me. I turned to Fred to ask if he had overheard what she said, but was interrupted by Florie's return. She thumped down the plates, distracting me from my contemplation of the stranger at the next table. The fried chicken smelled wonderful. Then she turned to the woman who had spoken to me. "Need anything else, professor? How about a little dessert?"

"No, nothing," said the woman, standing up. She collected her handbag and moved toward the cash register.

As she passed my chair, she looked straight at me again and said, "Be careful."

The others didn't notice, being busy with a debate about how much they could eat and still have room for pie. Betsy declared that she was willing to leave half her chicken on her plate if it meant she could have cherry pie. Fred, of course, said that he'd eat her dinner and his, and manage two pieces of pie. For a small man, he was perpetually hollow. He claimed it came from too many years of trying to eat inedible army food.

Their laughter and chatter shook me out of the anxiety caused by the stranger's remarks. I decided that she surely couldn't have meant that Sydney actually killed someone. She must have mixed up the man with one of his movie plots. People did that, thinking what they saw on the screen was real.

"Are you going to eat that?" Fred said, pointing his fork at my pile of mashed potatoes.

"Every bite," I declared. And I did.

When Florie came back to clear our plates and take orders for dessert, I asked her who the woman was.

"That's Professor Krosnowski," said Florie. "She teaches at Miskatonic. Knows all sorts of interesting stories."

"What kind of stories?"

Florie shifted the plates around so they rested on her hip. "All types. Quite a bit about the town and the families who built it. People like my grandmother's great-something granny. She was supposed to have been a Salem witch."

"There's more than a few of those around," said Fred, recalling Eleanor's claim when she first arrived.

"Reckon it's true," said Florie. "Women in my family have some peculiar talents, that's for sure."

"So were the Fitzmaurices one of these founders?" I asked.

"The Fitzmaurice family? No, latecomers they are. Arrived well after the Revolutionary War. Didn't even send the British packing in 1812," said Florie.

I thought about my parents, who hadn't arrived in Oakland until 1897, and wondered what Florie would call them. "So your family has been in Arkham longer than the Fitzmaurices?"

"Oh, yes," she said. "Earliest was Remember Wilson. She arrived in Arkham by the 1770s. Now there's Wilsons all over New England. Probably isn't a town within a hundred miles where I couldn't find some kin, even if it is only names carved on a tombstone."

"Really?" said Betsy. "Imagine knowing your history that far back. All I know is that my grandmother worked in a shirt factory and my mother decided that sewing wasn't for her. So she married a tailor. Said he could do the hemming at work and at home."

"Smart woman," said Florie. "Yeah, there's many in Arkham that know their family history. Sometimes a little too well, I think. Old grudges have a habit of lingering, if you know what I mean."

None of us had a good answer to that, since we all lived in a city where new people arrived daily, so we gave Florie our orders for pie. Three apples and one cherry for Betsy. The pie came out just as a number of people entered the diner. Suzie was released from her exile amid the greasy dishes. Both women bustled around the tables for several minutes.

Keeping her promise for coffee on the house, Florie returned to refill the cups and, as she put it, take a breath. She plopped the pot on an uncleared table and swung a chair around. "This is my break and if any of you have a cigarette, I'll thank you kindly for it," she said. "I'm fresh out."

Max handed over his case. Florie "la di dahed" when she saw the gold-plate engraved with Max's initials. Like his suits, Max's cigarette case was the best quality. He kept it stocked with Chesterfields. "Very pretty," she said, knocking out a cigarette with an expert twist. Fred provided the match. "My mother never did approve of ladies smoking," said Florie, "but then I never claimed to be a lady. I figured with you being theater type folk, you wouldn't mind."

We all assured her that we didn't. I never liked to smoke but it was common enough around a set. "Now tell me," said Florie. "What is Sydney doing back in Arkham?"

"How long has he been gone?" I said.

"Oh, it's been a long time," Florie answered. "He left in 1912, no, it was later than that. Summer of 1913. I remember that because my mother always claimed thirteen was an unlucky number and an unlucky year it was. Also it was right on a hundred years since the Fitzmaurice family built the first house."

"The house was built in 1813?" asked Max. "It doesn't feel that old."

"It's not," said Florie. "They cleared the land and started building in 1813. The woods and a little house burned down in 1818. Then the big house went in the 1823 fire. It was the second fire that killed the first Fitzmaurice, the one with the funny name who had been a soldier in Napoleon's army. They were lucky to save his portrait and papers. One of the maids got the children out with a handful of treasures that Fitzmaurice handed her. He went back for his wife and neither made it out. At least that's how my family remembered it. Took his son right out of the maid's arms and filled her hands with things, made his children carry his treasures too, so the story goes. Later the son rebuilt the house. Been Fitzmaurices on French Hill ever since."

"But Fitzmaurice died in the fire?" asked Max, clearly fascinated with all this gossip.

"Oh yes, he never came out. According to the maid, he went running up the stairs with his sword held high to find his wife."

"His sword?" I asked, remembering the blackened blade hanging beneath the portrait.

"Oh yes. They say that's all they ever found of him and his wife. Just the sword with his hand clinging to it."

"Just the hand?" squealed Betsy.

Florie nodded. "Everything else was burnt clean away."

Fred looked at me. "Didn't Sydney do that in *Winter's Rags*?"

"He did," I said. Max looked puzzled. I remembered that the studio sent him to us after that film. Sydney had just banished his second assistant and went a little wild over how he was going to tell a story in a new way. We'd filmed most of it on a stage, but Sydney wanted real snow and insisted on a day long drive into the mountains. Where we found mostly rain and rocks.

Betsy nodded. "That's the one where poor Selby broke his leg."

"He slipped," I said to Max, "and fell down a ravine. Fred and Jim pulled him out."

"And Jeany held him flat in the truck bed all the way down the mountain," Fred added.

That had been a true nightmare, with Selby moaning at every bump and me sure that we'd crippled him for life. He did have a nasty limp after that but found work in cowboy movies doing character parts.

"Well, my heavens," said Florie. "I never knew that filming was so dangerous."

"It can be," said Fred. "We try to keep it safe. But Selby was a fool, always just following Sydney's directions and not thinking about what he was being asked to do. I told him that the rocks were too slippery."

Fred worked harder than anyone to keep us safe. Besides being a wizard at figuring out the optical illusions that Sydney wanted, he wasn't afraid to point out when Sydney's ideas might cause problems. He nearly quit one time when Sydney wanted to send his hero up in a hot air balloon with no ropes anchoring it to the ground. Given that the actor didn't have any experience with flying, Fred refused to crank the camera unless a rope was attached or an experienced balloonist added to the scene.

"It's odd," said Betsy, "that Sydney would use something from his own family history, something like a dead hand."

"Sounds like Sydney to me," I said. "Renee always calls

him a magpie for stories. He picks up pieces everywhere and adds them into his films. It's part of his extreme realism. Don't you listen to his lectures?" Of course, *Winter's Rags* had been the most extreme of Sydney's attempts at realism and also one of the few flops that we'd made in the last five years. Renee's part as the mysterious wife of the lost soldier never made much sense. The audience was confused about the ending too, with the soldier vanishing into a fire while staring at the reflection of a hooded man.

"By the time Sydney starts talking about the scenario, I'm usually too busy writing down figures to listen to his lectures," said Max.

Betsy giggled. "Nobody can listen to Sydney all the way through. Remember the time that he started to lecture us about the daily torture of mediocrity and the lure of mutability. Nobody understood him."

"He got that from his grandpa," said Florie. "I remember him, toward the end. Old Mister Fitzmaurice used to rent a lecture hall and talk about his days in the theater. About how he knew the Booth brothers when he was young and how they were going to change the world. He'd go on and on about some play even greater than *Julius Caesar*, about something in Egypt."

I asked: "*Antony and Cleopatra*?"

Florie stood up and shook her head. "That doesn't sound right. It was two women's names. You'll have to ask Professor Krosnowski sometime. She'd remember. It's the same play that Sydney directed, his last year at the University."

"The one that caused a fire," I said, remembering the woman's strange comments to me earlier that evening.

"That's it," said Florie, grinding out the last of her cigarette in an abandoned saucer. "Back to work!" She collected all our dishes in a teetering pile. The bell over the door rang, and a young man walked in. Florie shrugged a shoulder at him, her hands being full of dirty plates. "Darrell, it's been awhile," she said. "These folks are working on that movie that you were talking about."

Darrell came up to us. "Are you with the Fitzmaurice production? Do you know Renee Love?"

I blinked at his enthusiasm as he pumped the hands of Max and Fred.

"Darrell Simmons, *Arkham Advertiser*," he said. "I'd be thrilled to take a few pictures for our paper. Especially Miss Love. She's a favorite." He blushed a little. "Um, I mean she's a favorite with our readers. Everyone knows that Sydney Fitzmaurice is from Arkham. They always show his movies at the theater. And, of course, Miss Love is a great star. I saw *The Net of the Siren* seven times. I hear that *Nightmare at the Circus* is even better."

Betsy smiled and pumped his hand right back. "It's a doozy," she said. "I played Miss Love's dresser. There's this scene where she rides a white horse round and round. Then the hero dreams that his death is riding for him. Everyone comments on that."

Fred and I exchanged glances. Besides the mishap of the mirrored costume, the actor playing the hero had been terrified of horses. Sydney kept making Renee ride straight at him until the poor man, shaking and sweating in his seat, finally yelled and ran away. None of us had been happy with how Sydney treated poor Rodolfo.

Once Darrell learned that Betsy was an actress, he ignored the rest of us and peppered her with questions. It was a relief. I never knew quite how to talk about Renee to a stranger like that, and always was afraid that I'd say too much. Or not enough. Betsy loved to "play the baloney card" as she called bantering with reporters. She spun fantastic tales of highly unlikely adventures. Betsy might have been just a bit player in 1923, but she had ambition and she could turn on a glowing smile when it was her turn to shine.

Betsy agreed to being photographed at the diner so Darrell could have a picture of the movie stars stepping out in Arkham. She beamed and twirled on one of the counter stools while Max, Fred, and I stayed in the background. Darrell even put her behind the counter with Florie, pretending to pour cups of coffee for a bewildered pair of old men trying to eat their dinner. Florie was very pleased with all the attention and reminded Darrell twice to send over copies for her and Velma.

As we walked out into the cooling night air, Florie had one last snap at Suzie. "See, told you that they'd be good for business," she said. "Next time, be polite when strangers come through the door. You'll get better tips, too."

Darrell held the car doors for Betsy and me, hanging through the open window to ask if he could take pictures at the Fitzmaurice house. Max told him to come by in a day or so, and he'd see what could be done.

"Oh, that would be swell," said Darrell. "My editor is going to love this. She's always after me for more society pages stuff."

"What do you usually do?" I said.

He paused, an odd look crossing his face that made him suddenly seem much older. "Well, there's stories in Arkham that not everyone likes to hear." He lifted his camera up. "Or see. I try to be honest. I think that helps anyone who runs into something that they don't understand. But my editor keeps saying folks want happy stories too."

Betsy reached through the car window. "Well Sydney's films aren't always happy, but they do have glamour. Wait until you see us in Jeany's costumes. We look swell."

Darrell blinked at Betsy's informality and then nodded. "Photos of Miss Love in her new costumes. That will be something."

"He better take a few of Lulu too," said Betsy as we pulled away. "Or we'll hear shrieking."

"I'll make sure that both of them are wearing something wonderful," I said. "And, Max, you better let Sydney know. He'll want his picture to be in the paper too."

We arrived back at the house to find it plunged into darkness. Going through the door, only a single candle lit the downstairs hallway. The multiple narrow mirrors lining the hall reflected the faint light and made our shadows overlap into a bulbous shape with elongated tentacles.

A shout from Sydney roused us from where we had paused in the doorway. "Fred!" he bellowed. "Is that you? Did you call the power plant?"

Fred led the way into the living room where the crew was gathered around a number of oil lamps. In the grate, a smoking fire, lit more for light than warmth, added to the flickering shadows around the wall.

"What happened?" I asked Renee.

"Sydney was talking about the script and all the lights went out," she answered. "We staggered about and found some candles. Paul tried to fix the fuse but failed. Then Hal went upstairs and fetched the oil lamps out of the bedrooms. After that, he, Paul, and Jim went out for a walk. I think they took a flask with them and some cigarettes."

"Sounds like those guys," I said. When things got chaotic, the actors were good at sliding out the door for a long smoke and quick nip. They'd return when things calmed down.

"Yes," said Eleanor, from her chair. "All very effective drama, that blackout. But we still haven't finished the scenario for tomorrow's filming."

"Are we moving past the entrance to the house?" I said.

"Oh, yes," Renee answered. "That's done."

I refrained from saying anything more, like, "Thank heavens." In the kitchen, I could hear Sydney, Fred, and Max mumbling something about fuses. Drawers clashed open and shut. Sydney yelled, "When am I going to have light again? I need light. Eleanor and I need to write. We cannot write in the darkness."

"I thought he liked the candles," I whispered to Renee, who rolled her eyes.

"Not after he stubbed a toe trying to walk across the room," she whispered back.

Lulu looked immensely bored. She teased her pug with the end of her scarf. "Filming seems so slow to me," she said. "Imagine taking a whole day to walk up a set of stairs."

"And there weren't even very many stairs," Renee murmured. I pinched her shoulder. Last thing we needed was to start a row again. She shrugged me off.

Eleanor spread out some notes on the table, shifting the lamp so she could see the pages more clearly. "Now that the doomed sisters Camilla and Cassilda have returned to their ancestral home…" she began.

"Are they doomed?" said Lulu. "Isn't one going to escape? The audience does like a happy ending."

"According to Sydney's notes, they are fated to disrupt the cosmos with their doom. That does not sound like a happy ending to me, dear." Eleanor squinted a bit more at Sydney's scrawl. "Although it's not clear that anyone dies."

Renee offered "Sydney doesn't necessarily spell out what happens after. He loved *The Turn of the Screw*. He thinks all endings should fire the imagination the way that James did."

"Oh, yes," Eleanor said. "I saw a copy of *Two Magics* in the library room. I always thought the governess was the most dreary of creatures. If it had been me, I would have locked both the brats in their room and left the house immediately."

"Perhaps she had nowhere else to go," I said.

"Any woman of intelligence can find some place else to go," said Eleanor. "By the time I was seventeen, I had learned enough to pack my bags and take the train to New York. Which must have been a great relief to Leiper's Fork. My family never knew what to do with me. Of course, they didn't approve of me reading Henry James or the Brontës. Indecent reading according to my mother. But then I'm sure that there were parts of the Bible that would have widened her eyes if she had ever read them."

"You didn't like *Jane Eyre* either, darling," said Lulu. "And you were positively vituperative about Heathcliff. How can anyone not adore Heathcliff?"

I tried not to show my surprise that Lulu knew English literature or could use "vituperative" in a sentence. With her wavy blonde curls and feathery scarves, I assumed that the *Argos* was as heavy reading as she ever did. Then I decided that I was no Sherlock Holmes, able to judge people correctly at a glance. I'd need to know more about Lulu to guess at her tastes in literature.

"I prefer Brontë to James," said Eleanor to her lover, "but you are right. Give me Louisa May Alcott any day, even though those March girls were damn Yankees."

"*Little Women,*" I said with a smile. "But not as good as *Anne of Green Gables.*"

"Interesting choice," said Eleanor looking at me. "Did you want to be Anne, red hair and all?"

"No," I said. "I like my hair. And my eyes." More than once in the orphanage, I'd been asked if I wanted to look different. Truth is, I never did. I knew who I was when I looked into the mirror, my mother's daughter.

Eleanor nodded. "Good for you. Too many women try to batter themselves into a shape that they can never have."

More crashing came from the kitchen and then a shout of triumph from Sydney. Someone must have found the fuses.

"So," said Eleanor, "Sydney wants a shocking scene that suggests the mansion hides many secrets."

"They could be forced to sit in darkness, waiting for the lights to come on," suggested Renee.

"That lacks a certain amount of suspense," said Eleanor.

"How about family portraits coming to life? A suggestion of ancient history haunting them?"

I looked up to the shadowy portrait of the first Fitzmaurice. His face was mostly bare. Jim sported luxuriant mustaches as the chauffeur. With his false whiskers removed and some shadowing on his cheekbones and around his eyes, we could make him into a fair match for the picture. An old coat could be dressed up with some braid and buttons to appear like the uniform jacket.

"I wonder if there's an attic," I said. "And trunks of old family clothes. We could use that to mimic the portraits. There's a couple of women in the other room."

"Sydney's mother and grandmother, I think," said Eleanor. "I noticed them too. We could move this gentleman into that room. Easier to have all three together."

"Betsy can be the younger woman and Pola the older," I agreed.

"Now how do we make them ghosts?" Eleanor mused, jotting notes on a blank page.

"Makeup. Cheesecloth. We stop the film and restart it. Fred can splice it together afterward. We sell the audience on the impression that they've seen more than we have shown. Sydney will have Fred concentrate on the reactions of Renee and Lulu," I said. Nothing new in these techniques but all of it reliable for building a mood of unease in the opening scenes.

"Yes," said Renee. "Lulu can scream."

"I can faint too," said Lulu, perking up and looking interested. "That slow crumple that I did for *His Bloody Hands*. Do you remember, Eleanor?"

"It made the audience gasp," said Eleanor. Seeing our skepticism, she added. "It did. Lulu can faint."

"Oh, good," said Betsy. "Our regular fainter Maggie stayed behind."

Suddenly it seemed like we could all work together. Even Pola, carefully counting her stitches by the fire, looked interested and cheerful.

Then the side brackets snapped on and we saw the dead bird.

CHAPTER SIX

A crow lay on the windowsill. When the lights were out, the black feathers blended into shadows. Pola stowed away her knitting. She walked over to it and looked down. "The neck is broken," she said. "It must have flown into the window."

"From the inside?" said Renee. She didn't get up. She never liked dead animals or birds. It was one of the reasons that we never kept any pets. We had a kitten once. Finding it dead on the back porch of Mrs Ryan's boarding house made Renee weep for a week.

"It probably flew in and then became confused. I'm surprised it didn't brain itself on one of the mirrors," said Eleanor.

Sydney, Fred, and Max returned from the kitchen carrying a triumphal bottle of wine and several glasses. The wine bottles had come up out of the cellar when we'd first arrived. Despite Sydney's assurances that his grandfather's stash was drinkable, the average was two bottles of vinegar to one bottle of mediocre red or slightly bitter white. At the rate we were progressing through it, we needed to find the local bootlegger soon.

"Problems solved," Sydney said. "Fred found the fuses. Max found the corkscrew."

"And we found a dead crow," said Renee, pointing at the cold mound of feathers on the windowsill.

Sydney went over to take a closer look. Unlike Renee, he adored dead things. His apartment was full of bits of taxidermy, some of it game that he claimed to have shot, as well as creatures turned into occult objects. Sydney even showed us a lion's head once, claiming he bagged it on a safari, but on closer questioning admitted that it was an old circus beast that he had stuffed and mounted

I had expected similar objects in the Fitzmaurice house. But other than a wistful grouping of poker-playing frogs under glass that had belonged to Sydney's grandmother, the place was remarkably free of dead things and occult relics. Perhaps Sydney's obsession with such objects had been picked up during his travels.

"Ah, a winged harbinger of death," said Sydney.

"A dead crow," repeated Renee. "You take it out."

He left the glasses on the table. Cradling the crow in his hands, Sydney seemed fascinated by the dead bird.

"Sydney," said Renee. "Eleanor suggested ghosts for the next scene."

"Excellent," said Sydney, still staring at the crow. "It is a good time to start haunting, with ways opening into the house. Max, I told you this picture would work better in Arkham."

We all looked at Max, who frowned at Sydney. "You said you could do this anywhere."

Sydney looked up from the crow. "Of course, I'm Sydney

Fitzmaurice, I can make pictures wherever I am. But this will work, Max."

"We need more costumes," said Renee.

"Something for Pola, Betsy, and Jim to turn them into ghosts," I said.

"Oh there's piles of old clothes in the attic," said Sydney. "Use whatever you find. Grandfather was an actor and never could throw away a costume. I stored a few things up there from my theater days at the University too."

"Wonderful," said Renee. "Now let's discuss how to make the library properly haunted. I like Eleanor's portrait idea."

Sydney opened a window and dropped the crow outside. "Humbert will clean it up in the morning," he said.

We poured the wine and found it drinkable, and spent the rest of the evening talking about how to haunt the Fitzmaurice house.

CHAPTER SEVEN

The next morning I sorted through the extra set of keys kept hanging by the back door and found some room keys. Two or three looked promising and I eased them off the ring. Then I climbed to the top of the house. The locked door at the end of the corridor, near where Pola and Betsy slept, did not lead to another room. Instead, opening when I tried the second key, it revealed a narrow little staircase leading upwards. "Attics," I said to myself with satisfaction. While playing croquet the previous day, I had spotted a small round window at the top of one roof peak. I had been certain that it marked an attic window.

Indeed it did. The attic stretched the length of the house, but only the one window gave it any light. The splintery boards of the floor were almost completely hidden beneath piles of boxes and broken furniture.

Remembering what Sydney said about old clothes and costumes, I looked for trunks. Shoving aside a crate of mismatched teapots, pitchers, and cracked saucers, I found a large old-fashioned steamer trunk. Although it was locked, someone had thoughtfully tied the key to a handle with a bit of string. I pulled it free and released a cloud of dust when I dragged the heavy lid open. Inside were a number of dresses and hats, all neatly sheathed in muslin. I set the cloth to one side, as it might be used in any number of ways, and pulled out the dresses. These were a near match to the style worn by Sydney's mother in her portrait. I picked one or two that could be easily altered to fit Betsy.

Worming my way through the boxes and broken chairs, I found a bulbous trunk, strapped closed rather than locked. It provided the skirts and blouses necessary for making the grandmother's ghost. The full petticoats that would have held the skirts wide were missing. But I could rig up something for Pola that would suffice for a short scene. Considering the grey and purple mourning colors of these skirts, I thought about draping the muslin over them to achieve a lighter, more ghostly effect.

A third trunk looked more promising for gentlemen's clothes, but it was locked and had no key. I poked through a few more boxes but nothing caught my eye. Eventually I grabbed a large wicker hamper with broken leather handles. Bundling my finds into it, I dragged the lot to the top of the stairs. With a little pushing and pulling, I thumped my way to the lower floor.

Fred came trotting up the back stairs as I maneuvered my basket toward my room.

"I thought you were rolling a body or two down the stairs," he said. "Or did you stuff it in that hamper?"

"Ghosts," I said with satisfaction. "We can dress Betsy and Pola with these pieces."

"What about Jim?"

"There's a man's trunk up in the attic. I didn't see a key but maybe you can get it open."

Fred patted his pockets and came up with a pocket knife, a screwdriver, and last night's corkscrew. "Probably can," he said. "Lead on, Macduff."

"It is 'Lay on, Macduff'," I said. We had held this discussion many times before.

"How should I know?" said Fred, as he always did. "My education ended at age twelve when I became a shoeshine boy."

"I thought you ran away to join the army," I said.

"I was so good at polishing shoes, the army drafted me later," said Fred. "To keep the generals all shiny."

Whatever his past, or because of it, Fred did know how to break a lock. After a few minutes of tinkering, he popped open the trunk. Inside were a stack of old leather-bound journals and an odd assortment of men's clothes. By age and style, it looked like the coats and pants of two different men bundled together. Unlike the women's clothes that I had found, these had been carelessly packed and were heavily creased. I spread them across the boxes, trying to find something that could be made into a uniform jacket for Jim. Nothing looked quite right, although one cutaway coat might work for Hal if we needed him to play a doctor.

Fred kept burrowing through the boxes behind the trunk. I could track him across the attic by his sneezes and the occasional swear word as he knocked into something hard or sharp. "Hey, Jeany, this might work," he said, squirming back into the small cleared space where I stood. In his hands was a uniform coat that looked to be of Civil War vintage. It was dark blue and the buttons were all missing. Stray threads hung from the sleeves and shoulders. Still, with braid stolen from a few curtains downstairs and some buttons from the other coats, it might do. I could cut into a woman's fur tippet that was in one of the other trunks and drape it across the shoulders to match the cape effect of the portrait.

"We'll need to hide Jim behind the women," I said. "It's a crude match."

"If we just show his head and shoulders, it will be fine," said Fred.

I looked around the attic. A broken picture frame about the same size as those downstairs leaned against an equally shattered chair. The outside edges of the frame were scorched but still visible were the same type of hieroglyphics as encircled the mirrors in the main hallway. The portrait in the center was hacked away but the oval hole gave me an idea.

"We could paint this up," I said, hefting the frame out of the stack of broken furniture where it rested. "And put Jim behind it."

"Shoot him through the frame?" said Fred. "Yeah, I like that. The frame is a close match to those downstairs."

"In the long shots, show the real painting," I said.

"And in close-ups Jim's head and shoulders," Fred nodded. "We could even have him move slightly."

"Then all the ghosts step off the wall into the room," I said.

"I think we film all of them through this," said Fred, holding the picture frame up and peering through it at my head and shoulders. "Film the paintings in the same spot. And then film them again outside the empty frame. It's a stop trick, simple enough."

Although the stop trick was an old technique, almost nobody could do it as well as Fred. In an earlier film he'd turned Renee into a tree and back again, when Sydney wanted a murderous dryad. By lining up the shot carefully and paying absolute close attention to the light angles and shadows, Fred could make anyone appear, disappear, or transform by altering just one or two elements in the scene.

"It will give Eleanor the look that she wants," I said. "But we need another stop trick later, when we film the scene with the mask. To make Renee's face appear and disappear. Too much of the same thing in one film?"

One of the things that kept the audiences guessing was never to repeat ourselves. It's why Sydney never did the same type of plot twice in a row, even in his sequels. If we had ghosts in one film, then it was sure to be mythological monsters in the next. Similarly, we tried not to use too many of the same scares. Shadows, stop tricks, a bloody hand, they were all good. But show them too often and the audience grew to expect it and even laugh at the effect. Fred and I joked one time that we should deliberately do some grotesque trick repeatedly, just to make the audience laugh. "I'm not sure that the world is ready for horror comedy," said Renee. But she would have been brilliant at it, with her ability to evoke laughter as well as gasps. It was something that Sydney never quite understood, as he believed that his terror pictures should be serious and evoke a breathless reaction in his audience.

Fred hitched the picture frame over his shoulder. "I'll take this out to the barn to paint," he said. "And think about the mask. Have you made it yet?"

"No," I said. "I have so many sketches, but nothing looks right."

"Something simple," Fred said. "That always works best." He was right. The more elaborate the prop, the more it could and often did look poorly made. Simple objects often photographed better.

I knelt before the trunk that Fred had forced open, rooting under the clothes and journals to see if there was anything else I could use. Something cold and metallic shifted under my hand. I reached in and pulled out a dull black mask. "Fred, look at this. It looks like an old tragedy mask. It must have belonged to Sydney's actor grandfather." It was so heavy that I couldn't imagine anyone wearing it, but it could have hung on a wall as a decoration.

Fred squinted at the mask in my hand. "It's not silver."

"Paint," I said. "Light colors. If the title card says it is a silver mask, that's what the audience will believe."

Fred nodded.

"We can make this look like silver," I insisted. "And make a second one out of silver paper that's transparent enough that a shadow of Renee's face can be seen through it. Especially with the right backlighting." With the light behind Renee but pointing towards the camera, the material should appear to glow around the edges. Twist the light a little to the side and a suggestion of Renee's face should be visible.

"Two masks," said Fred. "That's a good idea."

I stashed the basket full of old clothes in my room, intending to work on them later, and followed Fred out of the house to the small barn that currently stored our touring automobile and an old-fashioned lawn mowing machine. I'd seen the hired man, Humbert Welles, leading a mule up the drive two days ago to pull the creaky contraption and reduce the grass to a neatly trimmed length, suitable for playing croquet.

After mowing, Humbert led the mule away, back to the farm that housed it, but came by each day to see if "Mr Sydney" had any more work for him.

Humbert made the unlikely claim that his mother had named him for a prince. If she had hoped for something charming, she'd failed. He was, as Eleanor put it, "the most dolorous sort, who looked as if he spent his life sucking lemons and eating prunes." Tall too, topping both Fred and me by nearly two feet, and so skinny that Pola declared that he disappeared when he turned sideways. He had exceptionally knobby wrists and ankles, clearly visible with his too-short sleeves and trousers. Fred kept telling me that we could use him for a rendition of Frankenstein's monster if Sydney ever decided to film that story.

We found Humbert in the barn. He reluctantly agreed that there might be some white paint stored in the back that could be used for what we wanted. But why we wanted to paint up that fire-blackened frame and old mask baffled him. "Nothing but rubbish," Humbert rumbled above our heads.

"Props," I explained.

Humbert took the frame from Fred. Squinting at it, he shook his head slowly. "That went around the portrait of Mrs Fitzmaurice, the one that died in the fire."

"Sydney's mother?" I said. I hadn't heard that, but I was beginning to realize for all that Sydney talked about himself, he never said much about his family's long history in Arkham.

"Nah," said Humbert. "The first one. The one that died when the house burned down."

"We heard about that," I said. "The 1823 fire?"

"Yup. Nearly one hundred years ago exactly. The solstice fire."

"The solstice fire?" I hadn't heard that before.

"Yup. June 22, 1823. That's the fire where they found the first Mr Fitzmaurice's hand. And this picture frame, with the picture all burned up. She was supposed to have been a pretty little lady, all dark hair and wide eyes, like your Miss Renee."

"Ah," said Fred. "So they found this after the fire along with the old man's hand."

"And the sword," said Humbert. "That's still up at the house. And his picture too. That Mr Fitzmaurice made the maid take that out. But her picture was lost."

It was the story that Florie told. Apparently everyone in Arkham knew about the maid rescuing the Fitzmaurice portrait.

"Odd the frame survived the fire," I said, turning it over again to see why the wood hadn't burned. The feel of it, hard and cold, gave me a clue. "I don't think this is wood," I said to Fred.

"It was heavy," he agreed, taking it back from me and scraping a little at the charred edges. With an application of his pocketknife, he was able to lift enough paint off it to show the dull green metal beneath.

"Copper?"

Fred shook his head. "Maybe. Or an old bronze. It's strange, not like any metal I've seen before."

Humbert also took a closer look. "One of the first Mr Fitzmaurice's finds. Unlucky things he dug out of that grave in Egypt. Mr Sydney's granddaddy made quite a fuss about them. Went round and round the house collecting them up when I was a boy. Made me polish a few, too."

Fred took his knife to the mask, chipping off what appeared to be more soot than paint to reveal the same type of greenish brown metal.

"Humbert, how long have you been here?" I said.

"Well, now," he said, rubbing the back of his neck, "I've been working round the house since I could toddle. My auntie cleaned for Mr Sydney's mother and so did my other auntie. And my sister for a time, until she married that Innsmouth fellow. My cousin Florie never liked cleaning. She went to high school and got an education. Now she waits tables at Velma's."

"So there's artifacts from Egypt in that old house," I said.

"Yeah, quite a few. Couple times some professors came out with their students from Miskatonic University to take a look. Mr Fitzmaurice, the one that was Mr Sydney's grandfather, liked that. Sitting and talking to them about what an important man that first Mr Fitzmaurice had been and how he'd brought those treasures to Essex County."

"I wonder if this mask was part of the Egyptian find?" I said to Fred. "It doesn't look like anything I've seen called Egyptian."

Humbert shook his head at it. "Mr Fitzmaurice used to keep that in a drawer in his study. Said he had to hide it from the crows."

It sounded like Sydney's grandfather was stranger than his grandson. Neither Fred nor I could think of any response to that comment.

I said finally, "Do you think Sydney would be all right with us painting family heirlooms?"

Fred shrugged. "I doubt these are valuable or even from Egypt. The mask is probably an old stage prop. And even if the picture frame is old, it was pretty badly burned. Just junk. Sydney said to use what was in the attic. Besides, we can always clean the paint off later."

"Unlucky things in that house," said Humbert with one of his big sighs, looking at the objects that we had handed him. "Bad luck that rubs off on everyone, my aunties used to say. One of the students who came the most often went out to sea and never came back. During the War that was."

"Lots of men lost at sea during the War," said Fred.

"Anyone else?" I asked, beginning to feel very uneasy about the mask that I had just handed Humbert.

"Nothing's happened to other students, at least nothing too bad," admitted Humbert. "They all came back from the War. Couple even went to Boston to set up a medical practice. Hear others are trying to raise funds to explore Antarctica. They had a talk about that down at the library. Exploring the South Pole or some such thing."

"That's a long way from Egypt and New England," said Fred.

"Yup," said Humbert. "Can't see the appeal myself. Wouldn't mind going to Boston. But the rest is all too far away for me."

After leaving Humbert with the picture frame and the mask that he promised to paint before the end of the day, we walked back up to the house.

"They're a strange lot," I said.

"Who?" said Fred.

"The Fitzmaurices and the rest of this town."

"Isn't that what they think of us?" said Fred.

I stopped, looking at the lawn mowed so neatly by a machine that was twice my age, and down to the hedges that surrounded the property. Over the hedge top, I could see the occasional peak or gable of a fine mansion, houses that had been sitting on French Hill for one hundred years or more. But I couldn't see more than that. And certainly nobody could see us. It was as if we were all alone on an island, far away from other people, even though we were in Arkham. "It's all so old," I said.

"In Paris they'd laugh to hear you call this little town old," said Fred. "I went out for a walk one night, just a ramble because I figured this boy from Brooklyn ought to see what made everyone claim that we wouldn't want to go home again after we saw Paris."

"And what did you find?"

"It's old. Real old. True old. What Sydney would call ancient. And for once, he would be right. There's parts of New York that I thought were there forever. But you walk through Paris and you realize that everything we've built since George Washington crossed the Delaware is brand spanking new compared to the streets of Paris."

"So what?" I said. "That's Europe. It's supposed to be old. It's like my mother's stories of China, where you could visit your village's graveyard and find a hundred generations."

"Now wouldn't that be something?" said Fred.

"Maybe. Maybe not. My mother didn't want to stay there. And her family were happy to sell her to a bride merchant who was smuggling girls to Chinese men who couldn't get married here." They did not call it selling to my mother, but she saw her parents receive money from the man. When she talked to the other girls on the ship, she realized that they'd all been promised the same thing: a young, rich, handsome man from their village who would marry them and let them live like an empress. Being of a skeptical turn of mind, my mother doubted that many rich young Chinese men lived in America and wondered who they'd really have for her to marry. Instead she decided to run off with the tall Swedish sailor who made her laugh when he helped her practice her English on the voyage. She'd been happy to slip away from the bride merchant and make her way to Oakland. But she never dared write to her parents back in China or even visit San Francisco across the bay where there was a proper Chinese groom waiting for her. As far as I know, my father never wrote to his family in Filipstad either, to tell them that he'd settled in California with a Chinese bride and made his living working on the small ships that carried goods up and down the coast.

"That's it," I said to Fred as if he could hear me thinking through all my family history, the very small bit that I knew well. Being Fred, he waited for me to explain and maybe did understand, a little. "That's what's so odd about Arkham. Where we come from, Brooklyn or Oakland, nobody knows a hundred years of family history. Oh, they might know a parent's or a grandparent's tales coming from somewhere else. But they don't know their history back to when Benjamin Franklin tied a key to a kite and flew it through a thunderstorm. They don't have the kite sitting in a box in their attic, just waiting for somebody to talk about how crazy old Ben was."

"I don't remember seeing a kite in the attic," said Fred, trying to kid me out of my mood.

"Doesn't mean that it isn't there," I replied, remembering all the boxes and bags that we'd left behind. "But it gives me the shivers, how they all talk about these people long dead. Humbert, and Florie, and even Sydney. Talking about things that happened almost a hundred years ago as if it just happened. As if the first Fitzmaurice sat down with them and told them about losing his hand in that solstice day fire."

"Bit like being haunted," said Fred.

I looked around again at the garden enclosed by high hedges, and the tops of mansions like old-fashioned tombs looming in the distance. "More like living in the graveyard all the time," I said. "And the Fitzmaurices and other Arkham families never leave. They never want to go anywhere else." It really was like being trapped on an island, one where the past never let a person go.

"Sydney's grandfather left. Acted in New York, according to Florie," Fred protested.

"For a few years, she said. Then he came back and spent his time in that house looking at unlucky objects dug out of a tomb."

"According to Humbert. Who takes a pretty dim view of everything. And Sydney left too. For ten years. Now he's back," said Fred. "But he's only back to make this film. Then he's off to the next one. You know Sydney. As soon as it's in the can, he'll be dreaming up vampire ladies or ungodly doings in a crypt."

Fred did not see Arkham quite the same as me.

The hedges leaned in, I realized. Not a great deal. Just enough to make it clear that their purpose was as much to keep people inside the grounds as to protect the house from strangers. Or to hide the house from prying eyes. To keep the Fitzmaurice family and their doings invisible from the rest of Arkham. Except Arkham had a very long memory.

"I don't know Sydney," I said, and realized it was true. "I know the man that he's pretending to be. The one that the press wants him to be, the one that the studio wants him to be." The one that my sister said loved her. "I don't know the Sydney that Arkham remembers."

"And do you need to know Arkham's version of Sydney?"

"Yes," I said. "I think we do." Because a woman in a diner talked about Sydney killing someone. Because there was something wrong, very wrong, with the crooked shadows creeping across the lawn toward me. With the crows wheeling overhead and then streaming towards the woods pressed up against the back gate. We'd barely started filming but I felt like we were caught on the wrong side of the camera. That we'd all become characters in one of Sydney's horrible stories.

But I couldn't explain it properly to Fred.

"It's just the jitters," he said. "Get a few more days filming in and everyone will settle down, even Sydney. We'll know how it all turns out. Let's go move some paintings and set up the next scene. Time to put a few of Sydney's ancestors to work in the movies."

The shadows crept across the lawn. The house waited for us to return to it and start playing at hauntings within its walls. It was beyond foolish what we had done already and would do in the days to come, but it was all because we did not know enough about the Fitzmaurice family and Arkham then.

CHAPTER EIGHT

The ghost scene took a couple of days to stage but looked good by the time we were done. The paintings seemed ominous clustered together at one end of the long library room. Fred and Humbert did a little carpentry that created a false wall at one end of this grouping to hold the empty frame. Surrounded by other paintings, it deceived the eye at first glance, especially when somebody stood behind the wall and pretended to be a portrait. Paul and Jim shifted furniture around and moved in a few mirrors from the hall to reflect light from the windows. It set up much like we would at the studio, with the actors at one end and plenty of room for the camera and the rest of us behind it.

We stationed Pola, Betsy, and Jim behind the fake wall, peering through the empty frame, one after the other. Fred cranked the camera slow and steady, muttering at them if they twitched. The idea was to keep them as still as possible for this bit of fakery. Later Fred would cut the film between the long shots of the oil paintings hanging in what appeared to be the same spot and the close-ups of the trio so the audience would be convinced that the paintings turned into ghosts.

Betsy had the hardest time being still, as she was distracted by two Arkham visitors that morning.

One was Darrell, who shadowed Renee around the room, taking various photographs every time Renee paused. She wasn't happy about it. Renee wanted to concentrate on Sydney's directions as he went over his ideas for how the sisters would enter the library and be surrounded by their ghostly relations.

The other distraction was the violinist that Sydney hired to play during the scene. He'd read somewhere that United Artists were starting to use musicians to create a mood on their sets. She was a pleasant, round little lady who taught violin but also played the piano at the local movie theater, which was how Max had found her. She arrived at the house still in her Sunday best, complete with a new cloche hat, and clutching a well-used violin case.

The violinist, Virginia Murphy, listened patiently while Sydney insisted that he wanted a dreaming mood for the sequence. "It is not a nightmare," he said. "Not yet. The sisters are enthralled to see the ghosts of their ancestors. They teeter on the edge of terror, as will the audience, unable to deny the melancholy attraction of the tomb. Your music will convey that to the actresses, and they shall in turn create a living embodiment of the grief-stricken melody."

Like everyone encountering Sydney for the first time, Virginia seemed a bit overwhelmed. "Chopin?" she finally said. "His Nocturne in C Minor?"

Sydney shrugged. "If that is what you think is appropriate for ghosts."

She pulled out her violin and played a few bars.

Sydney turned to Renee.

"Does that evoke a haunting mood?" he said.

Renee crossed the room away from Darrell. "It's fine, but you know I don't need music to act," she said. Then turning to the violinist, she added, "Not that I have anything against your playing. You're very good. It was kind of you to come."

Virginia smiled. "I was so excited to be asked to work on a movie set. Everyone in town is talking about it since the *Arkham Advertiser* published that story yesterday. Florie told me about meeting you." The photos of Betsy pouring coffee in the local diner had dominated the front page of the little newspaper. "And, of course, Mr Fitzmaurice being back in town."

"Did you know Sydney when he lived here?" I asked.

Virginia continued to adjust her violin, trying out a trilling run of melodies. "Not really. I heard talk about the Fitzmaurices. Every time one of the pictures opened in the movie house, somebody would mention that Sydney Fitzmaurice came from an old Arkham family. And that his grandfather had been a very famous actor as well."

"Yes," I said. "Everyone seems to know about Sydney's grandfather. I've never heard anything about his parents." It was odd. Nobody ever mentioned anyone but the actor grandfather who was obsessed with family history and artifacts as well as the more distant ancestor who brought those objects to Arkham. It was as if the rest of the

Fitzmaurice clan were bit players in their own story. Except for Sydney. He would always insist on being center stage.

"No, I don't know much about the family," said Virginia. "I haven't lived in Arkham that long. You should ask Darrell. He writes the most curious articles, weaving the town's history into the news. Some of his stories read just like a Fitzmaurice picture."

I watched my sister dodge the eager photographer. "He's quite a fan of Renee Love."

"Oh, yes. I'd see him every time one of her movies played the theater. For the siren picture, I swear that Darrell sat in the front row the entire run," Virginia said. "I do enjoy a long run. Doing the same picture several times gives me a chance to adjust to the film. It's always much better the second or third time, when I know what's coming next."

She was right, of course. I'd seen movies done in small houses and in larger theaters where they were beginning to bring in full bands. Even with cue sheets, the music could vary wildly and the mood created didn't always match the action on the screen. Good accompanists, the best really, reacted to the film as it progressed. The worst were like that poor chap who played "Waltz Me Around Again, Willie" and "Love Me and the World is Mine" no matter what was happening on the screen.

Sydney had argued several times that the studio should pay for musicians to go out and accompany his movies from town to town, just to ensure that the mood was correct in every showing. They wouldn't do it, of course, but they did let him hire a composer and then printed sheet music to be sent around with the reels of film. The stunt had earned a certain press, especially since the composer famously jumped off a bridge and drowned after writing the music for *The Return of the Siren*.

None of which I discussed with Virginia. Instead we talked about the practicalities of living the artistic life. For as much as she adored playing the great composers, she was not above rehashing a ragtime melody or other popular song if it meant a payment at the end of the evening. "I teach and play for parties," she said. "Mostly University events. There's a few of us in town, enough for a quartet or a trio, if they want to add some dancing. Those professors, going round and round the room in a stately box waltz, it's something to see. There's one old dear, a very tall and thin Scot, with a darling plump German wife. They've been married almost fifty years. They always ask for a proper waltz to end the evening. And pay promptly, too."

"It must be nice," I said, "to live in a town where you know everyone. It's a bit like that in the studio, where we work with the same people all the time. Sydney's crew, they call us. But in Los Angeles, it seems like there's hundreds getting off at the train station every day. It's changing so quickly."

"Oh, you should see New York," said Eleanor, who left Sydney fussing over some business with Lulu. "When I got back from Europe, I couldn't believe the crowds and how they all seemed to have arrived yesterday." She turned to Virginia and held out a hand. "Eleanor Nash, writer. So here I am, having proposed that they see ghosts. Now we are all waiting for the ghosts to appear."

At her words, Virginia shivered a little. "How odd," she said. "I felt as if something cold brushed my back."

I felt it too. A chill, not like a draft, but more like some cold creature had settled on my head and then writhed slowly down my neck. Once, in the orphanage, another girl dropped a small frog down the back of my dress. The feeling was the same damp, cold touch. I tried not to shriek but whirled around, craning to glimpse my back in one of the omnipresent mirrors. Everything looked normal.

Across the room, the others made hesitant steps and glances at each other. Max, who had been moodily watching from an open door, probably calculating the expense of having a violinist on set, began slapping his back like a man suddenly overwhelmed by small creatures crawling across his skin.

Lulu screamed. Eleanor, who had been uneasily glancing over her own shoulder, twisted around. She strode over to her lover. "What is it, dear?" she said, catching Lulu's hands.

"Ugh," said Lulu. "It must have been a mouse. It ran right over my foot. I could feel its horrible little cold paws on my skin." At the edge of the room, Lulu's pug, Pumpkin, growled at something that wasn't there.

Sydney shouted for everyone's attention. "Right," he said. "Let's get started. The sisters enter the room. They hesitate in the doorway. Something chills them. A feeling of foreboding."

I shuddered as Sydney's words seemed to intensify the feeling of frogs and other creepy things crawling across my skin. The rest looked just as tormented. Only Sydney seemed immune.

"Where's that violinist? I need the music playing!" Sydney shouted.

Virginia lifted her violin and bow. Settling her instrument under her chin, she drew the bow across the strings in the same quick motions as before. But no melody emerged. Rather, it gave out an unearthly wailing noise.

Sydney blinked. "Not Chopin. But that works. Fred, begin. Renee. Lulu. To your places."

Virginia dropped her bow and said to me, "That's not what I meant to play."

"Try again," I said with as much confidence as I could. Just like the day that we arrived, I felt something, something unwelcoming, gathering in the shadows of the house. Something watching and judging, most unsatisfied with our actions and malicious in its reaction. Then I glanced across the room and saw Fred bending to the viewpiece, taking in the scene as the camera would see it. Beyond him, Betsy and Pola took their places. Jim, ordinary Jim, stepped behind the picture frame to play the ghost of an ancestor. It was all the very normal fakery of a movie set, a tale to cause the audience to shriek a little but no great threat to any of the actors I told myself, and hoped that I was not lying.

"Play. This should be fun," I said with greater confidence than I felt to the woman standing beside me.

Virginia nodded and with trembling hands began to play. This time the melody stayed true. The nocturne sounded throughout the room. Fred began cranking the camera, and its resounding clack nearly drowned out the violin. Renee entered first, heading to the end where the portraits hung. As the elder sister, Sydney informed her as she walked across the room, she must take the lead. "You are drawn to the picture!" he yelled. "You know that it reveals a terrible secret. A secret you long to know."

Lulu stepped across behind her. "You are frightened!" Sydney yelled at her. "You tremble in anticipation of what your sister will find. You fear the reveal of the stranger." Lulu stumbled a little and glanced at Sydney. "No, no," he yelled, "eyes on your sister. React, react, you stupid girl!"

"Well, that's the end of that," said Eleanor as Lulu froze in place.

"What did you say to me?" Lulu asked Sydney.

"Fred!" Sydney screamed. "Cut."

Fred stopped cranking. Renee walked back to her starting point with exaggerated care. Virginia wobbled through a few more bars of the nocturne, looked confused by the sudden lack of action and silence, and then stopped as well. We all waited for what would come next.

Lulu and Sydney lit into each other.

"Don't scream at me when I'm acting," said Lulu. "I'm trying to concentrate on my character. How can I do that when you're calling me names?"

"I am the director," Sydney reminded her. "You do what I tell you to do."

"I'm open to notes," she said. "You can give me notes when the scene is over. But during the scene, I'm working. Don't distract me."

Renee shook her head. "We do our notes while the camera is rolling. This isn't the theater where you need to stay silent for an audience."

Lulu stamped one foot. "This is ridiculous. That violin.

Sydney screaming. You walking off your line."

"I am never off my line," said Renee with chilly finality.

"Of course you are," Lulu returned. "You are supposed to be going to the first portrait of our ancestor, not the frame that Jim is hiding behind. The picture with the soldier in the stupid uniform."

"That is my great-grandfather Saturnin Fitzmaurice," Sydney said. I could hear his teeth grinding against his cigarette holder from across the room. "A descendent of French nobility."

"Well, Renee is supposed to be walking to his portrait. And why is she always entering first? And if she's supposed to be walking to it, why is the portrait over there?" Lulu pointed across the room to where the painting hung upon the wall, considerably to the left of where it should be.

"That's not right," said Fred, looking up from his camera. "I hung him with his ladies." By which he meant the old woman portrait of another Fitzmaurice, the one that Pola was playing in her broad skirts, and the empty frame that Betsy filled playing the young Madame Saturnin.

Sydney changed the story for the film, making out that his young and handsome nobleman successfully saved his child and wife, sacrificing his own life for love. At least that was how he told it to Darrell during the young reporter's interview. The part about Saturnin handing off his real children to a maid, insisting his portrait be saved, the wife burning to death, and Saturnin himself being reduced to a single charred hand, none of that came up in the tale that Sydney spun to Darrell. But he convinced Darrell that this movie was based on actual Arkham history. Darrell was nearly breathless with excitement about this "exclusive" for his newspaper.

"It's all a bit complicated, isn't it?" Virginia said to me as I whispered explanations of what was supposed to have happened next while Sydney and Lulu continued their argument.

"Sometimes Sydney changes things around. He probably moved that portrait" I said, although I couldn't remember seeing him near it at all. "Just to shake up the actors. He says it makes the reactions more real." But Sydney usually told Fred, so he knew where to point the camera. And I'd been by Fred for most of the morning and never heard any new instructions. It was all very strange.

Because now Monsieur Saturnin's real portrait was clearly exiled from the group, hanging some distance away from where we put it earlier.

"Who moved that picture?" Sydney roared.

Nobody answered. Looking around the room, everyone appeared confused. It made no sense for somebody to have moved that prop. It would have been physically difficult, too. The frame of Saturnin's portrait was made of the same metal painted over to look like gilded wood as the empty frame that we found earlier in the attic. The portrait made for a heavy burden, as Fred and I learned when we had shifted it about.

Darrell turned his camera on the portrait and snapped a few pictures. "Ghostly picture moves across the room, does it warn of doom to actors?" he intoned. Then he laughed. "That's quite a trick, Mr Fitzmaurice. You shook them up good."

Sydney looked confused for a moment, then a little shifty around the eyes. "Yes," he said, drawing it out as he considered both Dennis and Virginia, two outsiders who might tell tales around Arkham. "Never reveal all your secrets to your actors. That's the signature of a Fitzmaurice nightmare picture."

Darrell nodded eagerly, slinging his camera to one side and drawing out his notebook. "I thought so," he said with satisfaction. "Can you tell me more about what's planned for this picture? Is it a haunted house story? Is this the picture where you reveal the meaning of the hooded man?"

"Yes, darling Sydney," said Eleanor with a snap. "Do tell us what all this spookery is leading to."

"Isn't that your job, my dear Eleanor?" said Sydney. "Didn't your scenario call for the sisters to feel as if their eyes are playing tricks on them? That the ghosts of their ancestors are drawing them into a waking nightmare from which they can only be freed by a masked stranger."

Renee gave a little theatrical yawn. "Are we going to film the scene or discuss it? Sydney, if you want me to walk in a different direction, just say so. Don't make me hunt for that portrait of your ancestor."

Sydney shook his head and waved his arms in a way that he probably thought looked theatrical or authoritative. It always reminded me of a duck flapping its wings. He quacked a bit, too.

"Places, places, again. Fred," he shouted, "get ready."

Max grabbed the slate and chalk, scribbling the scene number and that it was the second take, and then held it in front of the camera.

"Action," yelled Sydney. Max whipped the slate away. Fred kept rolling, his hands as steady as clockwork on the handle of 242. No matter how flustered everyone else got, Fred always made the cranking of the camera look easy. I never once saw him miss a beat.

Renee altered her course, heading toward the portrait of the hussar, with Lulu trailing along behind her, and Sydney running parallel across the room, careful to stay out of camera range. "That's it. Go toward the portrait. Stretch out your hand. You feel as if he is about to speak, to impart great secrets if only you have the wisdom to hear his painted words."

Virginia, still looking a bit bewildered, whispered to me, "Do I start playing again?"

"You might as well," I said, although it was obvious that Sydney had forgotten all about the music teacher trying to accompany our film.

"Twelve cents a foot," muttered Max as he walked behind us. "How many takes today?"

"As many as it takes?" I said. Max winced at the almost pun.

Renee reached the portrait. She stretched up her hand. Darrell had packed away his notebook and was just watching her. It appeared that he was holding his breath. Renee's fingers lightly brushed the frame. She gave a quick little cry of pain, as if shocked by the touch.

At her cry, I started forward, almost committing the sin of getting into frame and ruining the shot. I felt a brief burst of fury, convinced Sydney was indeed playing tricks on us for a reaction. I don't know how he did the frogs and mouse feet, but he could have hidden a pin or something sharp on the frame to prick a reaction out of Renee. Directors did things like that. One even shot off a real gun on his set just to see the actors react. "How could he," I muttered, even though I'd never known Sydney to play such tricks on Renee before.

Unaware of the camera, Darrell yelled and lunged toward Renee, knocking my sister to the floor. After a brief, startled moment, we all started shouting as the portrait flew away from the wall. This time I ran toward Renee, no longer caring about the shot. The portrait of Saturnin Fitzmaurice crashed to the ground, crushing Darrell's leg under its heavy metal frame.

Lulu began to scream in earnest.

CHAPTER NINE

The doctor pronounced Darrell fit enough to go home. The leg was bruised but not broken, but she advised staying off it for a day or so.

"You've twisted that knee pretty badly," said Doctor Wills. A blunt-faced woman with a mop of frizzy hair twisted back into a bun secured by a pencil, she snapped her bag closed authoritatively. "However, you'll do."

"As long as my camera isn't broken," said Darrell, who had been more concerned about that than his leg.

We'd called the operator and she'd called Doctor Wills to the house for us. By the time the doctor arrived, Fred had Darrell settled on a couch in the parlor. A closer examination of the portrait showed no damage to the wire or the nail from which it hung. Nobody could explain how it fell on the young reporter. And no one admitted to moving it from one end of the room to the other. As for that moment when it appeared to fly through the air, well, none of us mentioned that either to the doctor or discussed it among ourselves. Darrell only said that he'd seen the picture move toward Renee when he'd jumped to intercept it.

I dragged Fred to the other room while the doctor examined Darrell and quizzed him about Sydney's instructions. He claimed, and I believed him, that Sydney never said anything about changing the scene. Which left me stumped. Why would Sydney play an elaborate hoax, especially one that might have endangered Renee, if it wasn't for a filmed reaction? For the first time, I considered if someone else had sabotaged the scene, perhaps to remove Renee altogether. I didn't want to believe that of Lulu or Eleanor. But nobody else would gain from Renee breaking an arm or leg, or even her head, when that portrait fell.

When Doctor Wills asked about the accident, Sydney came forward. He told her that a prop had fallen off the wall and struck a blow to Darrell's leg.

"I'm glad to see that you are still in practice," said Sydney, shaking her hand as she collected her things.

"Not many towns tolerate a woman doctor," she said with a shrug. "Of course, Arkham couldn't afford to be choosy after the typhoid epidemic of '05. They had trouble enough staffing the hospital. It's a decent practice now we've added that youngster McPherson to help out Simmons and me."

"Dr Simmons is making rounds too?" said Sydney. "I remember him calling on my grandfather."

"The old goat's over eighty," said Doctor Wills, "and he keeps trying to retire. But you know Arkham, never enough doctors. It's steady work. I'll send you my bill in the morning."

Max told her to address her bill to him in care of the Fitzmaurice house. "The studio will pay for any medical costs," he told Darrell.

"Won't be much," said Doctor Wills. "He'll heal quick enough. Come along, Darrell, and I'll give you a lift home. I've another patient out your way."

"I will be fine," Darrell said, waving away Renee's expressions of concern as he tried to slide off the couch. "It's been a real honor to meet you, Miss Love. And you, too, Mister Fitzmaurice. Your pictures are terrific. The way that your films show things that … that, well, I didn't know other people saw."

Fred and Max helped the limping Darrell into the doctor's battered Model T. The car belched a bit of smoke out of its exhaust pipe as it rounded the gate and took to the main road.

"Well, that's been exciting," said Sydney with a bit of a sarcastic laugh. "Now, shall we begin again? I'd like to get this scene done before it gets dark."

"Sydney," protested Lulu. "You can't ask us to go back into that room."

Sydney turned and gave her a patient look. "Of course I mean to finish this scene. The sisters must encounter their ancestors prior to discovering the mask."

At the mention of the mask, I heaved a sigh of relief that I'd found something suitable in the attic. All I had to do was make the lighter paper version to mimic it for Fred's trick shots.

"Yes, about this mask," said Eleanor. "What exactly is it meant to signify? Why do the sisters even want it?"

"Without the mask, the transformation cannot be complete," said Sydney. "It's all there in the script."

"And about that manuscript," said Eleanor, "it would

be helpful if you simply gave it to me. I could write all the scenarios."

Sydney waved her off. "First, let us finish this scene. Fred, where's Fred?"

"Here," said Fred, who had been hanging the portrait of Sydney's ancestor in the correct location for filming. "Are we starting from the top?"

"I think we must," said Sydney. "So many interruptions. Where is that violinist?"

Virginia stepped away from Sydney as he swung toward her. "I am sorry, Mr Fitzmaurice, but I must be going. I have a music lesson across town. Yes, that's it. A music lesson. One of my best pupils. I cannot be late." Despite her interest earlier, she now looked slightly desperate to be away. She kept edging toward the door as she talked.

"What's this? You are leaving? Surely we'd agreed that you'd stay until the scene was done." Sydney motioned to Max. "Max, Max, pay this woman something extra so she can skip her music lesson."

Max tried not to look horrified at Sydney's suggestion.

"No," said Virginia, waving off Max. "I must be going. I probably shouldn't have come. I was just so curious to see how a movie was made. And that's all been very interesting. But this house! Darrell's accident! When I was playing, it felt terrible. I really cannot stay." She continued backing toward the door as she spoke. "Oh dear, I thought all those things in your movies were just imagination. I didn't think a Fitzmaurice picture was truly scary."

Sydney looked a bit bemused by her statements. "Thank you," he started to say, but she didn't stop. Virginia hurried out the door, clutching her violin case under her arm as if one of us would snatch it away from her. I almost wished that I could have gone with her. I too had no real desire to reenter the room or watch the "ghosts" come to life.

Renee tapped Sydney on the shoulder. "I didn't like having music. It's a distraction. Let's finish this scene. We can always use the Victrola if you want more music later."

With a huge sigh, Sydney walked back into the other room. "No one understands me. No one appreciates me. Except you, my wonderful muse. You understand what must be done."

"Yes, yes," said Renee. "Let's just get through this scene. I don't like this room."

The room felt clammy and cold, as if it was the middle of winter instead of a pleasant June day. Outside, the crows set up their insistent cawing. Inside, our crew twittered at each other as we took our places. I helped powder Betsy and Pola, improving their ghostly pallor. Betsy stepped back behind the empty frame so Fred could film her full face and then, after a long pause, in profile. She kept the turning of her head smooth. Although I knew it was Betsy simply standing behind an empty frame with the center filled with gauze, the effect was uncanny. As if a ghost had peered through the frame and watched with deadly gaze as the two sisters walked across the room.

This time Renee walked right up to the portrait of Saturnin Fitzmaurice. She held herself still for one beat, two beats, and then stretched a trembling hand up to the canvas. Then, at Sydney's yelled instruction, she dropped her hand sharply and stepped back into the arms of Lulu.

The pair stood still, leaning a little against each other as sisters will at the end of a long day of sorrow, when the only thing that keeps them upright is each other.

Sydney yelled "Cut!" Renee stepped out of the pose.

Lulu turned to Sydney and said, "Now what?"

"We begin preparation for our next scene," said Sydney. "The discovery of the tramp in the woods. Then the nightmare of death. And finally the discovery of the mask." Eleanor looked intrigued by this recital and grabbed a piece of paper off one of the tables to jot down notes.

"Can't," said Fred, carefully packing up the camera, as I wondered how to tell Sydney that the mask was not ready yet. That I hadn't started the paper mask. "No more filming today."

"Why can't we film in the woods this afternoon?" said Sydney.

"Because we're short on film and the light's going," said Fred. "I need to go down to the station and pick up some new reels. Studio's last telegram said it would be arriving on the next train from New York."

"Twelve cents a foot," muttered Max.

"Then I shall go wash off this makeup," said Lulu, "and take a gloriously hot bath. Eleanor, can you take Pumpkin out for a short run? Poor darling has been waiting for me all day."

Eleanor glanced at the pug snoring in the corner of the room. "I doubt that dog knows the meaning of the word run, but I'll boot it onto the grass for a bit."

"Eleanor," fussed Lulu. "You're always so mean to poor Pumpkin."

Arkham Horror

"I'm a saint around that dog," said Eleanor. "Especially after it ate my best pair of gloves."

"That was not Pumpkin's fault."

"Oh, God, must I listen to the sins of a dog," moaned Sydney. "I am trying to make art."

"Such a lot of bother about a flicker," said Lulu.

At that fateful word, we all turned to look at Sydney. "Films are not just…" began Fred under his breath.

Sydney went for it with his full director's voice. "Films are not just cheap flickers, meant for a moment of quick entertainment! Movies have the power to rebuild the Tower of Babel and create a universal language. With the right picture, I can unite all the people of the world. They will see our work and understand the power that links us all. There will be no war, because we will speak the same language. We will all understand each other's deepest dreams and greatest aspirations. We will be united in our efforts to build the perfect civilization."

Lulu started to open her mouth, but Betsy, who was closest to her, trod heavily on Lulu's foot. At her squeak of annoyance, or possibly pain, Betsy whispered: "Hush. It's one of his best speeches."

It was, too. Sydney presented a dream of a world. A dream that began in a quiet movie house, with an audience waiting breathlessly for the first note of the organ and the first moment of light as the film began.

"I felt it once," said Sydney, "in the crudest of nickelodeons. I was broke, despairing, ruined in all the ways that a man could be ruined. I paid my nickel and wandered in to escape the rain. And there they were. All manner of people. Dock workers still stinking of their labor, washerwomen with hands so chapped and scalded that they bled onto their aprons, and the street's children who spoke no English. Waiting together for a film to begin. The piano was out of tune, the player atrocious. It didn't matter. We all came together in the darkness. Those who could read recited the cards to their neighbors; those who spoke English translated the lines to the friends that surrounded them. But that was not necessary. Speech itself was silenced into a more universal connection. The film itself, the images that glowed upon the wall in shadows of silver and black, that we all understood. We all laughed together. We all cried out with the same terror. We all wept as one. And when we stumbled out onto the street, we fell apart, each going back to their own sorrows and joys. But still we were connected. For we still held within ourselves that precious moment when we experienced each emotion as one entity, one soul. That is what a movie can do that no other art can. That is what we are creating here."

There was a moment of silence, then Betsy began to clap, and the others picked it up. For we did believe, we always believed that what we were making was a little different from all the other films being churned out by the score. Sydney was right. There were moments in his films that were unforgettable. Once experienced, a scene or a gesture would stay with you forever. Years later, people would talk about movies, about the thrills or the scares, and they would always conclude, "But it wasn't like a Fitzmaurice terror picture. That stuck with you."

We all knew that. And we all stayed with Sydney because

what he made was beautiful. And lasting. And we all, at that moment, wanted to be a part of what came next.

"The key," Sydney insisted to Lulu, who now looked as entranced as the rest of us, "is the right piece. I've been searching for that perfect movie, the one that will never be forgotten. The one that will be shown around the globe and open doors to worlds that we have never imagined. That piece is this picture. And the key to this picture will be the final sequence, when a beauty is transformed."

"I'm still uncertain how you expect that scene to go," said Eleanor.

"You will see," said Sydney. "We will create a perfect construction of terror. We will cause the audience to search their hearts. To pray for relief. And then, then they will be swept up into the shadow. The masked beauty will become them, and, like her, they will be transformed. Transfigured. Transported elsewhere and then brought back to earth again. United as minds have never been united before."

"Yes, but–" Eleanor said.

Sydney kept talking without pause. "The mask ripped aside to reveal the cosmos. The perfect mask for the moment," he said, swinging around to point at me. "Jeany's creation will set the final scene. It will be magic!"

I felt a moment of terrible doubt. Would an old stage prop repainted by Humbert really work? But it was only needed for a moment or so. Of course it would work, I reassured myself.

The others chattered with excitement about Sydney's vision.

"It's better than being on stage," Betsy said to Lulu, who looked skeptical. "No, really, how many people see you in a play?"

"Our theater seats nearly five hundred," said Lulu. "And Eleanor's plays run for months."

"Yes," said Betsy, "but even if a play ran for an entire year, the most people who could see you would be under two hundred thousand." That was Betsy, ever calculating numbers in her head faster than the rest of us could write two down and carry one. I liked that about her, the way she used numbers to explain bigger ideas. That, and how she believed the best of everyone, that they could be better than they were, even after they betrayed her. Very few in Hollywood, or anywhere, had Betsy's courage when it came to forgiveness. Certainly I could never forgive Sydney's later betrayals of our company.

"One picture can play in thousands of theaters," Betsy told Lulu. "There are more than twenty thousand movie houses operating in America right now. And every day they are building them bigger and bigger. Thousands of people in one theater to see you in a movie. That's millions of people who might see you in the same week."

Lulu's eyes began to gleam. She understood fame. And she'd forgotten about the frights of a few hours before. I could see that. I'd seen the same expression on Renee's face when Sydney began talking about acclaim and riches and all the other things that came with being a star in the pictures. It kept her coming back, even when Sydney was his most impossible. And I'll admit, I felt the same. Sitting in the audience and listening to them scream during a

Fitzmaurice picture and knowing it was our work that united them in terror was an unbelievably exciting feeling.

Max, this time, slid in the last word to Sydney's little speech, something he didn't normally do. "The studio is keeping a very close eye on how this goes," he said to Sydney.

"Do they doubt my talent?" said Sydney.

"No, of course not, your last two pictures were smashes," said Max.

"Of course," Sydney said. "There's never been anything like a Fitzmaurice picture in the history of the human race. I make movies that are the very height of diversion. The audience cannot escape the emotions, the very thoughts, forged in my world of silver shadows."

"Nobody's disputing your artistry, Sydney. But things are changing. The studio wants more control. Being so far away, in Arkham, it's making them nervous," Max said.

"Tell them to take a tonic," said Sydney. "I was wrong to think I could do this any place but Arkham. This is the place. This is the script. This time it will work."

"It's the expense," said Max.

"Dreams cannot be bought cheaply," retorted Sydney.

"Actually, Sydney," said Max, "that is what you promised them."

The dry finality of Max's tone made me wonder again exactly what Sydney was planning this time.

CHAPTER TEN

My mother talked about ghosts. But not as something that inhabited the house that you lived in. Rather ghosts were something far off, and part of the history that she had left behind. But if a light went out suddenly and left us in darkness, she would laugh and say, "the spirits have come to eat." When we questioned her about that, she said that her grandmother used that phrase whenever a candle blew out.

The spirits must have been very fat indeed at the Fitzmaurice house, for the lights constantly went on and off. Fred muttered at the fuse box on a daily basis, calling it a deceitful thing of beauty. Max had several long calls with the power company, who denied all malicious intent and inquired when last the wiring had been checked. The rest of the company, myself included, made sure to have candles or lanterns close to our beds with a matchbox conveniently nearby. The days were long, and the nights warm, so the inconvenience of finding a bathroom at midnight by candlelight was more a minor annoyance than anything else.

Still I found restful sleep increasingly hard to achieve. Every night, I dreamed of masks made of shadows, masks made of snakes, masks made of smoke, and masks made of silk that shredded into the webs of spiders. But when I woke and stared at the painted mask propped on my desk, the empty eyeholes stared back. Next to it was set its fragile paper twin, an equally unsatisfying prop. No matter how close these were to what Sydney described, I felt as if something vital was missing. Some otherworldly force, Sydney would say, except there was no such thing. "Props, just props," I muttered and pulled out my sketchbook to distract myself.

I tried to take my mind off the movie, sketching out costume ideas for future projects. Ideas I could present to United Artists and other studios. Ideas that would get me away from Sydney's horrid stories. Yet every night, I could draw nothing except a cloaked man with no face who nevertheless stared out from behind a masked woman. I threw my pencil across the room more than once, only to feel compelled to pick it up and start sketching the horrid creature all over again.

Eleanor seemed to have the same problem with her script. She typed page after page on a typewriter that she'd brought from New York. The clatter from her Underwood threatened to drown out Fred's darling 242 at times. Yet most of Eleanor's ideas were crumpled up and discarded as Sydney proclaimed that it was not quite what he was looking for or Eleanor herself would re-read what she wrote and sigh, "Not that shadowy masked woman and her cloaked friend again. That's such a useless idea."

By the following Saturday, we had barely filmed another page of the scenario, a slight scene where Pola played a visiting neighbor who gossiped about a magic mask hidden in the house. All the company was a little on edge and complaining about being cooped up indoors. Sydney proposed that we drive to the country. "A Sunday picnic in June," he said. "Just like my childhood."

Renee declined. She'd been suffering from headaches throughout the week and wanted to stay indoors and rest. On Sunday, I went to her room and asked if she wanted me to sit with her.

"No," she said, shaking her head with a wince. "It is just a headache. A day of quiet. That's all I want."

She did look pale. Her restless energy seemed diminished. She often wore herself out during filming, putting so much of herself into the performance that she could barely move by the end of the day. It was one of the reasons that she rarely attended or gave parties. The other, of course, is that we could never be sure when somebody outside our group would spot that she wasn't quite what she appeared to be. So Renee needing rest, and wanting to stay out of strong sunlight even with a group of friends, was not unusual. But it was rare for her to be this fragile when we'd completed so little.

"Do you want me to call the doctor?" I said. "I liked her. Doctor Wills seemed a sensible woman."

"I'm sure she is," said Renee, "but I don't need her. Go to the picnic. Enjoy yourself. I just need a few hours of uninterrupted sleep."

She lay back down on the bed with its fussy canopy

and piles of lace-edged pillows. Curled up in the center, she looked so small. I'd never thought of my big sister as anything less than ten feet tall, a warrior woman who protected me all my life. This picture did seem to be draining her energy at an alarming rate.

"Perhaps we should go home," I said.

Renee just waved one hand at me without opening her eyes. "We will. When this is done. It will be worth it. You'll see."

I wanted to argue that nothing was worth night after night of frustration, but then took pity on my big sister. I left quietly, shutting the door as gently as possible behind me.

After collecting a hat and stuffing my sketchbook into a large straw bag, I descended the stairs with some relief. Perhaps out in the country, away from the house, I would finally discover the proper design for the mask.

The touring car was filled with Sydney, Pola, Betsy, Paul, and Max. Lulu, Eleanor, and the pug named Pumpkin went in Eleanor's sporty two-seater. Fred had borrowed an old truck from Humbert for the rest of our gear, including two picnic baskets, several blankets, some old bolsters, and a ratty collection of golf clubs in a mildewed canvas bag. The latter had been unearthed from the back of the barn. Sydney thought they belonged to his university days. I squeezed into the front seat of the truck between Fred and Jim. Hal, like Renee, declined to picnic and waved us goodbye from a chair on the veranda.

Driving through the town, I remarked how pleasant, how ordinary, even quite pretty it was in spots.

"Yeah," said Fred. "Pretty as a picture postcard."

"Don't you like it?" I said.

Fred, the lover of science and all things mechanical, grimaced. "You're right about the shadows."

"The shadows?" I said, not sure what he meant. I didn't like the shadows at the house, the cold crooked patches of dark, but what did that have to do with driving through this pretty New England town?

"Noticed it when I was fetching stuff for Max," said Fred. "Some days, there's more shadows than there should be."

"It's probably because we are used to California sunshine," I said, because there was no sensible, rational reason to be worried by shadows. Even though I was.

"Yeah," said Fred. "That makes sense."

I wished again that this picture was over and we were heading home to Los Angeles.

Once we passed Arkham's boundaries, the road meandered pleasantly up and down the rounded hills. Everything was the new green of early summer. It was hard to imagine that redcoats and Colonial soldiers had once marched across these fields and peppered each other with shots. Fred had been reading up on the American Revolution, there being a lack of scientific literature in the Fitzmaurice library, and speculated now on how far we might be from the protests, riots, and other acts of rebellion.

"Wasn't that all closer to Boston?" I said. My knowledge of that time period was sketchy at best although I could remember Sister Martha reciting such names as Paul Revere and John Adams, with nearly as much fervor as she named the saints.

"Maybe," said Fred, shouting over the rattling of the truck. "Arkham seems to have missed a lot of history. No pilgrims to speak of, no revolutionary shots heard round the world. Nothing much ever seems to have happened here."

Jim snored on my right side. The man could, and did, sleep through anything. His ability to lean himself up against a piece of set and snooze until called upon to act was something of a legend.

"Perhaps that is why the Fitzmaurices settled here," I said. "Because it was quiet and safe." Except as I said it, I realized that the town never felt safe to me.

We climbed a hill, slowly. Fred ground the gears and shifted down. The touring car, although loaded with more people, made better time in front of us. Fred shouted over the engine noise about valves and engine power.

The road smoothed out and we started to talk about the next week's filming.

"Humbert is good with tools. As good as Paul," said Fred. "He's helping us build that box for Sydney's next big scene."

"Oh, the one that Eleanor was talking about at dinner?" I said. "The bed that becomes a coffin in the sisters' dreams. Did Sydney decide to do that next?"

"Yes."

"That's grim." I hadn't liked the sound of it when we had discussed it a couple of nights ago. It reminded me too much of my recent nightmares. There'd been a lot of talk about who would be trapped in the coffin and, after much discussion, it was decided that this would be Lulu's first big solo scene. Renee as the older sister had been the focus so far with the haunted pictures and even the major character for the minor scene of gossiping with the neighbor.

Eleanor proposed the bed sequence, because it was similar to something that they'd done on stage in New York and had gotten a lot of press at the time. Sydney liked the idea as it established that this was *the* Lulu, the screamer and scandalous darling of the New York stage. Renee expressed herself delighted to give the scene to Lulu and not have to sleep in a coffin.

"It will be a good trick when we're done. I'm taking a real bed and fixing up the coffin sides and a lid to slide up around Lulu. We should be ready by Monday. It will be a great scene."

"Well, let's make Lulu look amazing," and as I said it, I suddenly realized how to fix Lulu's hair and makeup so she appeared to be halfway between a sleeping beauty and a beautifully preserved corpse. I knew it would be gorgeous but terrifying, and Sydney would love it.

"You'll make it amazing," said Fred. "You always do, Jeany."

Fred's confidence cheered me considerably. Ahead of us, Eleanor tooted the horn of her car and turned onto a narrow lane after Sydney's group. We followed them to a meadow where the long grasses were intertwined with wildflowers. Butterflies and small birds darted about. Far off in the distance, the Miskatonic River glittered silver in the sun as it ran east toward the ocean.

Fred pulled the truck behind the cars. With a snort, Jim woke up and amiably lugged picnic baskets, blankets, and bolsters into place. Most of us collapsed around the largest basket, unearthing various sandwiches, cakes, cookies, cheese, crackers, cold chicken, and three jars of pickles packed earlier by Mrs Mayhew. Pola, as usual, drew out a bag of knitting as soon as she settled herself on a bolster.

After eating everything but one jar of pickles, we all sprawled in splendid post-feast repose. Fred grabbed Jim, Paul, and the bag of golf clubs. They wandered a little ways away and used the rejected pickles in place of the missing golf balls. Soon small bits of green were streaking across the meadow with a wet thwack.

I pulled out my sketchbook and began to doodle. Flowers and butterflies intertwined in geometric and angular shapes. I thought about how they could be printed as a border of a gown or beaded onto a scarf and sketched some more. As I turned the page to shade in a long stem of grass, I saw how other shapes formed between an outstretched wing and curling petals. Shapes that looked like angular skulls and rounded creatures of a vaguely aquatic nature. The shadows growing behind them turned into the shape of a woman, oddly blurred and masked, with a shadow that stretched in all the wrong directions. Behind her stood a cloaked man. I slammed the sketchbook shut and stuffed it into my bag, determined not to work any more that day. I truly hated the hooded man in that moment and never wanted to draw him or his mysterious companion again.

With a giggle, Betsy pulled Max off his blanket and persuaded him to walk with her down the hill to find a better view of the river. Pola shook her head at them and then took a finer wool out of her bag. She cast it on her needles and began to knit a pattern of interlocking circles.

"That's beautiful," I said.

"A shawl fine enough to pull through a ring," answered Pola. "In my hometown, every bride had one in her trousseau."

The others were asking how Sydney knew about this idyllic spot.

The meadow was part of the Mayhew farm, according to Sydney.

"We always came here for picnics," he continued, waving one hand in a lazy circle much as a king might describe his kingdom with a wave of a scepter. "I used to chase butterflies with a net."

"And stick them in a killing jar," guessed Eleanor. She lay back on a blanket, her face tipped up to the sun. Lulu nestled at her side, a large hat shading her face.

Sydney laughed. "Well you can't catch and release them. The net breaks their wings. I wonder what happened to my old butterfly collection. I used to have a hundred or so, all pinned on cards with the Latin names written underneath. *Papilio polyxenes* or the black swallowtail. The painted lady or *Vanessa cardui*. How very long ago that was."

"How very ordinary. To chase butterflies with a net," said Eleanor.

"I found them endlessly fascinating," admitted Sydney. "As a boy I believed all manner of stories about butterflies. That they were the souls aflutter from a cooling body, the psyche that emerges from the dead man's mouth."

"So this obsession with death began at an early age?" Eleanor gave him a doubtful look. "Or is that a story that you made up to impress the press?"

Sydney shook his head. "I was a precocious child and quite my grandfather's shining hope. The Fitzmaurices have always had a fascination with ancient mythology. Particularly Egyptian. My grandfather collected an extensive number of books on the subject. I devoured every tale that I could find in his library. Especially the ones about psychopomps."

"Pumps? Lunatic pumps?" murmured Lulu, but something about her smile said that she knew very well what Sydney was talking about.

"Lulu, don't tease," said Eleanor. "We had discussions with the most darling little professor from Bryn Mawr about the creatures that escort newly deceased souls from Earth and where exactly they escort those spirits to."

"The horrors of research for one of Eleanor's plays," said Lulu. "You thought the professor was darling. I thought she drank too much of our gin."

Sydney looked a little put out to be upstaged and plunged back into his explanation of how ancient civilizations had lists full of creatures that led souls, both dead and living, to a place somewhere outside the cosmos that we knew.

"A liminal space," said Sydney, staring hard at Lulu.

"Oh, one of those places," said Lulu, "where we are in space between one point in time and the next. A doorway, just on the verge of being open or closed or that moment in a dream when you take a step and haven't started falling yet."

"Well, yes," said Sydney, a little disconcerted.

"I don't know how she does it," Eleanor said to me, not without some pride. "As far as I know, she had no formal education, grew up in the back of vaudeville theaters, and her mother actually did put her in a lion's cage in a melodrama at the age of three."

"She most certainly did," said Lulu. "I remember it clearly."

"And you never read anything but the most dreadful romances and the stage papers," Eleanor said to Lulu.

"Now, that is not true," said Lulu. "I often read your dull reference books when I want to go to sleep quickly. How about that New England history tome with the impossibly convoluted sentences right beside my pillow back at the house? Pumpkin has chewed the cover twice and declared it virtually inedible."

Sydney tipped his hat further over his face to shade himself from the sun. "I gave my best occult histories to Eleanor for her work. Not for the pug's supper."

"Very tiny nibble," said Lulu. "Barely a scratch." Eleanor swatted her with her hat and mouthed "Behave".

To Sydney, Eleanor said, "Your grandfather was an actor. Quite famous, I hear."

"In his younger days," said Sydney. "It was all glories of the past by the time I was old enough to be interested. It was hard to imagine. That he actually knew the Booth brothers and saw them all play together at the Winter Garden. About how they had power, but didn't understand it. How John was a fool who thought he could change history with a gun when he could have done so much more."

"I would argue shooting Lincoln did change history," said Eleanor. "The death of the great man will do."

"So crude," said Sydney. "And, I don't believe a single

shot, no matter where it happens or to who, really changes the world. It may bend history for a decade or a generation, but things do slide back. Same old problems crop up again."

"How very cynical of you," said Eleanor.

"How very noble of me," said Sydney with a flash of a smile. "After all, I'm the first to say that violence is useless. Shoot a man, and another takes his place. Win a war and another war is just waiting around the corner to begin. A war to end all wars will never happen. Change, true change, must come from outside. A radical change driven by a new consciousness. Or the return of a very old one."

Eleanor shook her head. "There's no new consciousness. Our perception is formed by our experience. To create something that nobody has ever experienced is impossible, because we all draw from the same conscious or unconscious well of experiences."

"Isn't that what we have been doing with our films? Creating something never experienced before?" said Sydney. "My grandfather thought you could bring it forth with theater, with ritual, but that all goes back to an idea that has been around for uncounted generations. I cannot tell you the number of times that it has been tried. And failed. There's some very interesting stories about that, especially around Arkham."

"But what we are doing is a form of theater," said Eleanor, who was obviously becoming more intrigued with Sydney's proposition. I recognized it, of course. It was Sydney's idea of a universal language, much as Sister Theodora once argued at the orphanage. A way to end the division caused by the fall of Babylon.

"Film is something completely new and growing stronger every day," said Sydney. "A collective communication, understood wherever you go, made of electricity, light, and shadows, a visual medium that progresses straight into the mind, without any common language needed at all. I too tried the theater, based on my grandfather's recommendations, and found it sadly lacking. But luckily I made that discovery while still in college. Next I thought it would be the circus, that art known round the world. That failed too. But I am convinced now that it is the movies."

Lulu teased her pug with a bit of ham taken from a sandwich. "It must have been a happy childhood. Living here in Arkham."

Eleanor sighed, "Oh Lulu. That wasn't what we were talking about."

Lulu winked at me. I understood immediately that she knew exactly what she was doing. Not arguing with two intellectuals sparring over vague concepts. Just pulling them back to earth a bit. It was one of the reasons that I couldn't dislike Lulu. Sydney's speeches on controlling the common consciousness made as much sense as Fred's speeches about using radio waves to convey sound and pictures. However, Fred's ideas had some practical merit. Sydney, especially when he started on the occult and metaphysical, made my skin crawl. Somehow, with him, it sounded more like universal hypnosis than communication. I never liked the character of Svengali and a Svengali who controlled populations through film was an idea that I hoped Sydney never wrote into one of his films. It would appeal too much to the wrong type of people.

"What?" Lulu said to Eleanor. "I meant it. Sydney seems to have been blessed. To grow up in a large house. To come on picnics to a pretty meadow full of butterflies. It sounds much happier than my childhood. Don't forget my mother put me in a lion cage at the age of three."

"As you never fail to remind me," said Eleanor. "It was one melodrama that ran less than three weeks. And the lioness was toothless, according to your mother."

"I didn't know that," said Lulu. "But still, Sydney, you sound as if you had the perfect happy childhood."

"Happiness was never a particular goal of my family," said Sydney. "We were far more set on other things."

"That's an interesting question," said Eleanor. "What's more desirable? Happiness? Wealth? Fame? Power?"

"Doesn't wealth, fame, and power bring happiness?" said Lulu.

Eleanor sat up. "I used to think that. But now, I find myself less sure. I chased through Europe for stories, certain that being a war correspondent would be the path to fame. And all the rest that you listed."

"Eleanor, your stories were printed in the *Saturday Evening Post*," said Lulu.

"And that did pay well," said Eleanor. "Although our horrid plays, all full of blood and screaming, paid even better. Then we fell in love and that certainly made both of us famous."

"I'm not sure that was what Sydney meant," said Lulu. "But it hasn't been that bad."

"No, dear," said Eleanor, giving Lulu a quick kiss and hug, "there's been a lot of good in the last year. But it proves my point. Or rather makes one think. I've been rich, well, as rich as a writer can be, and famous, or at least infamous. And has it made me happy? At least as happy as a simple picnic, sitting in the sun, arguing about what brings happiness."

"But you haven't been powerful," said Sydney with a sly look sideways. The sun slid under the down-tipped brim of his boater and made his eyes gleam. "Not the type of power that true fame and fortune brings. Where you can ask for anything and be given it."

"That's making three wishes off a magic fish," said Eleanor. "Nobody should ever be able to ask for anything and be assured of having it. Makes them spoiled. Makes what you are asking for worthless."

Fred wandered back to the blankets, swinging his golf club at daisies in the grass. "Is there any ginger ale left?" he said.

I pushed the picnic basket closer to him with my foot, relieved to be distracted. "Look in there."

"What's the argument this time?" he said, nodding toward Sydney and Eleanor.

"Fame versus happiness, I think. Or perhaps power."

"I'll take happiness," said Fred. "If we can order it off some menu."

"Don't think that is quite what they mean." But I thought he had it right. I loved my work, but I never cared, as Renee did, who knew about it. I never wanted to be famous. At least, I didn't think I did. Renee occasionally accused me of lacking ambition. But it wasn't that. I wanted to design for the movies. I wanted to have people clamor for my clothes or put my drawings on the cover of *Harper's*. I just didn't want to have my picture taken by reporters or have people speculating about my love life in the gossip columns. I watched Renee manage that, and manage it well, but it meant hiding part of herself. That I never wanted to do. If happiness meant forgoing fame, I'd take that.

Eleanor was keeping up the argument with Sydney, despite Lulu's best attempts at interjecting a little levity. "Changing the world through your creation. That's every artist's dream. But no art has that power. To bend the world to the image that you want."

Max and Betsy wandered back to the blankets. Max, as always, looked pressed and tidy. Even on a picnic, he wore immaculately tailored trousers, jacket, shirt, and tie. Even his boater sported a broader ribbon than Sydney's. "What are you talking about?" he said.

"Which is the most desirable: happiness, fame, wealth, or power," said Eleanor.

"Wealth," answered Max without hesitation. "The rest all follow the money."

"You have a mercenary soul, Max," said Sydney. "Art is the power to change men's minds."

"What about the women? Oh, we're already in our right minds and so don't need to change," retorted Eleanor.

Max just smiled. "If you can pay the bills and still have money left over for luxuries, wouldn't you be happy? There's nothing more miserable than being poor."

"Quite true," said Sydney. "I was miserably poor once. Down to nothing more than a nickel, and I spent that to go to the movies. Wisest decision that I ever made."

Max shook his head. "Sydney, you have never been poor. You may have been out of money once or twice, but you have always known that you could come back to this." He pointed at the picnic baskets. "A house full of treasures, servants, the luxury of a lazy Sunday afternoon spent discussing what is the most important thing in the world."

Betsy looked startled at this outburst. We all were. Max never spoke out or spoke up around Sydney. That's why Sydney liked him better than the studio's last two assistants. Max just totaled the numbers and moaned a little about Sydney's extravaganzas before figuring how to make it all work out.

"Why, Max," said Sydney, his mouth half crooked in a condescending smile, "you sound like a socialist."

"Oh, not me," said Max. "What do I care about the masses? My grandfather might have subscribed to the *Workers Times,* but it was a waste of his money. It did him no good at all."

"Not a fan of Emma Goldman either?" asked Eleanor, citing the outspoken radical who had finally been shipped back to Russia. "I heard her speak once or twice before she was deported."

"I have no time for anarchists, socialists, or communists," declared Max. "Or any other radical. And as for the government thinking they can solve problems by simply shipping people out of the country, that's as foolish."

"Careful, Max," said Sydney. "Next you'll be saying that you disagree with Prohibition."

"You can't legislate people into being prudent, sober, or good, however you define good," said Max with some bitterness. "None of that works. All decisions in the end come down to the irrational and the emotional."

"In that," said Sydney, "we are in some agreement. Fear speaks directly to the irrational mind. Terror is the key."

Max sat up even straighter. Like Sydney, his face was shaded by his boater. Weirdly shadowed, like a black hood fell across it. Suddenly Max – sweet, note-taking, cost-obsessed, creased-pants Max – seemed like the figure of my dreams. It was the most ridiculous idea that I had ever had.

"Terror is the key," repeated Max.

Eleanor continued to watch the two men with a considering look. "Keys can be dangerous," she finally said. "Look at Pandora and what she found when she unlocked her box."

Lulu broke up this sobering discussion, rising with a shaking of her skirts and tumbling her dog into the grass. "Come along, Pumpkin," she said. "Let's take a walk and enjoy the sun." She gestured to Eleanor. "Want to join us or continue arguing politics?"

"Darling Lulu," said Eleanor, getting to her feet. "You are always far more fascinating than men arguing about power versus wealth." She wound her arm around Lulu's waist. The pair wandered down the same path that Max and Betsy had taken earlier.

"Want to join our game of pickle golf?" Fred asked me.

"Oh yes," I said jumping up, wanting more than anything in that moment to leave behind my new and disturbing vision of Max. "How do you score a hole in one?"

"Smash the pickle completely?" Fred wondered as he handed me a golf club. "Or maybe turn it into relish?"

Betsy grabbed another club and followed us. "Who wants to talk about boring politics," she said. "Everyone has tough times. Why not enjoy what we have now?"

So we left Max and Sydney behind to discuss terror and keys, when we should have stayed and asked more questions about Sydney's ideas. That night the electricity went out again. The nightmares began in earnest.

CHAPTER ELEVEN

We were hot and tired, and just a little sticky with pickle juice, by the time that we got back to the Fitzmaurice house. Lines formed outside the bathrooms. The hot water had definitely cooled by the time I could fill a tub. Still, it felt lovely to wash my hair and pull on my silk pajamas. I dropped into bed convinced I would sleep forever.

Instead I dreamed of coffins, masks, and endless rooms filled with smoke. And I was alone, terribly alone. I knew in my dream if I could find Renee or Fred, it would be all right. But they were gone. Everyone was gone. Mirrors reflected flames behind me and muddled the way. I came to doors that were locked or doors that opened into infinite darkness. Nowhere could I see a clear path out of the smoke.

Smoke smothered my screams. Muffled, blinded, lost, I wandered the endless and hostile corridors of the Fitzmaurice house. No matter which way I turned, mirrors blocked my way and taunted me with the reflection of a door, a door that I could not reach but that promised freedom and clean air.

I choked on smoke and despair. I never knew such sorrow, more bitter than when Renee held my hand and told me that our mother died. I never knew such terror, not even as a child, when the influenza pinned me helpless to my bed with fever and I was convinced that I would never be well again.

In the depths of each mirror swam the shadow of a woman, a strange and amorphous creature of coiling smoke, and a hooded man standing further away. I could barely see him. He was more of an impression, but I would catch greater glimpses of her the closer that I went to the mirror. Her hair spilled down her back, writhing like snakes. She was constantly walking away from me. When I would turn and hurry in the opposite direction, trying to catch a glimpse of her amid the fumes, I would confront another mirror and a vision of her retreating back.

The man never moved. Instead he watched us engage in this lunatic race, looking for the right way out of the smoke and fire.

Weeping with fear and frustration, I banged my hands against the mirror, almost as if the woman was on the other side of a window and could hear me. The creature slowed and then turned, presenting to me a perfectly blank face, an oval of polished silver that reflected flickering flames and my own frightened face.

I woke gasping and almost screaming, convinced that I could smell a fire. But there was nothing but darkness, a warm smothering darkness. As I groped for the matches and the candle beside my bed, I heard small cries and startled exclamations coming from the hallway. Finally a lantern shone outside the door of my bedroom.

"Jeany? Jeany, are you awake?" Renee stood there with her bedside lamp casting wild shadows up and down the wall. Her hands were shaking too badly to hold it steady.

"I'm here," I said, tumbling out of the bed and making my way to the door. I heard the crackle of paper underfoot as I trod upon my sketchbook. "What's wrong?"

"Nothing," she said. And then, almost in a whisper. "Old nightmares. Would you mind sleeping in my room tonight?"

I nearly made some sarcastic remark about how that would look, but then I saw her face. She was biting her lips to keep them from trembling. I had not seen such sorrow and worry in her face since the day we went to the orphanage. But the moment I came close enough to touch her, Renee straightened her shoulders and assumed that look that only big sisters can give to little sisters.

"I'm all right," she said. "But I dreamed that something was in my room tonight. A bird trapped in the house? I kept hearing wings. I swear I felt it fly past me. Please stay with me."

"Of course. Don't worry. I'm sure it's nothing." Dreams, I told myself. It was only dreams and dreams could not hurt us.

As we went down the hall, we found a number of the bedroom doors were open. Eleanor and Lulu were in the hallway, arguing about whether or not to go downstairs and find something to drink. "I just can't sleep," said Lulu. "But it's so dark on the stairs."

"That's why we have lanterns," said Eleanor, hoisting hers above her head. "Please remember that our mothers managed stairs quite handily in long skirts and with no electric lights."

"We never lived in any place big enough for stairs," muttered Lulu.

"There's a smaller stair here," I said, pulling back the chintz curtain that hid the back stairs. "You go right into the kitchen on this."

"There," said Eleanor, shepherding Lulu onward. "Let's go down and see what we can find. I might even manage to light the stove to make a cup of Ovaltine."

When we reached the kitchen, we found the stove already lit. Fred pulled a boiling kettle from the top. "Hello," he said. "Anyone for a hot toddy?"

"Dear man," said Eleanor, "do you actually have whiskey for that?"

"Hot water, honey, and Max's favorite bottle of scotch," said Fred. "I remembered where he hid it in the library."

Betsy and Pola came tumbling down the stairs next. "Oh Fred," said Betsy. "That smells wonderful."

Fred filled up cups with generous dollops of Max's imported scotch and hot water. Eleanor stirred in the honey and handed us each a toddy.

"It would be better with schnapps," said Pola, sipping her cup, "but a good thought all the same."

Hal and Paul joined us next, claiming that Jim's snoring had woken them up but looking equally glad to have a toddy pressed into their hands. Max was the last to arrive.

"Is that my scotch?" he said, eyeing the empty bottle.

"Here," said Fred, handing him a cup. "You'll find it medicinal."

Only Jim, who could sleep through earthquakes and thunderstorms, and Sydney failed to join the party.

"But what did wake us all up?" Eleanor asked after her cup was empty.

"I thought there was a rat in the room," said Lulu. "It was climbing on the bed."

"Not likely," Eleanor answered. "Pumpkin was still wuffling away on his pillow when we left. Even that dog would wake up if he smelled a rat."

"I smelled smoke," I said. "Or I dreamed I did."

"I thought I heard a bird beating against the window," said Renee. "Maybe that was what started my dream."

Renee spoke of mirrors that cracked while she tried to fix her makeup and reflected a scarred face. "It was a bird, a crow," she said. "A crow flew into the mirror and cracked it. Cracked me too. Like a porcelain doll face, shattering on the floor."

Pola admitted that she dreamed of knitting shrouds for all her family. Betsy bit her lip and said "I couldn't make the numbers work in my favor. No matter how I added it up, I couldn't save him." But she refused to say who she was trying to help.

Eleanor sighed and said, "I dreamed that I was surrounded by paper and none of the ideas in my head would come out as coherent words. Every time I started to write, it turned into blobs of ink that meant nothing at all. And all the time I knew I was dreaming and was afraid to wake. It seemed as if awakening would release even more terrible dreams lurking inside of my dreams. Those were my terrors of the small hours."

Lulu hugged her and Eleanor hugged her back. "All ridiculous," said Eleanor. "I've seen far worse awake and survived quite sane. No matter what the New York critics say about my scripts."

Paul wouldn't say what woke him, but Hal told of a nightmare where he was being chased by chickens.

Max reached for the scotch bottle and tipped the remaining drops into his toddy cup. "I dreamed that I was poor again," he said. "I dreamed of the steps leading down to my childhood apartment and how they always smelled of garbage and damp. And I knew if I went into that basement apartment again that I could never leave. That's frightening enough."

"Oh, Max," said Betsy and tried to pat his hand. But he turned half away from her and took a long drink.

Tidying up the kitchen, Fred said, very quietly, "I was back in the trenches. And a mortar blew my hands off."

I watched Fred's clever hands stack the cups neatly into the sink. I could not think of a worse nightmare. All of them had already lived their worst nightmare. More than ever, I hated the Fitzmaurice house and wished we were anywhere else.

But what could I say? That the house was haunting us? The script that Eleanor and Sydney hadn't even finished writing? The mask staring with sightless eyes at me whenever I looked up from my bed? We made up stories like this all the time. We knew that such tales were just tricks of light captured on film. No wonder Sydney slept peacefully above. He was the storyteller who directed these scenarios. Why would he be frightened? Why would any of us suffer from nightmares when we were the creators of terror?

CHAPTER TWELVE

I went into the pantry to fetch the bread and cheese as well as some leftover bacon. Fred found the skillet and between the two of us we made a hearty middle of the night meal for everyone.

We sat up the rest of the night, talking of the next scenes to be done, what we thought Sydney wanted, and where we intended to go when this film was over. Lulu and Eleanor wanted to return to New York. Hal still spoke of a chicken farm so eloquently that Paul offered to go halves with him. Turned out Paul had raised chickens as a boy on an Iowa farm, so that Hal's plans made more sense than usual. Fred, of course, had ideas for improving 242, this time centered on the sidefinder that he had built for the camera. He even talked of applying for a patent.

"I'd need help drawing it up, and filing the paperwork," he said. "But there's guys I knew in the army who do such things. Engineers."

"I can help you with any drawings," I said.

Conversations ended when we heard the rattling of the

dairy truck delivering the day's eggs and milk. Ethel arrived not long after with Mrs Mayhew and a couple of girls who did the Monday laundry and heavy housework. They chased us out of the kitchen with only a few words about the dirty dishes in the sink.

A second round of baths and naps followed, despite Sydney coming downstairs for breakfast and to chide us all for being unprepared for the day's filming. "If you slept normal hours…" he started but Renee stopped him.

"We don't all take powders before we go to bed," she said. "It was an uncomfortable night."

"Storm's coming," said Mrs Mayhew, passing through the dining room to direct some business around the polishing of mirrors. "You could feel it last night. That sticky heat."

"Yes, yes," said Sydney. "I'm sure that was all it was. A long day outdoors and a warm night. If we get some rain, everything will cool down."

"Solstice in a few days," said Mrs Mayhew. "Always brings bad weather. And trouble."

Sydney waved her off. "Nonsense. It's the best day of the year. The most light, the least dark," he said.

"That's why," said Mrs Mayhew. "Dark gets jealous. Tries to grab more than it deserves. It's a bad time to be opening doors. Worse time to be standing in doorways."

Sydney frowned at her and started to say something. But then he turned to Max and began talking about the scene to come, the coffin to trap Lulu.

Mrs Mayhew watched him leave the room with a dissatisfied expression on her face. She looked over the rest of us. Only the women were still lingering at the table.

"Some of you appear to have more sense than others," she said, looking directly at me. I glanced at the others, but they were occupied with letters, newspapers, or just peering with tired eyes into the bottom of their coffee cups.

"Thank you," I said to Mrs Mayhew, when nobody else responded.

"It's not my place to interfere," she said while gathering up the dishes left behind. Like Florie in the diner, she balanced a tray skillfully on one arm with all the plates neatly stacked on it. "It's not my place to gossip."

"Of course not?" I said, still unsure on why she was looking so hard at me and ignoring the others.

"Watch the mirrors," she said. "Count how many doors you see in them."

I glanced through the dining room archway into the long hall. We had moved the long narrow mirrors back into their original places after finishing the ghost portrait scene. One of the mirrors reflected the edge of the table, and Mrs Mayhew looming beside it. Except she wasn't a large woman. Taller than me, as most women were, but not by much. No, there was a larger shadow behind her, someone almost as tall as a man. I turned my head to look down the table, but nobody had moved from their seats and the angle was all wrong for that.

Mrs Mayhew didn't move herself, other than to watch me look over her shoulder, but she gave a little nod. "Sensible. You turn and count noses when you see people in a mirror. Keep noticing. It will help," she said. Then to the room at large, "More coffee?"

A murmur of denials ,but Eleanor asked where she could

find more paper for the typewriter. "I've finished almost all that I brought," she said.

"There's probably some in the library," said Mrs Mayhew, "or you can go into town. The stationers would have what you want. If it's just plain and not fancy, the five-and-dime would have it too."

"Let's go to the five-and-dime, darling," said Lulu. "I love a good small-town five-and-dime. There's sure to be something that I need and a half a dozen things that I don't."

Eleanor groaned a little but agreed to a trip. Betsy looked intrigued. I asked if they could fetch some notions for me. "Bits of trim and other things that I could use," I said.

"There's a five-and-dime?" said Fred, wandering back into the room to grab another slice of toast. "I need some wire. Maybe some nails."

"Don't take Fred," I advised the others. "He takes hours in those stores."

While we made plans for shopping, Mrs Mayhew slipped from the room.

After lunch we gathered in the long parlor where we'd filmed the scene with the ghosts. Paul, Hal, and Jim were all rigged out like undertakers with top hats, long black coats, and black gloves. All the outfits were taken from the attic and there was a strong smell of moth powder lingering around them.

Taking advantage of the long windows, Fred and Humbert placed the rigged bed in the center of the room and moved sun reflectors, made out of silvered canvas screens, around it. Lulu arrived in a long pale champagne silk negligee straight from her trunks. She'd brought several.

Sydney earlier rejected those with ruffles, fox fur, ostrich feathers, silk fringe, or ribbon flowers. This particular robe was the simplest of her collection, with only a few wide panels of lace for decoration.

"Mind you," said Lulu as we powdered her for the scene, "that lace came from Belgium before the war. They said it was made by nuns."

"I'm sure the sisters will be delighted that their work is in the movies," said Eleanor. "Are you sure about her eyes?"

"Yes," I said, painting a little extra arch onto Lulu's eyebrows. "Sydney wanted them emphasized." As I'd imagined the day before, Lulu looked even frailer, as if she was made out of porcelain, a doll or a corpse. But an exquisite corpse.

Betsy, who loved fiddling with makeup as much as me, took a long look at Lulu. "It's perfect," she pronounced. "She looks unearthly."

"Not too dead," said Lulu.

"No, no," said Betsy. "Just right. You'll match the ghosts from the earlier scene."

We lowered Lulu into her bed and arranged her hair so it became a blonde halo surrounding her. She looked lovely against the linen and lace draped pillows from upstairs. Betsy whispered to me: "What will Mrs Mayhew say?"

"Something unpleasant about making powder stains on the best linen," I responded, "but she's working for Sydney. He can talk to her."

Sydney leaned over Lulu to give her his instructions. "Wake up slowly. You have dreamed of strangers. Of gods in distant cosmos, vast beyond your comprehension, stirring in shadows. And, and… oh damn, what did you write, Eleanor?"

Sydney waved his hand at Eleanor, who handed him a scenario page. Sydney skimmed down it. "Oh yes, here we go. You wake in your comfortable, ordinary bed. You realize that your night terrors are simply dreams. Relieved, you stretch up your hands to pull down the sheet. But you cannot. You are trapped. You are tied to the bed by these simple luxuries that have so comforted you… Max, are those my monogrammed silk sheets?"

Max, who had been conferring with Fred about something, swung around. He glanced at the bed where Lulu was still lying, waiting for us to start. "Yes, Sydney, those are your sheets. You said she's trapped in a bed by the silk sheets. You have the only silk sheets in the house."

"Damn it, Max, what am I to sleep on tonight?" said Sydney. "You'll have to go out and buy more."

"Sydney, we will have to send to New York. Or you can sleep on cotton or linen like the rest of us until these are laundered," said Max. "And do not tell me to hang the expense. The whole point of filming in Arkham was that you could have the atmosphere that you wanted for half the cost of creating it in California. Remember?"

Sydney, who had been halfway through saying "hang the expense," just sighed. "What one sacrifices for art," he said and started to read from the scenario again. "You are trapped. You are tied to the bed by these simple luxuries that have so comforted you. You and the audience slowly realize that the silk sheets and lace pillows do not decorate a simple virginal repose."

Lulu giggled at the last. "Really, Eleanor, simple virginal repose?"

"It was late, my dear," said Eleanor. "And I was longing to get done. One puts in some words to fill the space and hopes to change them later."

"I like it," said Sydney. "Now will you all stop interrupting?"

I heard a muffled laugh from Renee but when I looked over my shoulder, she was innocently sitting in her chair, apparently helping Pola with her knitting. They would have a scene after this one and were partially costumed with towels around their necks to keep their makeup from staining their dress collars.

"Do you think it will take as long as the stair scene?" said Betsy.

"I hope not," I said. "We'll be here all summer at this rate."

Sydney growled and continued on, reading over the whispered conversations floating around the room. I was thankful that there was no Arkham reporter or violinist today to create even more distractions.

"Your silk sheets and lace pillows," bellowed Sydney above all the noise, "are the decorations of a coffin. You realize that you are trapped and about to be buried alive!"

Lulu pursed her mouth. "How can I be buried alive if there's no top to the coffin? Can't they just see me struggling? Oh, and you're not throwing dirt on me. Not this negligee! It's Belgium lace."

Sydney clenched his teeth against his cigarette holder. "You wake up. You look happy. You look distressed. You look terrified. Then the sides and top of the coffin come up and close around you! Can you do that?"

"Of course," said Lulu, snuggling down into the silk sheets. "Just yell when you want me to open my eyes."

"Fred!" said Sydney. "Max. Places. Now, begin!"

Max waved the slate in front of the camera to mark the scene and the take. Fred cranked steadily. Lulu remained absolutely still, looking beautifully asleep or perhaps even dead. The audience would not know at the beginning of the scene, according to Sydney and Eleanor.

"Now," said Sydney.

Lulu's eyes fluttered open. She allowed herself the faintest of relieved smiles, portraying the sister who had awakened from a disturbing dream to find it *was* only a dream. Then she shrugged one shoulder. Her negligee slipped, revealing a silken strap and bare skin.

"Show off," muttered Betsy as she mimed the same movement with her own shoulder. I was sure I'd see it in one of her future movies. Eleanor shifted to stand beside us to get a clearer view of the action.

Then Paul and Jim shoved on mechanisms that cranked up the coffin sides and lid built by Fred and Humbert. The coffin banged into place around Lulu.

"Thank God that nobody in the audience will hear that," said Eleanor to me. "About as scary as a trunk lid being snapped shut."

"Depends on whether or not you are in the trunk," I said. "What did you do in the theater?"

"Oiled the hinges and had the orchestra play extra loud," said Eleanor.

Fred straightened up from the camera. "Good enough. Take it apart, boys."

Jim and Paul pulled on the lid. Nothing moved.

"Oh hell," said Fred. "It just snaps loose from the side. Twist it."

"It's stuck," said Paul. "Stuck fast."

Muffled banging sounded through the room. Eleanor swore. "She's terrified of small spaces," she said. "We never left her in our box past the curtain banging down."

The banging from the coffin increased in its fury. Appalled for poor Lulu, I joined Fred pulling on the lid.

"Get her out," Eleanor cried. "Oh, please get her out."

I knew how Lulu felt. I once got locked in a closet by another girl at the orphanage. It seemed to last forever, even though Renee tore open the door only minutes later. I glanced up and those horrid mirrors reflected us all banging on what looked like a real coffin.

"Pull!" yelled Fred.

We all pulled. Even with all of us shoving and pushing, the lid of the damn fake coffin stayed firmly shut. The banging inside became more frenzied.

"Lulu, Lulu," yelled Eleanor, "keep still. We'll get you out."

Sydney broke off a discussion with Max about the next shot to wander over. "What's wrong?" he said.

"The coffin won't open," Eleanor panted as she twisted the lid.

Fred left the room running. The frenzied knocking inside the box continued and a wailing shriek rose from within. At least we knew Lulu wasn't suffocating. Fred raced back with a crowbar. He shoved Eleanor to one side and applied it to the coffin lid. Made of cheap wood, it splintered apart. Lulu rose out of the shreds of wood and tangle of silk sheets.

"I am never, ever doing that scene again!" she cried. Tears coursed down her face. Her makeup streaked her cheeks. No movie corpse ever looked more appalling.

And the mirrors reflected it all. Except, as I turned fully to the door, the mirrors were back in the hallway and there was no earthly reason I should see the room so clearly in them.

"Watch my sheets," retorted Sydney. "Don't snag them."

"Damn your sheets. Damn your movie!" Lulu clambered out of the wreck of the coffin and stalked across the room. There were bits of wood in her blonde hair and she'd ripped out at least one seam on the negligee. Eleanor hurried after her.

Sydney eyed the wreck of the coffin bed. "I don't know," he mused. "That has a certain Gothic charm. She wakes in the ruins of a coffin."

"I don't think we can get Lulu back," I said. I looked out the door. I could barely see the edge of the mirror or Lulu's passing as she stalked toward the stairs. The disorientation made me feel strange, as if I had taken a step and missed my footing. That odd fall that happens somewhere between waking and dreaming.

"Renee, darling, come here." Sydney motioned to my sister. "What do you think?"

Renee looked over the ruins of the bed as she would have looked at any set up in any movie. Props did fail, all the time. Walls fell down. Glasses shattered. Actors tripped over footstools. All of this was simply the stuff of an ordinary day of filming. I looked down at my shaking hands. Why was I suddenly convinced of some supernatural malice? It was ridiculous.

Renee discussed possible solutions with Sydney. She shone at this, the ability to quickly adapt a scene and get an extra thrill out of it. "Show one sister going to bed in the coffin and then show another rising from it?" she said.

Sydney nodded. "That's the ticket. Fred, can you cast a shadow across Renee's face to make the suggestion of the mask that is to come?"

Fred nodded and started to shift the curtains and reflecting walls about. Using one lamp, he was able cast a dark shadow across the pillows left disarrayed by Lulu's escape. "Like this?" he asked.

"Very good," said Sydney.

"I need to change," Renee said. "I have a robe that is similar to Lulu's upstairs."

"I'll help," I said and ran up the stairs ahead of Renee to fetch her white robe out of the closet. Once she joined me, I helped her take off her dress and placed the robe over the simple peach slip that she wore.

"No need to change completely into a gown and robe," Renee said. "Especially if Sydney's concentrating on my head and shoulders."

"Do you want to redo your makeup so it's closer to how we did Lulu?" I sorted through the brushes and pots on her traveling case. It opened out in three tiers, with trays stored above and below that were filled with makeup that Renee favored.

As she sat on the stool next to the dressing table, I widened her eyes and drew shadows along her cheekbones. Over Renee's shoulder, I watched us both in the mirror. The reflections looked murky despite the clear summer sunshine streaming through the lace-curtained windows.

"Are you sure about this scene?" I said. My lingering unease bothered me. It was just a failed prop. Horrid for Lulu, but nothing supernatural.

"Of course," Renee said. "More screen time is always good. Sydney and I were talking last night about the relationship of the two sisters, how the audience should see them as two halves of one personality."

"Why?"

"We make it unclear who the monster is until the end. It's all part of this grander plot."

"Have you seen this manuscript? Eleanor keeps complaining that Sydney won't show her the end."

"He hasn't told me everything yet," Renee admitted as I drew the line of her eyebrows to match the arch we gave Lulu. "But it's all about how a very human woman can be transformed into a goddess of shadows, a divine and terrifying creature, that opens the door into another world."

"And what happens to the sister that isn't transformed?"

"She's destroyed," said Renee, turning around on the stool to examine her face and plucking the brush from my hand to add a little more shadow along the line of her left brow.

"But would a sister do that?" I said. "Allow the other to be destroyed." Because sisters protected each other. That was what they do, I wanted to say to her.

"It's just a story." Renee smiled into the mirror. The curtain stirred in the breeze, and the shadows in the mirror moved with it. For a moment, it looked as if someone was peering over her shoulder, looking back at me. But just the two of us were in the room and it was too warm.

"Let's go," I said. "I want to finish this scene today." I wanted done with the horrid scene and all the rest to come.

Lace shadows draped across Renee's face as she turned away from the mirror. I considered a lace mask, a pattern rather than the pale smooth oval that Sydney described. Black lace, like a widow's hat veil, that dissolved to something more eerie. And I would lock the masks in my room back in a trunk in the attic. For some reason, I was starting to hate them, even though the pair, metal and paper, matched Sydney's vision so exactly.

As we descended the stairs, I discussed the possibilities with Renee. If she liked the idea, she could easily sway Sydney into changing his plan for the masked woman. He knew that she had a better eye for the small detail and what suited her characters best.

"Black lace," she mused. "That might work. But, Jeany, it seems so clichéd for one of Sydney's films. A dangerous woman in black lace. I'm sure we can find something more unusual."

"But isn't it all about the glamor?" I said. "Look how Lulu fusses over her lace trimmings. I thought that it should be a half mask, something that leaves your mouth free and visible. Something human that the audience can focus on. That's more intriguing."

"I don't know. Sydney has been so sure that it needs to be

a full-face mask. Something about that was what a priestess would wear."

"Are you a priestess? I didn't know that about your character."

Renee half turned on the stairs to look back at me. "Perhaps. You know Sydney. Vague, always so vague. But he said something last night about Camilla being descended from an ancient line of priestesses. Something about the real Saturnin's wife coming from Egypt and bringing that legacy to Arkham."

"That seems unusual," I said and wondered if Florie or Humbert knew about that. They seemed full of gossip about the early history of the Fitzmaurice family. If the wife had been Egyptian rather than French, surely someone would have mentioned it.

"Yes, something about Saturnin finding her in a temple along with a bunch of treasures. That's why he left France for America. As a French Hussar, descendent of nobility, he didn't have a choice. Nobody would have let him come home with such a wife."

"I cannot think he would have been that welcome in New England, either."

Renee descended the staircase with a laugh. "Oh, he probably just told everyone that she was French like him when he got here. Isn't that what America is for? Making up new stories about yourself? It's been going on a lot longer than Hollywood. However, I doubt Sydney got it right. You know him. Probably half the tale is from some Haggard novel that he read and forgot he had."

Perhaps she was right, my clever sister who never forgot

anything that she read. Perhaps Sydney had fooled himself into thinking some Haggard story was his family history. As for changing your history to suit your vision of yourself, well, nobody knew more about that than Renee.

Downstairs, we arranged Renee on the bed surrounded by the wreckage of the fake coffin. She was an even more beautiful corpse than Lulu. Suddenly struck by an unreasonable feeling of horror, I wanted to pull her out of the coffin. It was too deathlike. Once again, I nearly made the unpardonable mistake of walking into the shot and ruining the take.

Fred adjusted his beloved camera and peered through the sidefinder. "That shadow is falling all wrong," he complained to Sydney. "I can't see her face at all. It looks like a mess of black snakes."

Sydney also bent to the camera and then straightened up. "No, it's perfect," he said. "She looks as if she is covered in a mask of shadows. Just what I want."

Fred grumbled as he cranked, and every click sounded like a gunshot to me.

"Jeany," he said, and I nearly jumped to the ceiling, so concentrated was I on the strange attitude revealed by Renee's pose. "Jeany, would you move that pillow just a little to the left. I still don't think that her face is visible. Sydney, are you sure about this shadow?"

"Yes, yes, of course," said Sydney.

I readjusted the pillow under Renee's head as she smiled up at me. There was something about that smile, with her makeup so heavy upon her cheeks and brow, that made her look even stranger. I tried not to shudder as I fluffed her hair across the pillow in the same manner as Lulu.

Sydney caught a glimpse of her smile and told Renee to hold her face just so.

"That's my Camilla," he cried. "My lady of the shadows and doorways, my key."

The sun sank lower, and longer shadows crept into the room. For June, it felt ice cold. Even Renee began to shiver a bit between takes, despite being nearly buried under silk sheets and lacy pillows.

But Sydney was right. There was something mysterious and enthralling about her pale face surrounded by the ruins of the fake coffin. The black wood, white lace, and Renee's own elegant features blended in the shadows cast by Fred's cleverly placed lights. She appeared as much a ghost, or more, than Betsy and Pola from the first scene. While there was not a suggestion of blood, the entire scene reeked of violent death and resurrection. The fact that it was unclear whether it was a bed or coffin just added to the aura of sin.

This scene alone would earn Sydney his usual title of "king of terror."

Max certainly noted it. After the fifth take, he pulled Sydney aside to ask how long he intended to film Renee in bed and how much time that would take up on the screen in the finished film. "The ladies in Peoria won't like it," said Max.

"But everyone else will," said Sydney. "They don't pay for pictures that are sweet and safe. They pay to be enthralled. To have their emotions twisted about. A lovely lady, dressed for bed and surrounded by death, that sells. You know that, Max. The studio will tell Hays that everyone is clothed and we're really teaching morality to the kiddies by equating sex with destruction."

For the last three years, various church groups protested any theater that allowed young children to watch movies, especially those that were immoral – and what suggested immorality to those critics seemed to be everything that occurred in films, especially films like we made. There'd been testimony in Washington, DC, before Congress when one preacher had professed to watching hundreds of hours of films, documenting carefully each time a suggestive look or flash of skin occurred. The result had been a stunning stack of paper, thumped on the legislative desks. Now William Hays was out in Hollywood, promising to help the studios keep their pictures clean, but nobody quite knew what that meant. And everyone in the business knew that the movie producers and theater owners, not Congress or some church group, paid Hays a handsome salary.

Max muttered that if we kept on filming a girl on a bed, wearing nothing but her negligee, we'd get banned by at least one bishop.

"Banned by the bishop," Sydney chortled. "That's money in the bank, guaranteed."

Renee spoke up from the bed, "If you don't want me to really fall asleep, let's finish this scene. I've done horror, delight, desire, and panic. What next, Sydney?"

Sydney looked down at her. The shadows created by Fred's rearrangement of the curtains and lamps fell in stripes across her face. Some window left slightly ajar created a draft, and shadows stirred like snakes crawling across the bed.

"Utter stillness," said Sydney. "Eyes wide open but staring into the nothing that comes from the end of dreams. That moment when the dreamer begins to fall forward into the abyss."

Fred cranked the camera. The ordinary, simple sound of the whirring click of the film advancing echoed through the room like the beat of a funeral drum.

Suddenly I hated this scene more than anything that we had done. It reminded me of those horrible days after our mother died, when people came and went in our rooms, discussing how to organize our lives without giving us any voice in the matter. I clasped my hands around my arms and shook in my corner. I shivered so violently from the sudden invasion of memories that it was all I could do to keep from running forward and pulling my sister from that horrid bed. With each turn of the camera's crank, the cold increased, and my dread roared through my body like a fever.

I almost moaned with relief when Sydney finally called a halt for the day.

"Now for the woods," Sydney declared with satisfaction.

"What happens in the woods?" I asked Eleanor later that night.

She was scribbling on the scenario, sitting at the small table at the back of the parlor, while the others played cards and argued about their bets. As usual, Betsy was intent on winning all their spare cash.

"Dog bites man," said Eleanor.

"What?" I was distracted by watching Betsy flirt with Max and take the pot from Paul.

"I was reading one of Sydney's occult books, Anubis and all that. I had the clearest vision of a dog-headed creature carrying off a man at the command of a priestess. Only we will make it more vague, more horrifying than that."

I turned back to Eleanor. "We haven't made any costumes for a dog man. Would Jim play that role?" We had made a wolf's head once. Sydney hadn't liked it.

"No, it will be more subtle than that. The dog man will be a creature of shadow, never fully seen." Eleanor wrote this down as she said it. "Besides, I cannot wait to be out of this house."

"It can be harder, filming outdoors," I said, thinking of the problems that we had with seagulls during the *Siren* picture.

"Better than in this house," said Eleanor. "It's always so cold. I know many people don't like New York in the summer, but I love the heat. Even the smell. It just feels like life. This place is cold as…"

"As a tomb," I said. Eleanor stared at me and then nodded.

I looked through the door of the parlor. It shouldn't have been possible, but I saw Eleanor and myself reflected in a mirror. We both looked pale, with exaggerated eyes and mouth, like ghouls or ghosts.

I turned away, arguing with myself that this was just a trick of reflections, the flickering electric light.

When I looked again, there was nothing there. No mirrors were visible from this angle. None at all.

CHAPTER THIRTEEN

Two days later, we lugged all the equipment across the lawn and into the woods. Finally Paul Kopp had a part to play, a hobo who surprised the sisters as they walked on a wooded path. As Eleanor explained it, this character would at first be menacing as he begs for work upon the sisters' estate and then menaced by an unseen threat. Later the sisters would chance upon the hobo's bloodied and shredded coat blocking the garden gate.

Of course, that scenario meant we needed two coats. One for Paul to wear and one that was probably destroyed. The night before I asked Eleanor how the destroyed coat should look.

"Oh, like a wild animal attack," she said as she scribbled more details on the scenario for Sydney. "Something large and vicious with claws that snatch and teeth that bite. It's my jabberwock of a scene."

A search through one of the downstairs closets had turned up a number of dark men's coats of an age to have belonged to Sydney's grandfather. Men's coats being men's coats, there were two black coats of a similar cut. One I roughed up with an old metal file that I found amid Humbert's tools in the barn. That made it look like our tramp had been sleeping rough. As for the other, I stared at it for a long time, thinking about how an animal might attack a man. Would it come from behind, catching at his back and shoulders? Would it attack him from the front, ripping down a lapel and biting through the coat to his heart? How would the blood seep through the coat? Could I even make the blood show on the dark cloth?

When Fred wandered into the barn in search of a screwdriver or a wrench from some adjustment to the camera's tripod, I posed the questions to him. Being Fred, he gave it serious and careful consideration.

"Paul's a large man," he said. "So it would have to be a brave beast to attack from the front. Or one that was trapped and had no way out. I saw a bear maul a man because it could not escape."

"They had bears in Brooklyn?"

"Montana. I stopped on my way west, working on a ranch before I decided that cows were dumber than a kid from Flatbush."

"Your rail-hopping days?"

"Yes. Thought I'd take a peek or two at how the cowboys live. Didn't like it and kept going west."

"So, back to the bear mauling," I said, thinking that might be the size of creature that Eleanor had in mind. "How did the cowboy look after it was done?"

"Like a mess."

"And his clothes?"

"Not good. Not that anybody noticed. You tend to look at the blood and body bits."

I gagged slightly, but persisted. "If the coat is crumpled on the ground, could the camera pick up that it is torn?"

Fred squinted at the coat. "Not really. Maybe we should drape it over a bush?"

"Would a bear leave a man's coat draped over a bush?"

"Sydney's pictures aren't always realistic," Fred pointed out.

"It doesn't seem like a torn coat would scare the audience." I circled round and round the coat, throwing it in different heaps about the ground and then picking it up and shaking it out.

"Maybe that's what they could do?" said Fred. "Perhaps we could shred the coat and tumble it in a heap on the ground in front of the gate. The ladies can pick it up, revealing that it's been cut into pieces."

"A look of horror on their faces," I said, slowly because I was thinking it through. "Then Renee holds out her hand and we see blood dripping off it. Blood from the coat. That works and will be easier to show than stains upon the cloth itself."

Fred nodded. "What will you use for the blood?"

"There's syrup and lard in the pantry. I can mix something together that looks thick and drips slowly. Renee will hate getting it all over her hand."

"We all suffer for art, according to Sydney," said Fred. Rummaging through the tools, he pulled out the head of an old garden rake. "You can use this for claws."

We draped the coat over a couple of crates that we found

in the back of the barn. With file and rake, we attacked the coat, mimicking the catching of claws and the chewing of teeth. By the time we were done, the front of the coat hung in long shreds. We agreed that any tramp wearing it would be dead.

"Of course, it doesn't really explain why the coat ended up in one place and the tramp's body disappeared," said Fred.

"Let's hope the audience doesn't think that hard," I said. "Maybe we'll show Paul's body later on."

Humbert came into the barn to collect some clippers for trimming the hedge. He shook his head at my two coats and muttered about the waste of good clothing. "It's art," I said, but Humbert muttered all the more.

Fred made the adjustments that he wanted to the tripod. We hauled all the gear down to the far end of the garden, where a wooded gate opened into a small copse. The path was badly overgrown. When Lulu and Renee arrived, they both eyed the walk with trepidation.

"That will be murder on my stockings," said Lulu, pointing out with one toe and displaying an ankle nicely draped in silk.

"Could we film the scene upon the lawn?" Renee asked. "The tramp could lean over the gate and call to the sisters."

"No," said Sydney. He looked down at the pages clutched in his hand. "Eleanor's scene takes place in the woods. To the woods we go."

Eleanor frowned. "The setting isn't all that important. They could be standing at the gate."

"You wrote that they encounter a mysterious man upon a

wooded path," said Sydney. "That is what we are going to do."

"Sydney," said Max. "Is it that important?"

"I think it must be," said Sydney. "Max, things are stirring. But not enough. We need more now. Especially if we are to make the studio happy."

Max nodded. "Very well. Ladies, if you would." He swung open the gate and gestured to the path. "Let's let Sydney direct as he wishes."

"If I snag my dress or Lulu ruins her stockings, the studio pays for them," said Renee, a threat that could often cow Max, with his careful accounting of every penny spent. But this time he just shook his head and gestured at the path. With a sigh she led our small troop into the woods.

It was a little wooded plot, sandwiched between high hedges and fences of the French Hill estates. Back in Arkham's early days, there had been a smaller house on the property, according to Sydney, but it disappeared. An odd word choice, I thought. "How can a house disappear?" I asked Sydney as we walked into the woods.

"Oh it burned, like the big house," he said. "And the trees grew up around it. Trees like fire. Now it is a nice mix of pine, maple, oak, and hemlock. Mostly hemlock, according to my grandfather."

"Isn't hemlock a poison?" said Lulu.

"It's a poisonous wood," echoed Eleanor, pulling a shoe out of a muddy patch of ground. "Ugh, look at my shoe. And listen to those insects. What a noise."

"A poisonous wood," chuckled Sydney. "That's perfect. We'll have to put it on the title card. Nobody could quite agree on who owns this land and the pond in the center.

My grandfather said that one summer the nearby houses stocked the pond with fish for the amusement of small boys with poles. It was considered safer than fishing in the Miskatonic River. But the fish died. Now most of the estates keep their woods gates locked."

The crows flew from branch to branch, following us through the hemlock, the muttered cawing rising above the insects' drone like old men grumbling over our heads.

"When I was a boy," Sydney recalled, walking down the path, "I was often the only one playing in these woods. There used to be frogs there too. I'd catch them and put them in a jar. My grandfather said that they cut ice out of the pond in the winter and stored it in an ice house at the bottom of the garden. That's all gone now."

By the time I reached the pond, I felt unbearably hot and sticky. The woods exuded a moist heat that itched under my shirt and damped my collar. No birds sang in these woods but the odd hoot or caw continued as Fred set up the camera. Louder and more persistent was a humming buzz, more like flies around rotting garbage than bees. I kept expecting stinging insects, but none appeared. Just the horrible whining buzz that rose from all around the edge of the murky, weed-choked pond.

Sydney told Paul to emerge from the bushes at the edge of the pond, startling Renee and Lulu on the path. With much muttering, Paul pushed his way into the center of one large and prickly looking bush.

Fred set his beloved Bell and Howell number 242 in the center of the path. The sun filtering through the trees glinted on the camera's black enamel case. The adjustments that he made earlier to the Akeley tripod made him grunt with satisfaction. The Akeley GYRO head proceeded to pan and tilt as Fred cranked the camera. The resulting film, as we'd learned from prior shoots, would give the audience a disorienting view of the sisters as they proceeded to the pond. Despite Fred's usual application of care and grease, the gears whined louder than ever before, nearly drowning out all the other noises in the wood.

Paul crashed onto the path, forcing Renee and Lulu back toward the camera. With a dirty face and ragged coat, he made a fine figure of menace. The pair shrank toward each other as Paul held out a hand covered with a greasy, fingerless glove. My touch to his makeshift character. I remembered a drunk coming up to me one night as I got off the streetcar and headed to my apartment. He'd been a harmless old man, well known in the neighborhood for drinking bathtub gin and then begging a dime for coffee and a little something to eat. But that night, with his fingers bared by a torn glove, he'd startled me. I'd almost run away, but then Renee had come up behind me and spoken to him very gently, digging a quarter out of her purse and pressing it into his dirty hand. I'd been so proud of my sister then. Her kindness was well known throughout the movie community. She never turned down anyone who truly needed help.

I wondered if she remembered that night. Once again, as Lulu shrank away, Renee pressed forward, grasping Paul's dirty hand in her own. This time, and much against her real character, Eleanor's scenario called for Renee to throw Paul's hand aside and threaten to call the dogs if he bothered them again. Paul started forward as if to strike her. Lulu shrank back further, having established that the younger sister feared the world more than the elder. Renee flung out an arm in an imperious gesture, and Paul turned aside, now shrinking away from her.

"That's it," directed Sydney, "go back around the pond as if heading away toward town. The sisters turn back to their house but pause. They hear the sound of real dogs hunting in the distance. A sacrifice in blood about to happen. A way to open. Cut!"

"Now how will they know that?" said Max.

"Know what?" said Sydney, frowning at the bush bent by Paul's struggle to climb back into it.

"Know a blood sacrifice opens the way? Oh and dogs barking," Max said, with more emphasis on the former and the latter – canine howling – sounding like an afterthought.

"Title card," said Sydney. "And instructions on the score for the dog howl. I did tell you that we had to have a score made to send to all the theaters."

"Yes," said Max, a little reluctantly. "But the studio is wondering if that expense is necessary."

"Of course it is necessary," said Sydney. "Everything is necessary. If the studio wants results, if the studio wants *worldwide* results, we need a score to go with the film. That's crucial. It's all in the manuscript. The importance of music as the masked stranger descended into the darkness. How it called forth the shadows."

Eleanor had been standing with Lulu, discussing the scene and possible modifications to her reactions. Upon hearing Sydney's comments, she turned around.

"What are you talking about?" she said.

"The ending. How important it is that everything leading to the ending be as outlined in my grandfather's manuscript."

"About that manuscript…" began Eleanor.

"Your scenarios are marvelous," said Sydney, talking over her. "Just the right touch of foreboding. Paul, get further back into that bush. I want to try your approach to the sisters again. Come onto the path a little faster."

"Sydney, that bush is sticking to my coat," complained Paul as he repositioned himself. "I don't think I can escape any faster."

"Try," said Sydney with no sympathy at all.

Paul did multiple lunges out of the bush as Fred cranked the camera. Then they moved further down the path to show Paul stumbling away from the sisters portrayed by Renee and Lulu. Finally Sydney declared himself satisfied.

We walked up the path to the gate. I pulled the bloodied and ripped jacket out of my basket. I draped it across a bush for the first pass at the scene.

Renee and Lulu walked up to it, hesitated, and then recoiled from the discovery.

"No," said Sydney. "That's too tame. Try again, but with more terror upon seeing this evidence of a terrible accident, a mauling by a wild animal."

Three more attempts left Sydney as dissatisfied as the first try. I couldn't blame him. I had already suffered the same doubts. The unexpected discovery of blood was terrifying. It was just difficult to show. At least in a way that would make some type of horrid sense to the audience.

"Perhaps we should move the jacket?" I said. "Have it across the path so it blocks the gate. Renee or Lulu could pick it up to make it clear that it is ripped."

I explained my idea of dripping blood, but without much hope. Renee, predictably, protested getting her hand smeared with a sticky mixture. "Besides, we've done that before. At least twice," she said to Sydney. "Let's be different this time."

I couldn't disagree. I hadn't liked the idea much and I liked it less the longer we stood in the woods. Splashing blood about, even fake blood, seemed like a very bad idea.

Oddly, Sydney agreed, although not necessarily from the same trepidation that the idea gave me. "Just splattering gore about, that sounds like a Tod Browning film, not a Sydney Fitzmaurice," he said. "Just act as if you see blood. We don't need to show it to the audience."

They tried again, but Sydney waved them back down the path. "That's not right either. Put it on the gate itself."

"Why would it be on the gate?" asked Renee. "What animal would leave it in such a place?"

"Push the back against the gate, as if the man backed up against it. That he was literally ripped apart just steps from safety," Sydney said with satisfaction.

After that, I affixed the jacket to the gate by slinging it over my shoulders, pushing back against the gate as if something was charging up the path at me. Something so terrible that I would rather turn and face it than fumble with the lock. The wood gate scraped against my back. I felt the rough wool coat catch on the boards of the gate. Turning, I shoved the material so it truly caught on the top of the gate.

Pulling away, it looked like a sad empty scarecrow dangling in front of us.

Once again Renee and Lulu approached the now filthy coat. They recoiled from it as if the tramp himself stood in front of them.

"That's it," Sydney said. "As if you stand accused of the man's murder, as if your banishment led to his doom," he continued, reciting from Eleanor's scenario.

Renee stood proudly, as if the man's fate failed to move her, while Lulu cringed away from the gate.

"Cut! Perfect. My vision exactly," said Sydney.

Both Renee and Lulu slumped a little. The buzzing in the woods sounded louder and more angry than before. With some relief, I pulled open the gate into the garden. I couldn't wait to leave the woods. For once, I wanted to return to the house. At least there were no insects there.

A large brown dog came charging up the path, with a man following after him shouting: "Duke, Duke, come back here, you mutt."

The man behind the dog was a scruffy sort, dressed in an old worn suit and battered hat. Over one shoulder he had slung a guitar.

We all started to see a real tramp appear in the woods.

"Hello," he said, upon spotting us. "Didn't mean to scare you."

With the rest dumb with surprise, I stepped forward and held out my hand. "Hello, I'm Jeany."

"Pete," said the man. "And this here is Duke. He's a good dog, don't let his looks fool you."

Eleanor followed my lead. She shook Pete's hand and

patted Duke on the head. "He looks like a very good dog indeed," she said, with that croon that true dog lovers get in their voices. It did go a long way to explaining why, for all her jibes to the contrary, Eleanor was nearly always the person who walked Pumpkin and made sure that the pug was fed.

Pete looked over our heads at Sydney. "I heard you were back, Mr Fitzmaurice," he said. "Didn't expect to see you in the woods."

"I'm surprised to see you still wandering around Arkham," said Sydney. "How are you doing, Ashcan Pete?"

The man shrugged. "Well enough. Always something to do, something to see in Arkham. Duke was just certain there was something new on this path. Guess he was right."

Duke was sniffing around the gateposts and the ruined coat that still swung from one corner of the wooden gate. The dog let loose a howling bark, which made me start. The dog's deep baying sparked off the cawing and rustling of wings in the trees above us, the ever-present crows of French Hill.

"Oh hush, Duke," said the tramp called Ashcan Pete. "Nothing here at all."

Max stepped forward to shoo the dog away from the coat, trying to drive Duke off with a flapping of his hands that just made the hound wrinkle its brow at him.

"Oh, for goodness sake," muttered Eleanor, stepping around Max. "Duke, go with your master. Go on. Go home!" The last was said with a firm emphasis on home.

Pete chuckled to see the dog retreat from Eleanor's onslaught. "That's right, tell him straight. Can't shillyshally with that dog. Come here, Duke. Come here, now."

With a whine, the big dog backed away from the coat and followed his master down the path. Above them the crows kept up a raucous cawing.

Sydney frowned after the pair as they wandered off. "I wonder how he got in here," he said. "The woods are fenced all the way around. He must have cut across the back of one of the other estates."

"Does it matter?" said Renee. "Are you satisfied yet?"

"No, it needs something else," Sydney said. "Something more."

Eleanor gave the birds in the trees an unhappy look. The cawing was so loud that it drowned out the buzzing in the bushes. "Maybe they could be attacked by crows?"

"No!" cried Lulu. "Eleanor, this is a Paris coat. I'm not getting bird mess all over it."

Sydney nodded. "That's an idea. Fred, how can we stage that? Max?"

"Perhaps one of the guns from the house?" Max said. "You could fire it off. That will scare them out of the trees and Fred could film them flapping around."

Renee frowned. "And we can wait inside while you do it. I agree with Lulu. I do not want to be cleaning bird mess out of my hair."

She rarely spoke so forcefully with Sydney, but I knew that she did not want to see Sydney kill one of the crows with this silly trick. Dead animals always upset her.

"We can scare them into flying about, and do it without any birds getting hurt," said Fred. He too had caught the distress in Renee's voice and knew how much she hated to see animals suffer. Once, back in Hollywood, he had helped me find a good home for a canary given to Renee by an admirer. She loathed caged birds, but we couldn't just set it free as she demanded. The poor thing had had its wings clipped, something that I didn't tell Renee. Instead, Fred found a very nice old lady who lived in a little house across the street from him and had always wanted a canary to brighten up her living room.

Fred adjusted the camera so it was pointing nearly straight up into the trees where the restless crows paced back and forth on low branches, ruffling their wings and croaking at us. "Use the shotgun but fire away from the trees and don't hit any of them. We don't want dead birds raining down in the shot."

Renee winced, and Sydney looked thoughtful. "Well, one or two…" he began and then stopped at a glare from Renee.

"If we tossed some bread or other food on the path…" I said, hoping to hurry the scene along. I wanted out of those woods. "…we can lure the crows down. Then scare them into taking off. Like pigeons in the park. Less dangerous than firing off a gun, anyway." I pushed for a decision. Sydney was capable of standing around all day, and the woods were closing in on me like Lulu being trapped in the coffin.

Fred agreed with me. "You could flap that coat at them."

Max went up to the kitchen and brought back a couple of stale loaves. The crows didn't seem to care for the bread, keeping up their cawing and ignoring our efforts to coax them. So Max trudged back up to the house and returned with aging sausages that somebody had bought for lunches but nobody liked. The smelly, bloody meat brought the crows out of the trees to battle over the bits. Fred cranked the camera, capturing the vicious fighting over the sausages, which Sydney pointed out could be taken for actual human fingers.

"Hays will certainly censure us if we say that," I said, feeling slightly queasy. Sydney was right. It did look like the crows were tearing something living apart.

"We do not have to title it that," Sydney said. "Just drop some hints to a few reporters about the scene where the crows dismember a dead body. Of course if anyone asks directly, we just say we did some wildlife filming of birds eating stale bread and old sausages."

But when I flapped the coat at the quarreling crows, the contrary birds simply hopped or skipped out of my way without taking to the air. Now the birds decided the bread was to their liking and the trees were a boring place to be.

After a couple more unsuccessful tries, I turned to Sydney. "Now what?"

"Rock salt," said Sydney. "We can get some from the kitchen and load the shotgun with it. It will make a bang and a sting, but no dead birds. That should get them back in the air."

"You don't need us to film this," said Renee, who already retreated halfway up the lawn with Eleanor and Lulu. "I'm going back to my room."

"I'll walk up to the house with you," said Max, "and bring back the gun."

Lulu and Eleanor decided to take their car for a drive,

since Sydney's efforts to direct crows seemed likely to account for the rest of the day. The pair strolled around the corner of the house, heading to the barn where they stored their car next to the touring automobile that Sydney had leased.

"Well, at least you have not deserted me," said Sydney to Fred and myself. And somehow, I could not leave, much as I hated this little patch of hot, muggy woods. I felt like I was stuck trying to get this right. As if something had to happen now so we could resolve the rest of the film.

Max brought back a shotgun which Sydney loaded with rock salt. "Step away, Max," Sydney said as he took aim at the crows. Max and I sheltered behind the gate. Fred started cranking. Sydney let off the shotgun. There was a tremendous bang and an even greater cry of outrage as the crows took to the air in a black cloud.

Then the cloud turned in midair and began a murderous dive toward Sydney. With a shout, he dropped the shotgun and lit out for the house, running ahead of pecking, clawing birds. Max plunged after him.

Fred swung the camera to follow them, still cranking and muttering a great deal. I ducked behind Fred, but the birds showed no interest in us. We apparently had earned some protection by being the dispensers of bread and sausages, while Sydney had been the god of rock salt and noise. Max should have stayed with us.

Sydney and Max reached the kitchen door and plunged through it. It closed with a great bang. The cloud of crows flew straight up in the air, wheeled a few more times around the chimneys, and then settled down on the roof.

We could hear their discontented croaks from across the lawn.

Fred cranked a few more feet of film and then stopped. "That will work," he said with quiet satisfaction. "We can splice that into the beginning, a great ominous cloud of birds flying around the top of the house."

I thought about how it would appear on the screen. "But it could be even better," I said. "if we splice scenes of the crows throughout the film."

"Every time the sisters venture out of doors, we show the crows watching them," said Fred.

"And peering through the windows at them," I said.

"The audience will be terrified of birds by the time they leave the theater," Fred chuckled.

I grinned. It was a great idea, better even than Eleanor's scenario or one of Renee's little edits. One of those touches that made a Fitzmaurice film famous. I suddenly felt a bit more charitable about being stuck in the woods. But not enough to stay any longer.

The crows continued to pace across the rooftop, muttering and watching us.

"They carry the souls of the dead," said a voice behind us.

I gasped and whirled around. Humbert was standing by the gate with a rake over his shoulder.

"Heard Mr Sydney firing at them," said Humbert. "He used to do that as a boy. Take the gun into the woods and pester the crows. Then run back into the house. One time, they caught him. Down there in the woods. Pecked him bloody. Had to call the doctor for stitches and all. Bet he remembers that."

"He didn't seem to worry today," I said, watching the crows finally fly away from the roof and toward town. Off on their own crow business.

"Crows remember," said Humbert. "Crows have long memories. Better than bees, says my aunt. Comes from carrying ghosts around in their beaks."

"Ghosts in their beaks?" I said. I hadn't heard that one. Although I recalled Sydney talking often enough about birds being guides to the realms of the dead. "Psychopomps," I remembered suddenly. "Eagles, cranes, owls, ravens, and crows. Sydney bringing back those weird feather bits and saying they prevent hauntings."

"Yeah, Jeany, all those feathers for *Death is a Woman*," said Fred.

"Plumed hats," I said, remembering how Sydney had wanted us to place different types of feathers in Renee's hats. He bought a stuffed owl for the set, because it was supposed to represent some goddess. Renee had hated that dead bird. "And we couldn't find a crane feather, so we used an egret. So Sydney was furious, although nobody would know the difference."

Humbert watched us with his usual dour expression, but his tone was mild when he added. "Don't know nothing about pomp birds. But crows fetch ghosts out of a house, says my aunt. If you let them. Nobody ever let them into that house. That's why the crows are always so mad at the Fitzmaurices."

With that pronouncement, Humbert ambled away, off to do something with the garden.

I waited for Fred to break apart the camera and tripod,

and then took the tripod from him. We started toward the house, discussing Sydney's odder beliefs when it came to beaks and feathers. We were almost at the house when Fred looked over his shoulder and said, "But where's Paul?"

CHAPTER FOURTEEN

We searched for the rest of the evening. It started simply. Walking up to the house, looking casually for Paul, certain that he had slipped by us and returned to his room while we were messing with the crows. But we could not find him.

After dinner, with still no sign of Paul, everyone grew a little more worried. Except Sydney, who said that Paul must have wandered off somewhere for a smoke and would turn up soon. Max kept looking at Sydney in the strangest way, but mumbling that he must be right. After all, what could happen to a man on a warm summer afternoon in a neighborhood like French Hill?

The days were getting longer, and it was still very light in the early evening. Fred and I decided to search back in the woods. "Maybe he fell?" I said as we walked, remembering that movie shoot where we broke the actor's leg and had to ride down the mountain with him. Of course, there we saw him fall. But perhaps it was something like that.

"Or he walked out at a different place. It can't be just the one gate at the Fitzmaurice house," said Fred. "That tramp.

The one with the dog. He didn't come through the gate, he was already in the woods when we got there."

"Of course," I said, very relieved. "There's probably another gate or break in the hedges, and Paul went out that way. Only…" Only it wouldn't have been more than a mile in any direction to get back to the Fitzmaurice house. So where had Paul gone?

Fred pushed open the gate at the end of the garden. We walked through it into the hot, sticky woods. The crows were settled on the branches above us now, and the hideous insect buzzing was louder than before.

"Only what, Jeany?" said Fred.

"It's not a very big woods," I said as we walked through the green shadows cast by the trees. "Even if he walked all the way to the far end."

"Maybe he didn't feel like coming back to the house," Fred said, ambling along beside me. His hands were thrust deep in his pockets and his cap was pushed all the way on his head. By the clinking sounds he made, I knew Fred was fidgeting with something in his pockets, probably some bolts and nuts or loose coins. He always did that when he was worried.

"Nothing has gone right on this shoot," I said, which was probably what we were both thinking at that moment.

"No more a disaster than usual," said Fred. "Stuff happens, Jeany. Nothing ever works as smooth as we like."

It was true. And it wasn't. Effects did go wrong all the time. But we didn't all wake from screaming nightmares at the same time. People didn't break legs from props that flew off the wall or get boxed into coffins.

"It feels like we're cursed," I said, and I wasn't joking.

We reached the pond. It looked as dismal as it had before. More so with the shadows creeping around the ends as the sun went down. The water was murky brown with dead leaves floating on top of it. The tangle of weeds on the edge was rimmed with a green slime as the roots trailed into the water.

"Think little Sydney really went fishing here?" said Fred, picking up a pebble and tossing it into the pond. It landed with a deadened plop, and few sullen ripples spread out across the water.

"What would you do with anything you caught in that?" I said.

"Knowing Sydney, he stuffed any fish and mounted them on the wall."

I smiled. "I'm not sure that you can do that with a fish. Besides, he said all the fish died."

Fred poked around the weeds a bit, scuffing at them with his shoe. Neither of us felt like touching any of the plants growing in this dank little wood.

"There's another path here," said Fred as he walked around the bush in which Paul reluctantly hid earlier.

"Where does it go?" I said.

"Not back to the house. Looks like it heads to a different part of the woods. Probably where that guy with the dog went."

"Ashcan Pete," I said. "His name was Pete and the dog was Duke." I circled round the bush to the spot where Fred stood. I saw a thin little path leading through the trees. As we went along it, I started to see paw prints in the damp earth. Pete and his friend had passed this way.

"How can the woods be so wet?" I said to Fred. "It hasn't rained for days."

"Underground springs?" he suggested. "The water for the pond has to come from somewhere."

"But it's at the top of a hill," I said. "Doesn't water run downhill? Why does it collect here?"

"Jeany, I'm from Brooklyn. What do I know about nature?"

"Didn't you spend time with cowboys out west?"

"Only long enough to know that I didn't like cows." Fred stopped. We'd reached a place where the path widened into almost a circle of trees and a bare patch of ground. A few bare stones poked through the tangle of tree roots and weeds.

"Wasn't there supposed to be a house in these woods?" said Fred. "One that burned down."

"They have a lot of fires in Arkham," I said, considering the tales of how the Fitzmaurice house also had burned down and been rebuilt by Sydney's ancestors.

"Like anyone from San Francisco can talk about fires."

"Oakland. It's not the same," I said.

I wandered around the bare outline of walls that no longer existed.

"Looks more like a hut to me," I said as I traced that square. It was tinier than our first apartment in Los Angeles. "Must have been one room only." A large pile of rough-cut stones lay at one end. "Chimney? Fireplace?"

Fred shrugged. "Maybe. There's more paw prints here."

There were. Circles of overlapping prints, huge and splayed broader than my outstretched hand, with deep gouges in the dirt as if the dog had dug around the base of these ruins. Huge gouges really.

"How big was Pete's dog?" I said.

Fred was poking around the other end of the clearing. "Huh? Dog-sized. Not a little thing like that pug of Lulu's."

The paw prints, the claw marks, looked bigger to me than any normal-sized dog. Almost the size of a man's foot or hands. Some of the gouges in the dirt seemed different. Those looked like the mark of a man's hands, a man who had been digging his fingers deep into the muddy earth to try to avoid being dragged by something. I remembered in one of Sydney's movies that we made marks like that in the dirt, to indicate that the hero had been carried off by the ghoul that stalked him.

"Fred," I said, backing away from the edge of the house. My palms felt sweaty and my voice sounded harsher than normal. "Did you come down here today?"

He walked back to where I stood. "No. I don't think anyone went further than the pond."

"Sydney didn't ask Paul to set something else up for filming. Like a man being dragged away by dogs?" Sydney had that habit of asking anyone who was nearby to do a task, whether or not they usually did that. He might have drafted Paul into setting a scene for later shooting. I hoped he had done that.

Fred shook his head. "Eleanor talked about showing the tramp being dragged off by a giant dog. It was in one of her scenarios. Sydney liked it but Max said that it would be too expensive to hire a dog. You'd need a trained animal to do that. Something like Duncan's Rin Tin Tin."

I'd heard Warner Brothers was filming a movie with Lee Duncan's big German Shepherd as the star. Sydney had been very dismissive of it. "Why would people want to watch a dog run around in a film?" he had asked. "It's only interesting if the dog attacks people. That might be worth it. Friendly family dog turns mad wolf and terrorizes town."

"So no faking up some dog paw prints?" I asked Fred. "So Sydney could have his dog bites man to death scene?" I pointed out the prints that I'd spotted. Fred frowned at the marks, also measuring them against his hands. When he straightened up, he looked as green as I felt.

"Sydney liked the whole idea with the sisters just discovering the bloody coat," Fred repeated, but I couldn't tell if he was trying to reassure me or himself. "He thought it worked better."

"Sydney kept talking about a blood sacrifice too," I pointed out, even though I wished I hadn't remembered that.

Stepping gingerly around the pawprints, we found where the path continued to spiral amid the trees. By then we should have reached the far edge of the woods, but the path twisted and turned so much that I could not tell where we were. I knew that the other houses of French Hill were only moments away, just hidden by the heavy growth. Hemlock, Sydney had said, the woods were full of hemlock. Full of poison.

"What's that?" said Fred.

Something was hanging from a tree branch high above our heads. It looked familiar. Getting closer I could see it was a man's coat, shredded and torn and draped across a high branch. A coat very much like its twin, the coat that I had left behind us with Fred's camera equipment. This one, this coat, would be the one that Paul had been wearing when he disappeared. The base of the tree seemed deeply gouged with claw marks.

I clutched Fred's arm. "Do you think?"

He looked wide-eyed at me. "Can't be. It's broad daylight. There's houses all around. A man won't be eaten by a mad dog in the middle of a neighborhood wood. A dog could never drag him into a tree. That's something cats do. Like lions in that film."

I remembered that film. I'd gone with Fred because a woman had shot much of the footage with her husband and, besides, I wanted to see a real lion in Africa. Not some sad old circus cat stuffed and mounted in Sydney's study. Fred had gone because the filmmakers had their camera eaten by bugs and that, according to Fred, had led to the invention of his beloved metal monster.

"No, of course not, there's nothing in New England that would drag a man into the trees," I said. "Except Eleanor said it would be a dog man who would kill the tramp."

A man savaged by a dog-headed man, a beast that could climb a tree like a lion. Except that was just a silly idea of Eleanor's. Just an idea to scare the audiences after we turned it into silver light and shadows on the screens of their movie theaters. It wasn't real. But the mound of black cloth hanging off that tree branch looked exactly like Paul's coat.

"It was probably thrown up there by children. Someone

playing pirates," I said, even though I remembered what Sydney said about all the other houses locking their gates into the woods and forbidding their children to play here. I walked forward to check closer. To prove that it was not the coat that I had refitted to Paul's broader frame just a few hours earlier.

That's when I stepped into the pool of blood.

CHAPTER FIFTEEN

I knew it was blood as soon as it soaked into my shoe. The thick, sticky quality of the liquid, not like water, and how it stained the leather. We went to a slaughterhouse once, Fred and I, just to see how blood spattered and pooled in dirt. We went because Sydney said that the blood we were splashing around on a set didn't look real enough. So we looked at real blood in a variety of places. We went to a morgue and talked to a coroner about how blood looked at a crime scene. We knew a lot about blood, probably too much.

I screamed and backed out of the pool. Fred came running to me.

"Jeany, what is it?" he said.

I scraped my shoe against a stone, again and again, trying to wipe it clean. "It's blood," I whispered, not willing to say it too loudly. I don't know why. Maybe because I was afraid of attracting the attention of whatever spilled that blood in the first place.

"Can't be," said Fred. But he leaned over the pool of

liquid and tapped it with one finger. He recoiled. Pulling a handkerchief out of his pocket, he wiped the liquid off his finger. It left the rusty brown stain of congealing blood on the cloth.

Fred looked at me. I stared back at him. Neither of us willing to say what we were thinking.

Finally I said, "It's probably an animal." Although I did not believe that.

Fred said, "Dog, maybe? Dog fight, couple of pets that ran off home afterward."

Neither of us sounded convinced.

Then a bark sounded, the bark of a big dog, and a man's whistle answered. Fred and I stepped closer together and turned to face whatever was coming.

Duke charged into the clearing only to stop at the sight of us. He put his nose down and started sniffing along the ground, imitating a bloodhound that we once filmed. That hound, the one in the movie, had been sent to hunt for a man falsely accused of murder. I couldn't guess what Duke was looking for.

The dog circled around us until he got to the base of the tree with the deep claw marks going up its side. Duke whined a little and backed away. Another sniff took the dog nearer to the pool of blood that I had disturbed. That earned another whine, louder and more distressed.

A man's whistle sounded again. The tramp, Ashcan Pete, strode up the path toward us. "Duke," he called. "Get away from there."

On spotting us, Pete tipped his hat. "Sorry, folks, still working on Sydney's project? Didn't mean to disturb you again. Duke just turned tail on me and came back here again. He gets agitated like that sometimes. Goes looking for trouble. Bad habit for a dog. Or anyone."

"It's all right," I said. "We're looking for a friend, one of the men that we were with earlier. Have you seen him? He's about your size and was dressed like a..." I stopped, not sure how to say bum or tramp to a man who obviously slept rough himself, to judge by the condition of his coat and trousers.

"Dressed like a gentleman of the road?" said Pete with a bit of a smile. "Saw that one of you was playing at that. Dangerous thing to do in these woods."

"What do you mean?"

Pete tapped his leg, and Duke ran over to lean against his master. The man ruffled the dog's ears. I had the impression that he was thinking carefully about his next words.

"There's spots here in New England, odd places," Pete said. "Where you can go off the road and end up where you don't want to be. Works the other way round too. Some things come creeping out that shouldn't be here at all."

Fred shook his head. "It's a small wood in the middle of a grand old neighborhood," he said. "How can something happen here and nobody notice?"

"Didn't say that they don't notice. Don't talk about it. Nobody in Arkham talks about it. But Arkham, Kingsport, and a bunch of other places, there's thin spots. Duke's got a nose for that. Nose for trouble." Pete patted the dog with a loving thump and was answered by an enthusiastic tail wag.

"I don't understand," I said. Blood on the ground, claw

marks on the trees, thin spots. None of it made sense. "What do you mean?"

"Just that there are places that you shouldn't go. Not alone, not looking for something, not hunting down paths. People disappear doing that in Arkham. You should ask Florie."

"Florie? At the diner?" I said.

"Yep. Her family has been in Arkham a long time. She hears things. She remembers things. Me, I just took a wrong turn and have been a bit stuck ever since. Of course, I found Duke and that's something." Pete looked around the clearing. "Going to be dark soon. I'll walk you two back up to the gate. Safer that way."

"But we need to find our friend," I said, not wanting to stay but not wanting to abandon the search for Paul. "And we found something. Blood." I pointed at the spot where I never wanted to step again.

Pete looked where I was pointing. He kept a firm grip on the back of Duke's neck. "Could be blood. Could be an animal got loose here and killed something. Not necessarily your friend. Look, I'll walk you back to the gate and then I'll take a little search around town. I know the places that man can go drinking when he's got a thirst. Likely your friend is in one of those joints."

Fred looked as troubled as I felt. "I've known Paul to go on a binge or two, but not when he's working. He's always been reliable."

"We should keep looking," I said. I hated to stop our search even though I felt as if I was being pushed out of the woods. Not by Pete, but by the trees, the buzzing insects, the rotting smell of the place, all crowding in on me like one of the nightmares that kept dragging me out of sleep in the middle of the night. Above us, the black coat swayed like funeral bunting on the branch.

"If Paul is not back by morning," Fred said. "We call the cops."

"Could do that," Pete agreed amiably as he practically shoved us back on the path and walked us toward the Fitzmaurice gate. "Not that the cops have much luck around here. Arkham's a strange town."

"I believe that," I said.

Pete smiled more broadly at me. "Florie said you were one of the clever ones. Well, she'd know."

Florie again! I resolved to go back to the diner as soon as I could. I wanted to talk to Florie now.

The shadows were deeper on the path. Once or twice a bush rustled, which was odd because there was no wind at all. I pretended that I didn't see the odd shapes created by some of the shadows. Shapes like a dog-headed man, hunkering down and loping on all fours like a wolf, only to stop and stretch, and stand like a hunched-over man in the shelter of the hemlock. Duke bared his teeth and growled at the nothing in the bushes, and it remained hidden.

Pete and Fred started talking about airplanes. Pete had no desire to fly in one. Fred wanted to take a camera up in one. "Did you see *The Skywayman*, some of the stunts that they got? But they filmed from the ground," said Fred.

"The pilot died," I said. It had been a horrible wreck a couple of years ago, killing both the star of the film and his co-pilot. Of course, their studio just rushed it into release with plenty of headlines in the press promising a final close-up of the killer crash. Sydney had seen it and reported his disappointment in the whole thing. He said most of it looked false because the studio had used models rather than actual footage for many of the "death defying" parts. "Why would you go up in a plane to be killed?"

"Planes are safe enough," said Fred. "And getting safer all the time. I've talked to some of the barnstormers. They can do tricks without any trouble if they are given time to set up and rehearse. It's like us. They make it look worse than it is, to give the audience a scare."

I had my doubts about that. But luckily Sydney had never liked how airplanes looked in films and never expressed any interest in doing a movie with one.

By the time that we reached the gate, I was almost convinced that Paul had just gone out for a snort on the town. But not quite. The voice in my head that I didn't want to listen to kept insisting that it had been blood on the ground and claw marks on the tree where we'd seen what looked like Paul's coat.

Pete shoved the gate open. Duke, with a happy tail wag, bounded through and across the lawn. We walked more slowly behind the dog. Pete came last. He turned and gave one more long look down the path. Then he shoved the gate shut and lowered the latch to lock it with a decisive snap.

"That's a bad place," Pete said. "The Fitzmaurice men could never resist it. But it's a bad place to get lost."

"Sydney said that he loved those woods. That he liked to go there with his grandfather," I said.

"Florie says he liked to throw stones at hornet's nests," answered Pete. "Lots of men in Arkham are like that. Shove a stick at something to see what will happen. Doesn't make it a good idea."

We bid Pete goodnight and trudged back to the house. "Tomorrow," I said to Fred, "you can take me to the diner again. I need to talk to Florie."

Fred looked up at the flock of crows that seemed to have returned to permanently settle on the roof of the Fitzmaurice house. The birds spread across the eaves like a giant ink blot.

"I think you are right," he said.

CHAPTER SIXTEEN

The next morning, Max told us that everything was all right with Paul. "He's taking the train back to California," he said.

I was only halfway through my morning coffee. Another horrible night had filled my head with nightmares. I woke with all my bedding, pillows included, in a tangle on the floor. The nightmare left me shivering and sweating with a horrible pain in my neck because I'd been curled up on a nearly bare mattress. There had been no fire in this dream, that I remembered, but something had been chasing me through the woods. My dream featured trees that dripped poison from stone leaves and giant insects, bigger and blacker than crows, that filled the skies with buzzing wings.

Gulping a couple more mouthfuls of coffee, I listened to the others question Max about Paul. Most importantly, how he knew that Paul was going to California and what did that mean.

"He got a job," said Max. "He called from the station and asked me to ship his stuff."

"He just took off in his makeup and tramp clothes?" I asked. That made no sense at all.

"No, of course not," said Max. "He came back here while we were still down at the gate shooting at the crows, and washed up. Found a telegram offering him a part in some project of United Artists and took off. I think he wanted to avoid Sydney. Well, you know how Sydney was about Maggie leaving. Paul just grabbed a couple of shirts and his razor kit. Then he asked if I could send his trunk later as he didn't want to deal with it. It's all locked up and ready to go."

Jim, who was stuffing his face with bacon, just nodded in agreement. Hal, who was eating with more dignified bites, said, "I noticed that his things were missing from the bathroom and closet. His trunk is still in our room."

"I didn't hear the phone," said Eleanor.

Max shrugged and took a bite of toast. "It was a bit later, when Jeany and Fred were out in the woods. I picked up the receiver just before it rang. I was in the hall, about to make a call to the studio, but when I picked it up, there was Paul on the other end instead of the operator."

It made sense. Paul always had been a bit distant with the rest of us. He might take off without telling anyone. Even if he'd promised to work with Hal on his chicken farm.

We heard a clatter on the stairs that meant Sydney was sweeping down to breakfast. Renee was eating up in her room, as was Lulu. Renee stayed upstairs because I'd washed her hair and set it in pins that morning to give her a proper curl for the day's scene. Lulu probably was eating in bed for the same reason. Being half dressed and made up did not do much for glamor over breakfast. Besides, both leading ladies had taken to avoiding Sydney in the mornings. He was either too cheerful to bear before coffee or equally gloomy and insufferable. We never knew which, and it seemed to be triggered by the state of the previous day's filming or whatever discussion that he'd had with Eleanor about the state of her scenarios.

"Hush," said Max. "Don't say anything more about Paul. I'll tell Sydney later. But he's not going to like losing him. You know how he gets when someone poaches one of his actors."

"Well, I know how I get when that happens during a show. How does Sydney react?" said Eleanor.

"Furious and unforgiving, and the rest of us will be questioned for days about our supposed lack of loyalty," said Hal. "He dislikes it most in the middle of a shoot. The last time was the young man who fell down the mountain."

"Selby didn't leave," I said. "He broke his leg and had to stay in the hospital."

"Exactly," said Hal. "Max should keep quiet. Sydney might not even notice for a day or two. Paul doesn't have any specific scenes coming up."

"I won't notice what?" said Sydney as he came in and dropped into his chair with a dramatic wave of the arm at Mrs Mayhew and her coffee pot. "Eggs, bacon, and very well-done toast," he called to her. "With the good marmalade. Not honey. And butter, don't forget the butter."

"Butter and marmalade are already on the table," I said, shoving them toward Sydney. Mrs Mayhew poured Sydney a cup of coffee and filled the rest of our cups to the brim.

I sipped mine a little to gain enough room for more cream and sugar.

"You won't notice that Renee and Lulu are breakfasting in bed in preparation for their big scene," said Eleanor with a wink at Hal. "Or resting from yesterday's activities. Lulu was up and down all night. She swears that she was eaten alive by mosquitoes and ticks in your woods yesterday. Not that I could find a mark on her."

"And I'm sure you looked closely," said Sydney.

"Every inch of her pearly white body," said Eleanor. "Honestly, Sydney, you are as bad as those New York reporters. Not that calamine does a thing for my romantic mood, but I stood ready with a jar of the stinking stuff."

"So she can film today?" said Sydney. "No bug bites showing?"

"You have a heart of gold, Sydney," said Eleanor. "Such compassion for your actors."

"I have a film to make," said Sydney, "and a studio to please, don't I, Max?"

Max had buried his head in the financial section of a Boston newspaper as soon as Sydney had entered the room, but he looked up at Sydney's comments. "We are making progress and that pleases the studio," he said.

"I live to please the studio," Sydney replied. Mrs Mayhew returned with his breakfast and placed the china plate carefully in front of him. "Excellent, excellent. Nothing like a hearty breakfast before a hard day's work."

Sydney was definitely in one of his jolly moods, which meant that he liked yesterday's filming. I was a little surprised. I thought he'd still be upset about the crows.

After all, the birds had chased Max and him into the house.

"What are we filming today?" asked Betsy.

"Just a couple of simple scenes. A lull before the real terror starts," said Sydney. "You dressing the sisters for a dinner alone in the dining room. The dinner itself. A knock on the door that you answer, only to find no one there. It's all building up to the entrance of the masked stranger."

"No party scene?" said Betsy. She loved the party scenes and being able to do a little extra cameo as a flirtatious maid or guest.

"I thought about it," said Sydney. "I discussed it with Eleanor."

"Endlessly, darling," said Eleanor.

"But we've done those so many times," said Sydney. "I wanted this film to be different. This film *will* be different. The audience will feel as if they are trapped in the house with the sisters and as anxious as they are to escape it."

"But not for a party," muttered Eleanor. "Women cannot be appeased with a simple party, a few drinks, and a pretty gown. They also want power, as our battle for the vote proved. Now we must show that we can use it wisely. We have been kept isolated too long, now we move into a new way of thinking. The sisters step forward into a new world and a new power after being imprisoned by their family's past. That is the current that carries this plot, that is why a party would be all wrong."

Betsy started to say something, then didn't. Obviously there was no winning such a dispute with Eleanor when she framed it like that. Whatever Betsy said, she would either fail to uphold the ideals of those who fought so hard to get women the vote, or label herself as far too easily appeased or too quickly distracted by pretty gowns. I gave Betsy a sympathetic glance. I couldn't figure out the correct answer either.

Eleanor's intellect was formidable. I admired her greatly. She also scared me a little. Which was unfortunate, because she could be the kindest of souls. If I had told her of my fears earlier, the outcome of that summer might have been different.

"We need the isolation of the old house, the anxiety of the sisters to leave their past behind," said Sydney. "They move to a new place and leave behind the shadows of the old. They remake their world as we will remake ours. Besides, it is much easier to frighten an audience with an empty room."

"A completely empty room?" questioned Eleanor. "Cannot be done. There's nothing frightening about that."

"Perhaps not on stage," conceded Sydney. "But it works on film. Didn't it, Jeany?"

I laughed. It had worked. It was a trick that Renee and I came up with to fill a spot in a film where not much happened. Of course, Sydney didn't like it at first. But when he saw how the audience reacted, he claimed it as his own invention.

"We had a scene in the *Witch Woman of the Woods*, where the heroine has to run away from the house into the woods. But why would she do that?" I said, echoing Renee's early arguments against the scene. "Wouldn't a house, even a spooky old house, be safer than running through the forest at night? So we show her enter the house, very afraid, very uncertain. She stands in the hallway looking into an empty parlor room. The audience sees it from the heroine's viewpoint. Just a long, long look through a half-open door at a nearly empty room. Just a chair and the edge of the table."

"No dripping blood, no headless corpses?" said Eleanor.

I shook my head. "Nothing. Everything is completely bare and simple. And we kept the camera on that empty room for a full minute." One minute of staring at nothing can seem like eternity in a crowded theater.

Eleanor caught that and nodded. "Long enough that the audience starts to fidget. Papers rustle. People start whispering."

"People always whisper at the movies," said Betsy. "They are reading the title cards out loud to their friends. But it was a long time with nothing happening."

"That was the beauty of it," Sydney picked up. "A moment of absolute stillness with an audience trained to look for frantic action by those silly Keystone pictures and all the rest."

"A long moment," agreed Eleanor. She looked intrigued by the idea. She was a very intelligent woman. "Then what did you do to make them jump?"

"Slammed the door," I said.

I still remembered the satisfaction of that spectacular hard push after sitting behind the door for a minute. The bang of the door, not that anyone could hear it, and Fred's triumphant call of "Perfect!" as he finished the shot.

"In the theater, the organ supplied the pop of noise, the sound of the slam," I explained. "And Fred had shot so close that it was like the door slammed right in their face."

"Clever. Bet that made them jump," said Eleanor.

I nodded. "It did." The night that Renee and I snuck into the back of a theater to watch, one man yelled so loud in surprise that he nearly frightened us. He certainly caused the rest of the audience to gasp. After that, nobody wondered why Renee as the sweet heroine turned around and ran off into the woods not to meet the terrible witch, but to become her. That was the other twist that kept the audience talking as they streamed out of the theater and into the night. It also marked the end of Renee playing sweet heroines in the movies.

"It's funny," I said. "That scene. The house was very similar. The way that the woods ran in the back." We'd filmed at a mansion that one of the studio heads had built up in the canyons. Sydney had picked it because there was a long lawn in the back that led to a tall iron fence and a gate opening into a wooded ravine. I remember Renee running down the back steps of that house and to the gate to disappear into the place of evil enchantment that changed the heroine forever into the witch in the woods.

"We use bits of our life to inform our stories," said Sydney. "And we are drawn to stories that inform our lives. Like dear Renee, forever transforming herself into something that she is not."

That made me look up. As far as I knew, Renee had never discussed her complicated history with Sydney. Or that I was actually her sister. But given their intimate relationship over the last few years, he probably guessed that she wasn't completely who she said she was. Was this a hint that he knew enough to keep her secret or a threat that he knew so much that could harm her?

"I watched a few of your older films," said Eleanor. "I have friends in the business and they were able to get a hold of the reels for a private screening. I did not see the witch movie but I saw the siren and the vampire. Both were surprisingly good. Renee truly transforms herself. At one moment, you are sure that she is innocent, perhaps the victim, and at the next she's a woman of such power, even of evil. Lulu, as much as I love her, cannot do that. She is always just Lulu. She can hold your eye. She can make you care about her character. She can be unforgettable in scenes. But she can never be anyone other than Lulu."

I knew what she meant. There were two kinds of actors, both equally at the top of their game. One disappeared into their parts so completely that you could not believe it was the same person the next time that you saw them. But each time you saw them, you believed in that role so completely that you couldn't look away. The other also caught your eye but always by playing a variation of the same person. If they strayed too far from that character, you didn't really believe it. Chaplin was like that. Always the Tramp, and you loved him for it, but never truly anyone else.

"But Lulu being Lulu is exactly what I want," said Sydney. "Today we will film them preparing for the dinner, tomorrow the dinner itself, and then we'll record Lulu's scream. The scream that will shatter the mirrors and release the masked stranger."

Fred looked up from his breakfast at that. "You didn't say anything about shattering mirrors. Do you mean the ones in the hall? Aren't they old? Valuable?"

"You cannot break those mirrors," said Sydney. "No, I want to record Lulu's scream. And film her screaming, of course. Then film dozens of mirrors shattering. As if mirrors are breaking around the world. As if doors are opening everywhere. Then we will do the scene with the masked stranger."

Fred sighed. "Dozens of mirrors. Breaking. Cracking and falling apart?"

"No, no," said Sydney. "An explosion of glass. Can't you use dynamite or something?"

Fred swore. "You want to put us all in the hospital? Sydney, we are talking about exploding glass. Is Lulu or Renee going to be anywhere near it? And if we do explosions indoors, we might burn the place down. It's not safe, you lunatic." Fred only called Sydney insane when he was truly worried. They had these fights once or twice before. The one time Fred backed down, Selby broke his leg.

"No, no, Fred," soothed Sydney, obviously recognizing that he had pushed a bit too hard. "You can set it up wherever you want. Buy some cheap mirrors, rig an explosion, film the results. We'll edit it in."

"We can use the back lawn," I said. "Down near the fence."

Fred grumbled a bit but finally agreed. "I can rig it. But everyone must stay in the house. I hate explosions."

"What about you?" I said.

"Somebody has to crank the camera," said Fred. "Humbert and I can rig up some type of barrier, just poke the lens through. Yeah, I can make that work. But, Sydney, between that and setting up the equipment to record

Lulu's scream, it's going to be a few days."

"That's fine," said Sydney. "We're nearly to the end. As long as Jeany has our mask done by the solstice, we'll be all right."

"I have a couple of masks," I admitted.

"But I need time," said Fred. "Explosions!"

"You have eight days," said Sydney with a snap of his teeth as he crunched through his marmalade-dripping toast. "You can be ready by then."

Fred muttered more about explosions, screams, and working for lunatics. "We've got just over a week," he said. "That's not nearly enough time."

"Of course it is," said Sydney. "We used to do an entire film in a week. Have you all gone soft? We can do this. Jeany, bring me the masks now."

"The solstice?" said Eleanor, saving me the need to respond. "Is that when we get to see your finale?"

"Ah, yes," said Sydney, finishing up his toast with one last bite. "The longest day of light, the shortest night, the perfect time to finish filming. It will be marvelous. Don't you agree, Max?"

Max mumbled something and folded his paper. He stood up. "I need to phone the studio," he said. "Let them know everything is proceeding on schedule."

As he left the room, Betsy turned to me and said, "Isn't anyone worried about bad luck?"

"What do you mean?"

"You know. Breaking mirrors. Seven years of bad luck."

I shook my head. "I don't think Sydney believes in bad luck. At least not for him."

But it was odd. Sydney was superstitious. Renee once laughed at him for walking out of his way to avoid a black cat. Maybe he did not know that breaking mirrors caused trouble.

Later I learned the truth. That he did not care what luck he brought down on the rest of us. And that he was not the only one with that attitude.

CHAPTER SEVENTEEN

Fred tried different ways of blowing up mirrors in the barn. The constant sounds of shattering glass reverberated through the house, to the point the indoor mirrors seemed to be humming in sympathy. I hated going down that hallway more and more each day. I felt like I had to apologize to the mirrors for the multiple deaths of their brethren. I also wanted to break them all every time I caught a glimpse of a crooked reflection out of the corner of my eye.

Humbert mumbled a lot about the waste of good hay, as Fred used the bales normally reserved for the grass-cutting mule or for mulching the garden as barriers to keep exploding glass from hitting him.

I tried to escape my woes once or twice by watching these tests, but Fred always chased me out with stern warnings about the dangers of flying glass and putting an eye out.

"And what will you do if you lose an eye?" I asked.

"Only need one to peer through the viewfinder," Fred answered far too nonchalantly.

At the house, when Fred did come back from the barn to film the scenes that Eleanor created, things became even messier. Of course, Sydney's assurances that we would only film one or two more scenes before the solstice quickly dissolved into a rush to get several new ideas into the can.

Perhaps it was Lulu or perhaps it was Renee, but neither were thrilled with doing little more than getting dressed for a dinner and then having the dinner alone in the house. They felt it didn't give them much scope to show off their best talents, despite Sydney's reassurances that the finale would be worth it.

"If this is all that the audience has to watch," said Renee on the first night, "they will either fall asleep or walk out." After spending a day watching Sydney direct and then change his directions while Betsy fussed with Renee's curls, the ones that I had already perfectly set, I had to agree.

"Our audiences expect a shock a minute," said Renee. It was a slogan that one of the theaters had used about an earlier film, one where we made the actors jump out of dark corners and rigged props to drop from the ceiling. "This is going to become the snore a minute film if we don't add some terror."

Eleanor became an unexpected ally. "I have to agree," she said. "When we do my horrid little plays in New York, I'm careful to ladle out the blood as thickly and as quickly as possible. You don't want the audience to stop and think. That's the worst thing that can happen to a horrible shocker. Otherwise they'll start wondering why a perfectly healthy young woman doesn't run screaming from the monster luring her to her doom."

"Exactly," said Renee. "Only in this case, it is why don't two bored young ladies leave their lonely house? Sydney, we are not filming Chekhov. Something has to happen."

"Spare me fickle, spineless, drifting people," said Eleanor. "You are right. The sisters should be actively courting their fate, however Sydney wants to arrange the end. Let's make something happen."

But Eleanor's ideas, while exactly the type of frightening and bizarre that Renee wanted, created the next accident.

Eleanor rewrote the dinner scene to include a lightning bolt that struck a guest through the window, slaying or at least maiming the poor man that the sisters have invited into their home.

"How do I do that?" said a much-beleaguered Fred, who was still searching for a mixture to create the proper explosion of mirrors as well as trying to borrow a microphone and other equipment from the University to record Lulu's scream. We all checked the calendar and were aware of time swiftly running out. The solstice was only a couple of days away.

"At our theater, we'd use a prop man," said Eleanor. "One who did a flash of light across the table and a rumble of a thunder sheet. Of course you need sound for that effect."

"We can write noise into the cue sheet for the accompanist. I hope this only shows in large theaters with good musicians," muttered Fred. "We have enough instructions to keep an orchestra busy. But we need something else."

In the end, he decided to use an old-fashioned flash powder. "Lycopodium powder," he said to me, showing me the yellow mixture. "The magician's friend. There was even a French fellow who tried to run an engine with it. Makes quite a flash."

"Where did you get it?"

"That five-and-dime, the one where Lulu wanted to go shopping? I found it. More of a hardware store than some. Even has a bunch of old men hanging in the back around the stove with bad coffee and lots of ideas of how to make and break things," Fred said. It sounded like his description of heaven. "I've been talking to them about different ways to break the mirrors. He had a number of minor explosive mixtures to try."

"Is it safe?" I said.

"Probably not," Fred sighed, "but it's better than some of Sydney's ideas. He wanted me to electrify the candlesticks and actually shock Hal when the bang goes off. Thought it would get more of a reaction."

"Not again," I muttered. Sydney did something like that in a past picture. A mild shock to make the actor jump. Fred had been furious when he'd found out that Paul had rigged that up for Sydney. It was like the balloon without any ropes. It never occurred to Sydney that someone could get hurt. It was one of the many reasons I appreciated Fred watching out for us. And, with Paul gone, I couldn't think of anyone else who could create a stupid trick like that for Sydney.

"Let's just tell Sydney that the bang will be so loud, everyone will jump," I said.

Sydney decided to film the scene at night, to make the flash at the window stand out more with the electric ceiling lights off. We broke out the stage lights that we'd brought from Hollywood to light the characters from the side. The room became a tangle of cords and wires that made Fred snap at everyone.

Then we discovered the real problem. Fred couldn't light the powder and crank the camera. He was too far away. With Paul gone, we lacked anyone that Fred felt was experienced enough to handle such a volatile effect.

"I think we should call it off," he told Sydney.

"No," said Sydney. "I like the scene as Eleanor has written it. We keep it. Can't Jeany or Max light the powder?"

Fred looked horrified at the thought. I hoped it was the idea of Max bumbling with a match and an explosive powder that bothered him. I knew I could do it, but I also had to be across the room to flip the switch on the lights and plunge the room into darkness after the flash. We'd already rehearsed it a couple of times. I knew the cues better than anyone.

As for the rest, Betsy was playing the maid, Pola and Hal were the guests, Jim also was serving, and Renee and Lulu were the hosts.

"Eleanor?" I suggested, because putting fastidious Max in charge of an explosion wasn't workable. And he needed to wave the slate in front of the camera so we could keep track of the takes, anyway.

Eleanor flatly refused. "I hate explosions. Fire. Loud bangs. Reminds me too much of my war days."

"But you wrote it into the scene," I said.

"Of course, you always give the audience something that terrifies you," she said. But she continued to refuse to help with the scene.

"If it is a loud flash and bang," said Lulu, "she won't even watch. She'll be busy writing up a new way to kill my character while we are playing the scene."

"Mister Claude," said Fred. "He could do it."

"Who's Mister Claude?" I asked.

"A stage magician who talked me into buying the powder. He's on the Orpheum circuit but visiting a friend in Arkham. He was picking up things for his act," said Fred, who explained this magician was a fellow fan of small-town five-and-dime stores. "He should know how to handle it." Fred patted his pockets and found a card. "He gave me his card and wrote his hotel phone on the back. Said he'd be interested in seeing how we made movies."

Mister Claude proclaimed himself charmed with Fred's invitation to set off an explosion on a film set. I liked him immensely when we met. If there was ever a man that looked like a stage magician, it was Julius Claude. Even in a simple dark suit, he gave off the aura of wearing a tuxedo with all the trimmings. I almost expected him to produce a dove from his pocket.

"I've often thought that we magicians could use more of the new technology in our shows," he said, looking over Fred's beloved camera with much interest. "There's possibilities in this."

"And we're going to take more and more of your audience every year," said Sydney, sweeping into the room. "Good to see you, Claude, it's been some years."

Apparently, Sydney knew more people in Arkham than we were aware of.

Mister Claude nodded. "A long time. You came to me about an act for your circus."

"Not my circus," said Sydney. "It belonged to Lucinda. Her grandfather had started it and it was a bit run down by the time that I arrived. I tried to build it up. But the time for circuses, vaudeville, and theater is past."

"Indeed," said Mister Claude. "Sally will be heartbroken when I tell her. She's just booked us into six months of playing the Orpheum Circuit."

"Still have that assistant?" said Sydney. "You are a lucky man."

"And the Fitzmaurices remain very unlucky men. I heard about Lucinda's disappearance and the circus fire."

"Tragic accident," said Sydney, moving away from us. "Although nobody knows what happened to Lucinda. They never found a body."

It was a bewildering exchange. Sydney always acted like he'd been away from Arkham for years and didn't know anyone in town any more. Although this sounded like the two men met in Sydney's fabled circus. The circus that left Sydney broke at a nickelodeon in San Francisco, looking for a new art form.

"Mister Claude," I said. "If you come this way, I'll show you where we want to create the flash."

"Please call me, Julius, Mister Claude is my stage name," he said with a courteous shake of my hand. "After all, we are fellow entertainers. And your name is?"

"I'm Jeany, Jeany Lin. I work on the costumes and makeup. Actually, I design the costumes. And the props, and do other things when we need someone."

"A talented young woman," said Julius. "Much like Sally Alexander. My act would not work at all without my assistant."

"Then you are lucky to have her," I said.

"Yes, indeed, although I don't think she always believes me when I tell her that. Is this where you want your flash?" We had gone out the kitchen door and circled back to the window outside the dining room.

We looked into the lit room. "Yes, right here," I said. "They will come in, sit at the table, make some conversation, and then Renee will say that she is waiting for the stranger. That's when you light it. When you hear her say 'I am waiting for the stranger.' Bang goes the flash and I turn out the lights."

"I did not know the actors spoke in the movies. Nobody can hear them."

"They say the lines. At least in scenes like this, where they are supposed to be making conversation. They used to talk all kinds of nonsense, but then lip readers in the audience would report to others what they said. If it was too foul or too silly, it would make the papers."

Julius chuckled. "I can see the embarrassment."

"So they speak the lines or close enough to the lines that will appear on the cards. Sydney insisted on that line: 'I am waiting for the stranger.'" As I said it, I felt a cold touch on the back of my neck. A whisper of a breath sounded in my ear. Once again, I had the feeling of being watched that walking down the hall of mirrors always inspired in me.

The magician noticed my shiver. "You should be careful," he said.

"What is it about this place?" I said.

"Arkham or this house?"

"Both?"

He made a gesture with his hand. A small white card appeared between his first finger and his thumb. He handed it to me. It was a simple pasteboard card with the name Professor Krosnowski on it.

"I know her," I said. "She was at Velma's. She spoke to me. Florie told me her name."

Julius nodded. "I am not surprised. You should talk to both of them again. Those women understand this town. They can help you."

I remembered the tramp, Ashcan Pete, had given the same advice about talking to Florie. I'd meant to go back to the diner, but Sydney had added extra scenes and I gotten caught up in the filming. I mentioned this to the magician.

Julius looked down at me. "Ashcan Pete knows this town and its people. If he thinks you should talk to Florie, you should do so. I also recommend seeking out Professor Krosnowski before the solstice."

"Why?"

"There's something here," he said. "You seem like a sensible young woman. And one who has seen too many stage tricks for me to misdirect you."

"I've only been to magic shows a couple of times. Fred likes them. He says there's a lot of tricks that we could learn, that we could use in the movies."

He chuckled again. "Indeed. I think we could learn from each other. But be careful. There's something about this house, about this family, and, I must admit, about Arkham that is not a stage illusion. I am convinced that there is real magic here. Or at least forces that cannot be easily explained."

His face was half in shadow and his voice, a deep baritone, sounded too serious for me to dismiss him out of hand. But could I believe a stage magician who claimed to know real magic when he saw it?

"Why are you telling me this?" I said again.

"Because little more than five years ago, Sydney Fitzmaurice came to one of my shows. He stayed afterward to ask me about some things that I had said. It was patter, the usual mystic mumbo jumbo that most magicians use in the act. Sydney heard something in my speech that caught his attention."

Sydney liked magicians. I knew that he often went to shows. Renee used to go with him, but magic acts bored her. Also she disliked the stage magician's common practice of hiding birds and rabbits in their clothing. She felt it was unfair to the poor creatures to be stuffed up a sleeve or trapped in a hat.

"Sydney heard me speak some phrases that I learned from a French friend who had died in the War, a man who often spoke of magic as real. So Sydney came backstage with a manuscript that he claimed came from his grandfather. A very odd play, apparently written by the grandfather when he was a young man. But the heroines spoke phrases that were even older than that, phrases very similar to those that I spoke. Sydney thought this was tied to ideas, rituals, that his family had stolen long ago."

I had a suspicion that this was Sydney's manuscript that he kept promising to Eleanor and then hiding from her. It sounded like he'd been doing that particular trick for longer than we'd known.

Julius shifted so the light spilling out of the windows illuminated his face more fully. He looked very serious and much older than he had appeared in the hallway only moments before. "Sydney was very secretive. He wanted my knowledge and he would give nothing in exchange for my advice. But it intrigued me that he claimed Arkham as home. This town intrigues me. I've found the occult library at the University is extensive. A strange thing to discover in a small New England town and enough to bring me back whenever I have engagements nearby. But I understand the dangers. Do you?"

"I can't leave," I said, as troubled as I was by this and the earlier discussion about the Lucinda who had disappeared. Was that the woman who the professor thought Sydney killed? No, she'd spoken of a student. "I have… friends in this company. I cannot leave them." I had to protect Renee. I could not abandon the rest of the company, not friends like Fred and Betsy.

"You may need to make a choice," said Julius. "Lucinda wanted what Sydney offered and failed to take the danger in account."

"You mentioned her before," I said. "Who was Lucinda?"

There were shouts inside the dining room. Sydney barked out instructions for the coming scene. Time was running out. I had to go to my place, or the scene would not work.

"Lucinda was more a creature of the air than the earth. She lived between the two," Julius said. "An aerialist in a small circus. Sydney promised her the moon, stars, and all the rest. He worked as a ringmaster for a season. He tried to create a spectacle with the show. He dressed them all in mirrors. He strung mirrors around the tent, so when Lucinda flew, it seemed a dozen women took flight."

I heard Fred calling me, but I needed the end of this story. "What happened? Please, tell me."

"Sydney came to me, asking for a magic that I did not have," Julius said. "I do not know what he did that night. But there was a fire. It destroyed the circus. And no one ever saw Lucinda again."

"Did he use a mask? Did he put a mask on her?" I said. Then, in response to Fred's shout, I called back, "I am coming. Just a minute."

I asked Julius again. "Did Sydney ask you for a mask?"

"No," said Julius. "He did not ask me for a mask. But I heard that Lucinda had a new costume. One that included a silver mask that reflected the audience, that reflected the flames, when she flew."

Time was up. Sydney was shouting again. "Thank you, thank you," I said as I ran back to the door. Florie, I was thinking, I need to talk to Florie. "You know what to do."

Julius waved in acknowledgment and shouted to me as I ran. "So do you." Then, just as if he was a mind reader as well as a magician, he said, "Go see Florie. She can tell you more."

I reached my spot before Sydney exploded. Fred was already behind the camera. The actors were all in place around the table. Renee looked lovely and, as Sydney exclaimed, otherworldly in a pale shimmer of a dress that I had sewn for another film but we had never used. Lulu appeared young and more pretty than beautiful in a lace dress that I had fitted to her earlier that morning. It was cut from one of the dresses that I had found in the attic and well suited to the character of the younger, shyer sister.

Betsy and Jim whisked around the table, very smart in servant costumes that we had brought from California. Hal and Pola both wore their usual dress-up clothes, a little more formal than they had for earlier scenes, but easy modifications had turned them into a country judge and his wife, out for a dinner with a pair of young ladies.

Eleanor was not watching. I remembered what she had said about her dislike of loud bangs. No doubt she was in her room for rewrites.

"Places," shouted Sydney.

The actors sank into chairs or, in the case of Betsy and Jim, began leaning over the "guests" as if they were serving the nonexistent food in their dishes. A few minutes of meaningless chatter was made to fool the lip readers: "How was the weather? Did it seem too cool tonight? Can I have soup? Thank you for the soup."

After enough of this for Fred to get his establishing shot, Renee spoke the one line that would appear on the title card: "I am waiting for the stranger."

Bang! Julius lit the flash powder. The bright light flooded into the room. I threw the switch that doused all the lights.

CHAPTER EIGHTEEN

Hal was alive, but barely. Max calmly called the operator and asked for Doctor Wills to be sent out to the house. Then he sat in a corner, taking notes and talking quietly with Sydney while the rest of us moaned about what a bad luck picture this was turning out to be. When the doctor arrived, she took one look at Hal and called for an ambulance.

"What happened?" I asked Fred after the ambulance came and went.

"I think he was shocked," said Fred, who promptly crawled under the dining room table. I crawled after him as quickly as I could.

"Shocked? How?" This couldn't have happened. We'd checked everything. Fred had checked everything. Hal couldn't be heading to hospital.

Fred pulled up a cable that had run under the table, leading to one of the big lights that we'd brought with us for night scenes. "I don't know how," Fred said, running his hand along the length of cable. "There's nothing wrong here. An arc of electricity like that, it should have fried these cables. And the fuses should be destroyed."

"What do you mean? The lights came on."

"Yes," said Fred. "The lights came on. The fuses worked. After a huge arc of electricity, like a bolt of lightning, strikes Hal. Jeany, that's not normal."

We crawled back out. Fred checked each of the lights in turn. Then he went to the kitchen to look at the fuse box. He found nothing.

We spent the rest of the night going over and over the scene. Nothing made any sense. It should have been as safe as safe could be. It was like the picture that had fallen off the wall or the coffin that closed on Lulu. Simple tricks, the type that we always used, that kept going wrong in this film.

Neither of us dared to speak of Paul. Of blood in the woods or the feeling of something truly wrong.

Well past midnight, we gave up. I dragged myself upstairs, almost too tired to sleep. As I walked past Renee's door, she called out to me. She was sitting by the window, peering out in the darkness. As I came up to her, I could hear the scratch of claws up on the roof.

"Those crows," said Renee. "Still out there."

I pressed my face to the cool glass and let my eyes adjust to the faint moonlight. Dark shapes were visible along the edge of the roof. They bobbed and weaved about, and I could hear the faint mutter of birds waking briefly and then returning to sleep.

"They are not doing anything," I said to Renee.

"No," she said with a shudder, turning away from the window. "They never do anything. They're just there. Like sentinels. Watching us. Waiting for another disaster to happen and somebody to die this time."

I couldn't bring myself to speak of Paul. He was in California. Max told us that Paul was in California. I couldn't bring myself to speak of the pool of blood in the woods or the terror it woke in me.

I'd never heard my sister sound so depressed. Usually I was the one who worried. Who was sure that something we'd done wouldn't work out. Renee just knew she would succeed, that she would become a star, that we would find a place to accept us even though we weren't everything that we said we were.

"It's just crows," I said. "They can't hurt us."

"I hate this house," said Renee. "It wants something from me."

"Renee!" I said, although I had felt the same for days. "It's a house. It doesn't have feelings."

"Are you sure?" said Renee, her voice barely above a whisper, her body slumped in defeat in front of her mirror. "Ever since we went into those woods, I've felt something terrible has happened. Something horrible will happen. Then the house will eat us up. Keep us trapped here forever."

"Renee!" I said again. This was too close to my nightmares. The house engulfed in smoke and flames while I wandered forever through its interminable hallways and was forever caught in the endless reflections of the mirrors downstairs. "We can walk out the door right now. Call a cab and go to the train station like Paul. We don't have to stay."

Renee looked shocked. As shocked as I felt as soon as I said it. But there wasn't any reason to stay. Let Sydney finish the picture without us. We could go back to Los Angeles. There were always more pictures, other directors, and nothing, nothing, was keeping us here.

"I cannot leave Sydney," said Renee. "We have to finish this picture."

"Why?" I said. "We've done enough for Sydney. You've made him famous."

"No," said Renee. "He made me famous."

"No he didn't," I said, suddenly as furious as I'd ever been with my brilliant, beautiful, genius of a sister. "You're the one who thought up the best tricks, the best way to fool the audience into thinking one thing and showing them another. You came up with all the twists, like that empty room. You made Sydney's ideas better and bigger and more amazing than anyone else ever could."

"More than you, with your clever costumes? More than Fred, with all his camera tricks?" said Renee. "More than Pola, Hal, Jim, Paul, and Betsy, with all the characters that they've created? More than Max with his notes and constant calls to keep the studio happy?"

"Yes," I said. "There's dozens like us in Los Angeles. Hundreds more every day, getting off the train and dreaming of work in the movies. But you are the star. You are the one that makes each picture unforgettable."

Renee grabbed my hands and squeezed them, that clasp of an older sister to a younger, the way that she had on the first night in the orphanage, and on the night that we decided to run away.

"Sydney gave me that chance, he let me be the leading lady. Not the treacherous fortune teller screaming curses or the wicked harem girl plotting to knife her master. The only roles that a half-Chinese girl from Oakland would be allowed to play. But Sydney didn't care who I was, what I was, he made me a star."

I shook my head. "You would have been a star without him."

"No," said Renee. "He got us all here, he made us the best at what we do. Scaring the audience, making them dream a nightmare, giving them a memory of something that never was and never could be."

"You sound just like him," I said. "Quoting bits and pieces that don't mean much if you stop and think about it. Renee, there's something wrong here. We should go home."

"No," said my implacable sister. She sat down at the mirror and peered into it, much as she had looked into the night-dark window earlier. What she saw in her reflected eyes seemed to satisfy her. "There is a way forward. We can finish. There's just the final scene with the mask."

I thought of the silver mask and its paper twin lying in my room. There was something about it that continued to bother me. The more that I stared at it, the more I could see the shadow of a face behind it. But not the face of an ordinary woman. The face of a monster, something both organic and metallic, something both hideously of nature and created by an alien science that I didn't want to understand.

But I couldn't tell that to Renee. That was a thought generated by nightmares and not an idea that I wanted to discuss in a house that creaked and groaned around us as dozens of crows slept, muttering crow dreams on the roof.

"I need the mask," said Renee. Her voice sounded peculiar now, an echo of her normal decisive tones.

"Not yet," I said. "We aren't filming that scene yet."

Renee kept staring at her reflection. A shadow stirred in the mirror. I looked over my shoulder at the bed curtains. That impossible canopied bed that she'd claimed from the very first night. No drafts moved the draperies. Renee continued to gaze into the mirror and the shifting reflections, which looked like a creature underwater rising to the surface.

"The mirror is key," she said. "Terror is key."

"Renee," I said, laying my hand on her shoulder and resolutely not looking into the mirror. "What are you talking about?"

She started a little under my hand. Renee blinked like someone waking up. "Finishing the picture. I saw Sydney's manuscript finally. He showed me it tonight."

"Oh, so you know how it will end?" I said. "What happens to the sisters?"

Renee was looking back into the mirror. "What? The sisters? I guess so. It's so much more than that." Her voice drifted off. If her eyes hadn't been wide open and staring so intently at her reflection, I would have thought she'd fallen asleep where she was sitting.

"But what is Sydney trying to do?" I resisted the urge

to shake her. Or at least spin her around on her chair so she was no longer looking at those fluctuating shadows in the mirror. It had to be the curtains, or perhaps the crows outside the window, that were causing those agitating shapes. I refused to see a dog-headed man crouching in the corner of the reflected room. When I looked back over my shoulder, it was just Renee's enormous traveling truck occupying that part of the room. When I looked back to the mirror, it looked as if three creatures stared out at us, or a three-headed dog man with snarling mouths.

"What was in Sydney's manuscript?" I asked.

"An ending," said the now sleepy sounding Renee. "An ending of everything normal."

"That sounds horrible," I said as firmly as I could. I liked normal. I liked simple days with friends, chatting over coffee, pinning up hems, sketching ideas in my book, or eating breakfast. I liked Fred being incapable of passing anything mechanized without wanting to tear it apart. Or Betsy counting cards in her head and gleefully pulling in the pot. Or Pola knitting blankets for all the babies of her acquaintance and Hal trying to decide if chickens and eggs would be the best strategy for early retirement. "I like normal," I said out loud. "I don't want it to end."

Renee swung away from her mirror with a yawn. "I'm so tired. I think I'll sleep until noon. Only a few more days until we finish the picture." Her voice shifted again. It was as if she was playing every possible version of my sister, of the persona that she had created for herself when we ran away so long ago. Now she was the daring Renee again. "We should do something amazing, darling. Maybe take the train to New York and shop our way through the city. How would you like that?"

"But, Renee," I said. "What about Sydney's manuscript? What was the end?"

She climbed into the bed, shaking her head. "Don't worry. It is good. Very good. Sydney's right. It will make us famous. Max says the studio is going to be so happy with this picture that we'll be able to do whatever we want."

"And what do you want, Renee?" What do I want, I asked myself. I had no answers.

As I turned off the lamp by Renee's bed, she stirred and said, "Jeany, can you cover the mirror? Please. Just throw a towel over it."

I picked up a shawl from her chair and dropped it over the dressing table mirror so it was covered completely.

Renee gave a sigh of satisfaction and rolled on her side, presenting her back to the mirror. "Thank you," she murmured. "I hate waking up and seeing those reflections. They watch me. I wish they wouldn't."

CHAPTER NINETEEN

The next morning, after checking on Renee who was still heavily asleep with her back to the covered mirror, I found everyone gathered in the parlor. In one corner, Eleanor sat on the sofa with Pumpkin on her lap, looking very wan, leaning against Lulu's shoulder and muttering in her ear.

Lulu finally shook her head and snapped, "Darling, don't be silly. It was an accident. Nobody knew poor Hal would be hurt."

"But it is exactly…" Eleanor started, but Lulu shushed her with far more force than I had ever seen her use.

"It's nothing," she insisted. Then she spotted me and waved me to her. "Jeany, did you see a bolt of lightning come through the window last night?"

"No, of course not," I said. "There was the flash. Mister Claude set that off." I closed my eyes, trying to picture the scene exactly as it happened. "I turned off the lights and then there was a flash across the table. Fred thinks it was one of the cables. That something sparked or there was an electric arc."

"Like the animals, two by two," said Lulu.

"No," said Fred, coming up behind me. "An arc discharge. Or voltaic arc."

Lulu and Eleanor both blinked at how that sounded in Fred's Brooklyn accent.

"He reads science magazines," I said.

"A little lightning bolt. A short-pulse electrical arc. But I can't find what caused it," said Fred. "I thought one of the cables was loose or torn. That might explain it. Why would it ground in Hal's body…"

"Fred!" I said as Eleanor looked sick and Lulu fussed over her with consoling little pats.

"There's no reason a spark should arc like that between the candlestick and Hal," said Fred. "There was nothing touching the candlestick to cause that to happen."

"Exactly as I wrote it," Eleanor said again. "Lightning comes through the window, strikes the candlestick, and then strikes down the old man. All because he is moving the candlestick to see the sisters more clearly."

"But Hal didn't touch the candlestick," I said. "He was supposed to rise from his chair and lift it after the big flash. Just after we switched the lights back on. Then he would have mimed a heart attack and dropped to the floor. That would have been the next scenario to film. But he hadn't touched the candlestick yet. I'm sure that he was just sitting in his chair, waiting, when I flipped the switch."

"I didn't see him move," said Lulu, "although that flash was so bright, I had sparks in my eyes. But it looked like there was just a fizz of electricity going from the candlestick to him. Without him doing a thing."

"A fizz?" said Fred.

"I don't read science magazines," said Lulu. "Sort of a hiss. Like an electrical snake leapt out and bit him."

Eleanor moaned a bit more and dropped her head into her hands.

"Eleanor," Lulu said, very stern. "For all your claims of being descended from witches, you cannot make things happen just because you write them down. Not even little curses. If you could, half the reporters in New York would be lying dead by now."

Eleanor raised her head and looked at Lulu. "I never wrote about the reporters. But I did write that scene with the guillotine."

"That was not your fault," said Lulu very firmly, not like her usual tones. Then, to Fred and me, she said, "It was the very first of our terror plays. Eleanor had a script that she found in France. She adapted it for me."

"Horrific happenings in the French Revolution," said Eleanor, with a resigned sigh. "Murder, mayhem, suggestions of lewd acts, even greater suggestions of diabolism, and a finale with a guillotine. Innocent girl loses her head while the howling mob watches. We called it *Reign of Horror.*"

"Sounds like a script that Sydney would love," I said.

"It didn't go over very well with the critics," said Eleanor. "We hired a magician to provide the final scene with the guillotine, but it never worked like I wanted. So we kept making changes in rehearsals. Which just leads to disaster, as you know. Opening night was the worst. The damn thing stuck halfway down. There's Lulu on the chopping block and nothing happens. So we cut the lights, dropped the curtain, and prayed everyone would think that was how it was supposed to go. But we were slaughtered in the papers."

"So Eleanor rewrote the scene that night in absolute fury," said Lulu, "and turned it around so that the magician is suddenly and permanently maimed by the very guillotine that he meant to use to destroy the heroine."

"And what happened?" I asked.

"Exactly what I wrote," said Eleanor again. "The stupid apparatus collapsed. Lulu walked away unscathed. But the stage magician, that poor man, lost his hand."

"But that was an accident?" I said. It had to be an accident. Bad things don't happen just because somebody writes a curse down.

"Gouts of blood and screaming accident. We dropped the curtain even faster. And had fabulous reviews the next day. Everyone wanted to come to our theater. But we never did *Reign of Horror* again," said Lulu. "Eleanor did get her wish. Revenge and fortune, all at the same time."

"That makes it sound like magic," I said, trying very hard to sound skeptical. Except there had been all those hints from Ashcan Pete, Julius, Florie, and even Darrell, that magic existed in Arkham. And if it existed in Arkham, why not New York?

Eleanor looked at me. "I have always been very careful since then to, well, not be angry when I write. My grandmother used to say that it was anger, hate, and other terrible emotions that led the women in our family to black magic. She was always preaching about it. How our wicked witch of an ancestor was burned in Salem for cursing her neighbors and the rest of the family fled south. But that wickedness went with us, even unto the seventh generation, as per my hysterical old granny." Eleanor's sophisticated drawl had dropped into a more blurred cadence, one that I recognized from Southern actors and actresses. Not quite Dixie, but close.

"Eleanor," said Lulu, draping her arms around her. "You are the least wicked woman that I know."

"You didn't mean to hurt Hal," I said.

"No, of course not," said Eleanor, "not at all. I quite adore him and love discussing chickens with him."

"Well, then," said Lulu.

"But I was angry when I wrote that scene," said Eleanor. "I've been angry, just brimful of hateful anger, every time that Sydney teases me about that old manuscript of his. I wanted to show him."

Lulu fussed and petted Eleanor some more. Eventually Eleanor agreed that the whole incident was just an accident. The pair decided to go for a drive, pleading a need to get out of the house.

"Would you like to go to the diner?" I said to Fred, who had sat silent, even slightly stunned through Eleanor's story.

Fred looked at me oddly. "Did Eleanor just confess to being a witch? Do you believe her?" he said, as if I should have reacted more than I had. Except by now, someone telling me that magic might be real seemed like old news.

"I need to talk to Florie again," I said to Fred. "We need to do that if we're ever going to understand what is going on."

Before we left, I hunted down Betsy in her room. I was worried about Renee and her strange behavior the night before. I asked Betsy to check on Renee.

"Of course," said Betsy. "I was going to start writing to other studios. This is the last picture that I'm making with Sydney." She rummaged through her trunk for stationery and envelopes.

"But what about Max?"

"Max is Max," said Betsy with a sigh. "Cannot help loving those three worry lines in his forehead but I don't like how he goes along with everything that Sydney says. He's just a studio flunky."

"Are you sure?" I said. There were times in recent days when I felt Max had more agency that we originally thought. That maybe he told what Sydney to do, and Sydney listened.

"It's always about the studio. Nothing but how the studio trusts him to get things right and the studio knows that he'll do what is necessary. I don't think he even cared that Hal was hurt," said Betsy, and she looked heartbroken at that thought.

Although I hated to agree, I had noticed how cool Max had been through the whole accident. It had been shocking to see Max making notes in his notebook as the ambulance came and took Hal away. And what about Paul? He'd been so unruffled about Paul even before Paul phoned him from the train station. As if he hadn't cared that people were disappearing.

"I'm glad that Pola went with Hal," I said. She'd grabbed her bag of knitting and climbed into the back of the ambulance last night. As far as I knew, she was still at the hospital.

"Yes," said Betsy. "And I'm not sure that they'll be back. Pola said something to me about how as soon as Hal is well, she's taking him back to Anaheim."

"What's in Anaheim?" I said.

"Her brother, and his chicken farm," said Betsy with a slightly hysterical giggle.

It shouldn't have been that funny, but it had been a terrible night. I started to giggle too. "So Hal will find out which comes first, the chicken or the egg?"

Betsy collapsed with a shriek of laughter. A shriek with a razor's edge of hysteria to it. Arkham started to fray even our most determined, hopeful player.

I heard Fred shout up the stairs. "We need to leave," he called.

I met him in the front hall.

"I need to swing by the University to pick up that microphone that they are lending me," Fred said. "We record Lulu screaming and then shoot the final scene as soon as the sun sets during the solstice tomorrow."

"Not another night shoot?" I said. "Not another shoot right after Hal's accident?" What was Sydney thinking? None of us were ready to start filming again.

Fred nodded. "Candles down the hallway, flames flickering in the mirrors, and Lulu screaming at the entrance of the stranger."

"And who is playing the stranger?" I said. It had been vague in all the discussions so far.

"Jim, he's the only actor left," said Fred. "Sydney wants him in the hood."

"The stranger is the hooded man?" I said. That was odd. The hooded man usually showed up earlier in a Fitzmaurice film and never had much to do with the actual plot.

"Yes," said Fred. "Guess the hooded man finally gets something to do. Make Lulu scream."

"Jim wore the hood and cape in the last film, so I won't have to make any changes," I said. As the tallest of our three regular actors, Jim made a fine skinny hooded man with the cape going all the way down to his ankles.

As we passed through the main door out of the house, I glanced down the hallway. The mirrors were playing the same tricks that I'd noticed the first day in Arkham. Showing other rooms in impossible angles. I couldn't see either Fred or myself in the reflections, but I could see through the open doors of the kitchen to Mrs Mayhew arguing with the cook about something. Both of them had hands waving in the air like witches trying an incantation over the cauldron. But I suspected it was just a discussion of the soup for lunch.

The mirrors also showed Sydney and Max entering the library, with the rows of books behind them like dark bricks in a cemetery wall. A wall filled with the dreams of dead men encased in gold-tooled leather bindings.

Betsy had joined Eleanor and Lulu in the sitting room, as if none of them could bear to be alone. Eleanor was still pale, and Lulu was watching her with narrowed eyes. Betsy was writing busily at a desk, planning a future far away from all of us. Max would miss her once she was gone, I thought. But Betsy was also right in thinking that he'd never notice her until she was gone. He was too busy trailing after

Sydney, trying to be like Sydney, from his well-tailored suits to his fancy cigarette case.

I looked for Jim, but he was the only one out of sight. Perhaps because he was sitting in the window seat. Knowing Jim, he was probably napping upright.

Fred tugged at my shirt sleeve to get my attention. "Are you coming or going?" he said, while I stood frozen halfway in and halfway out of the door.

"I don't know," I said. "That's the problem. I don't know where we are going next."

"Velma's Diner first," said practical Fred. "It's almost lunch time. You'll feel better after a sandwich."

"That's your answer to everything," I said. "More food."

Fred nodded. "It's a simple answer but it works most of the time."

Velma's was busy, but nobody paid much attention to us. All the booths and tables were full, so we sat at counter stools. After a few minutes, Florie swung by with a coffee pot in one hand and a pair of menus in the other. She slapped the menus down in front of us.

"The movie folk," she said. "But less of you than last time."

"Just us two," agreed Fred. "How's the turkey sandwich?"

"Not bad, but the roast beef is better," said Florie. "Less of you at the Fitzmaurice place too. Hear the woods have been playing tricks."

I must have started, because she put the coffee pot down and patted my hand. "Can't keep secrets in Arkham," she said. "At least not for long. Got one missing, one in the hospital, and one sensible enough to walk herself out of that house, or so I hear."

"Paul went back to California," I said. "Hal's in the hospital and Pola's with him."

"Smart woman. Knitters nearly always are," said Florie, leaning on the counter with her notepad like she was taking our order. "You sure that one of you went back to California?"

"Yes, Paul went back more than a week ago," I counted the days since we had filmed in the woods.

"Guess that's why Mrs Mayhew had Humbert take his trunk up to the attic, then," said Florie.

"No," I said more slowly. "Max shipped it out. Didn't he, Fred?"

Fred nodded, but Florie just shook her head.

"Florie, how do you know about the trunk?" I asked.

"Humbert," said Florie. "He's kin. Besides, he eats here regularly enough. Heavy trunk, he said. Lots of things for a man to leave behind."

"Paul is in California," I said, more firmly. "If not, where would he be?"

"Now that," said Florie, "is a very good question." Somebody further down the counter shouted for more coffee. Florie picked up her pot. "So, turkey or roast beef?"

"Roast beef," Fred said.

"Turkey," I said.

Then, after she walked away, we both looked at each other, remembering the clawmarked tree and the man's coat waving from the branches overhead.

"And that was definitely blood on the ground," I said to Fred as we waited in a noisy, crowded diner for the world to stop spinning out of order.

Fred shook his head. "We don't know it was Paul's blood. Max got a phone call from him."

"Max got a call from somebody saying he was Paul," I said. "Remember, he said that he picked it up and there was Paul. That the phone hadn't rung yet."

"So?" said Fred.

"What if it was Sydney, on his extension upstairs?" There were two phones in the house. The main one was on a little table downstairs just outside the library door but there was another in the little study just off Sydney's bedroom. It had been installed for his grandfather, Sydney told us, after the old man had trouble going up and down the stairs. He used it to talk to Mrs Mayhew downstairs as much to call out, so Sydney said.

Florie slapped our sandwiches in front of us. Fred took a big bite of roast beef and chewed thoughtfully. "Wouldn't Max know it was Sydney?"

"Sydney's good at imitating voices," I said. "Remember last year, at the cast party, when he did everyone, including how you talk about your camera 242 and Betsy's giggle when she slaps down her cards?" It had been a little uncanny, listening to Sydney parrot our pet phrases and vocal expressions back to us. His imitation of Paul asking to borrow a cigarette off Hal was particularly good.

Fred chewed some more but he didn't disagree that Sydney could have pulled off a quick conversation as Paul. "But why?" he said. "Why would he go to the trouble?"

"So we'd stop looking for Paul," I said. "Because if we knew something had happened to Paul, we might stop working."

"We'd never stop filming," said Fred, a little shocked at the idea.

"Why? Why do we keep going? Is a movie so important that we have to finish it, no matter what?" I said. "Even if it kills someone? Because that's what the studio expects us to do."

"Jeany!" Fred said and then stopped. Because I was right. That was what the studios expected. There was money in movies, lots of money and more every day, but only if new movies kept coming out and kept getting bigger, kept getting better, kept bringing people into the theater. Like Eleanor's play where the magician lost his hand. Like the film where the plane crashed. People might have been shocked or even horrified, but as Lulu said, the reviews were smashing.

"Accidents happen," said Fred. "But we don't get paid if the films don't get made and keep getting made. That's all that's happening. Maybe Sydney is cutting a few corners, but not more than usual."

"What if Sydney promised the studio something truly shocking?" I said. "Like that flyer film, where the pilot died."

"Nobody planned on that," said Fred. "It was a night landing and they made an error."

"But their studio still released the film," I said. "Sydney quoted the *LA Times* about it, 'what is gone in the flesh will live forevermore on the screen.'"

Directors cut corners, studios cut corners, everyone wanted something more and the business folks didn't really care what happened to the artists as long as the films were released and tickets sold. Fred was sticking his head in the sand if he thought Sydney and Max were immune to such pressures.

Fred shook his head. His sandwich was nothing but crumbs on this plate. I had barely touched mine as I considered all the ways that Sydney might do something truly horrible to the cast.

"I don't see how these accidents could be anything but accidents," said Fred, more slowly than before. I could almost see the thoughts tumbling through his head. Thoughts too terrible for a nice man who just liked to invent things. "It makes no sense that Sydney would ruin his own work."

"There's something strange about this script that Sydney has," I said. "And this ending with the hooded stranger. I think he promised the studio something terrible."

"Jeany, the studios, all the studios, are getting more and more nervous about moral codes, church protests, and civic investigations," said Fred. "If Sydney did anything dangerous, anything wrong, that might cause the studio to abandon this project. That's why we've got Max. To keep an eye on Sydney. Not just watch the expenses, but to stop Sydney from causing the type of trouble that might land us in the newspapers in the wrong way. They don't want another Fatty Arbuckle."

Florie whipped by us again, and eyed my uneaten sandwich with disfavor. "You should eat that," she said to me. "You are going to need your strength."

"Why?" I said. "What's happening?" I still didn't agree with Fred's assessment and was trying to think of ways to talk him into taking my point of view. Except he was right:

nothing had happened that couldn't be labeled an accident, except the possible disappearance of Paul. And that was so vague, so uncertain. I needed more proof that Sydney was planning to create the accidents. That he had deliberately set out to harm the actors to terrify his audience.

And, if that got out, who would work with Sydney again? Would he risk losing his whole company, I asked myself. I shook my head. Of course, he wouldn't lose his actors. Hundreds of would-be stars were getting off the train every day, looking to become rich and famous in the movies. Look at Lulu, look at Renee, intelligent women still following Sydney's directions, even as others were harmed nearby.

Florie slapped down a bill. She looked with greater satisfaction at my plate. I'd managed to eat my entire sandwich while considering how I could prove Sydney such a villain that I could make Renee and all the rest abandon the picture.

"We should talk to Max," I said to Fred.

"Why Max?" he asked as he dug change out of his pocket to pay Florie.

"Because he's nervous about what the studio thinks. He's always nervous about that," I said. "If we can convince him that the studio heads will be angry about Sydney's plans, we might get the picture halted."

Fred tipped up his cap as he scratched the back of his head. "Maybe," he said. "But if the accidents haven't upset them yet, there's not much we can give them."

"There must be something more," I said.

Florie brought back the change and thanked Fred when

he told her to keep it as a tip. "Have you talked to Professor Krosnowski yet?" she said to me. "She's a bit worried about you."

"The professor that was here the other night?" I said. "Mister Claude asked me to talk to her too."

"Good advice," said Florie. "You can find her at the University this afternoon. She's teaching today. Try the English department first. If she's not there, then she'll be in the stacks, looking for some dusty old book."

Fred settled his cap more firmly on his head. "I'm heading to the University for a microphone. You could talk to the professor while I'm picking that up," he said.

I nodded and asked Florie, "What classes does she teach?"

"The nasty kind that people like," said Florie. "All about murder, and devils, and curses. Only she calls it poetry and literature. Writes, too. Mostly local history – she just changes the names so nobody recognizes their family in it and calls it fiction to stay out of trouble. If anyone knows what Sydney Fitzmaurice is up to, it's the professor. She's got a powerful dislike of that man and his movies. Rants about him every time a Fitzmaurice picture plays at the movie house."

"But why?" I said, being more than a little tired of vague warnings. "What did Sydney do?"

Florie put down her coffee pot and leaned over the counter to whisper in my ear. "She says that he murdered a girl with magic. On the summer solstice."

CHAPTER TWENTY

During the drive to the University, Fred and I debated the possibility that Sydney might have killed someone. Fred didn't believe it. I almost didn't. Not the way that Florie said. It was Sydney, who I had known for years. He was flamboyant and self-centered and more than a little careless about how his ideas might impact someone else. But murder? Sydney's style was selfish. He put people at risk and probably didn't care if people got hurt. But it was stunts that he could justify as risky but worth it. It was pretty common throughout Hollywood. But deliberately murder someone? That was harder to imagine, but this summer, I was starting to imagine it. And then I thought of Renee and groaned. How was I going to convince her that Sydney was so dangerous?

"And what did Florie mean, a murder with magic? A magic trick that went wrong? Like Eleanor's guillotine?" said Fred.

"I don't think Eleanor likes to think of it as her guillotine," I said, remembering the upset woman that we'd left behind at the Fitzmaurice house. "But I could see Sydney setting up a trick and not being too careful or thinking it through. Like that balloon that he wanted to use. Or directing Selby off the mountain."

Fred nodded. "I cannot see it. Not like shooting or stabbing someone."

"No," I said. "But Mister Claude mentioned something. About a circus performer. One that went missing after Sydney set up a new act for her."

A woman of the air, wearing a mirrored mask, who reflected the flames, as I recalled our conversation. So much like how Sydney described his masked stranger in this movie. Too much like it for my comfort.

"Maybe this professor knew her too," said Fred. "And that's why Mister Claude wanted you to talk to her."

I nodded. That made sense, and apparently both Mister Claude and Professor Christine Krosnowski knew Florie. "I think that all the news in Arkham isn't in the newspapers," I said. "I think it all goes through Velma's Diner."

"Good diner is hard to beat for gossip," agreed Fred.

When we got to the University, Fred was sent in one direction to collect his microphone while I went in search of the English department. We agreed to meet back at the car.

I found Professor Christine Krosnowski in a tiny closet-sized office in the English department. I slid through the partly open door and took the one seat in front of the desk. Behind her was a peeling wall calendar and a bucket with a mop.

"The janitor and I share," said the professor, with a glance at the bucket. "I work days. He works nights. As you can see, I'm highly valued by my colleagues."

"But why do you work here?" I said. It was an odd conversation. It felt like we fell into talking like old friends or at least recent companions. Except we had nothing in common and had only met once, very briefly, at Velma's Diner. "Couldn't you teach elsewhere?" I honestly wanted to know, even though it was the least urgent question that I had to ask her.

"One of the Seven Sisters?" the professor said. "Probably. But Miskatonic has its charms. Especially the library. And teaching leaves me plenty of time for writing. For the pulps." She smiled a particularly wicked smile. "Which does make the old dears on the academic side rather livid. Except they can never prove, never want to prove, that I'm writing about them. So they give me whatever class that they don't want and the worst office on campus. Not that I care. Not as long as I get paid for my teaching and access to the more… shall we say… off-limits areas of the library."

"Florie said that you wanted to see me. So did Mister Claude," I said.

She tapped one finger on the desk. Thinking about what to say next, I guessed. Her face was a little severe but not unfriendly. As a teacher, she must have been one of those with eyes in the back of her head. I met a few nuns like that back in Oakland. The teachers who always gave the impression that they knew exactly what you were thinking and were pondering how best to open your mind to greater possibilities.

"What do you know about magic?" said the professor.

"Stage magic? Like the kind that Mister Claude performs?" I asked.

"No," she said. Tap, tap went the finger. Pay attention was the message, I guessed. "The real stuff. Magic to open doors. Magic to let things out."

"Thin spots," I said, remembering the conversation with Pete in the woods.

The professor tilted her head and pursed her lips. "Deliberate openings, not just natural occurrences. The Macedonians brought it into Egypt with Alexander. Or the Macedonians found it elsewhere and carried it back from further north or further east. It's not like Napoleon's savants understood what they found."

"Napoleon's followers," I said. "Like the first Fitzmaurice."

"Yes, that one," said the professor. "He went to Egypt, following Napoleon's orders, with a whole gaggle of men, called savants, to study history, especially the ruins related to Alexander, another military man dedicated to conquering the world. Some say that the savants went seeking magic to make their general stronger. Almost found it too. But Napoleon abandoned them to go back to Europe, and they started bickering among themselves. Eventually Saturnin Fitzmaurice returned to France, but the wrong way round the Mediterranean, going east, going north, following some map of Alexander's conquests. Picking up items all along the way."

"Sydney's grandfather thought everything was taken from an Egyptian tomb," I said. "At least that's what Humbert says. And Sydney."

The professor shook her head. "There's been a number of people at the University who talked their way into old man Fitzmaurice's parlor to look at his 'treasures.' A hodgepodge of history, one of them called it, a magpie's picking of loot."

It seemed the magpie approach was Sydney's family heritage, I thought, and told the professor about Sydney's own collecting of strange objects from occult shops and bits of stories from everywhere.

"Too many like that. No scholarship. Just collect to collect. But Saturnin Fitzmaurice finally crossed the wrong people in Europe. He fled all the way to Arkham. With a wife who was a priestess by all accounts. Of a religion far older than even the pyramids."

I shook my head. "That's not what Sydney says. He's descended from French nobility." I remembered the stories, the quotes given to Darrell the day he came to the house and had his leg crushed under Saturnin's portrait.

"Descended from a Marseilles wharf rat who deserted the French army and jumped ship for a country as far away as he could get with a stolen bride and artifacts," the professor said. "You shouldn't believe what people say about themselves. Always check your facts." The last sounded like a piece of advice that she gave her students regularly.

"Everyone in the movies invents a new biography," I said, and I wasn't trying to excuse Sydney. But I wasn't sure what she was driving at. What did she really know that wasn't very ancient history?

"It's a very American thing to do, reinventing yourself," said the professor. "But murdering women with magic.

That's a Fitzmaurice trick, and one we need to stop."

"This is about the circus performer," I said. "Mister Claude told me about her. But she died in an accident. Or maybe died. Nobody ever found her body." It could not be murder. It was about taking risks, about causing accidents, about… I was terrified and babbling in my head. Because if Sydney was a murderer, he was in a house with my sister. My sister who was not acting anything like herself when I left her last night.

"Lucinda," said the professor, mentioning the same name that Mister Claude had. "She came later. She was his second victim. The woman that I knew, my student, died almost exactly ten years ago, performing that atrocious ritual that Saturnin brought to Arkham. The solstice ritual of the masked Camilla, to bring forth the hooded Stranger."

"But that's the character that my… that Renee is performing," I said. And inside my head, I was screaming, and Renee was not with me. Renee was in a house with Sydney. And Sydney, if he believed what the professor said that he believed, was beyond dangerous.

"Camilla isn't a name," said the professor, lecturing me as if we were in a classroom instead of a closet and she wasn't discussing murders happening to real people. "The Camilla is, as far as I can tell, a title. The title of the head priestess. The Cassilda is the secondary priestess, the one that opens the ritual with a bird-like scream, according to the notes that I've seen. But that old man, Sydney's grandfather, turned the whole ritual into a play back in the 1850s. A couple of French savants did that in Paris as well. Ended badly there too. Fitzmaurice tried to peddle his version to the Booth brothers before the Civil War, but they never produced it. The brothers fell out. Fitzmaurice moved back to Arkham, where he kept trying to sell various members of the University on performing his ritual."

"The professors here? But didn't they think that was dangerous?"

Christine Krosnowski snorted. "That wouldn't worry my Miskatonic colleagues then or now. They tried at various times to get hold of the manuscript for the University library. Orphaned young, Sydney became his grandfather's pet. A more spoiled brat of a rich man's son..." She sighed. "And handsome too. Still is, I hear."

"Some people think so."

The professor nodded. "I had a student, a young woman who wanted to be a writer and an actress. Violet had so much talent. Sydney talked her into adapting the old play that he found in his grandfather's papers. She brought it to me, in bits and pieces. Asking my advice. And, to my regret, I encouraged her to work on it. It was all about masks and strangers, a woman calling forth a hooded man. Bringing the stranger to our world through a doorway in a mirror. Every time I read what she had written, I'd have terrible nightmares. The dreams lingered for days."

"That's what we've been filming," I said, not that I wanted to confirm her fears. Why hadn't the professor stopped Sydney then? Why was I going to have to do something now? "A movie about two sisters, waiting for a stranger. Only there are mirrors that explode and a silver mask."

Christine Krosnowski sighed. "Then he's still at it. Just like his ancestors. They've tried before. Several times.

Always on the summer solstice, always between the thirteenth and twenty-eighth year of a century, in five-year intervals. In Sydney's case, 1913 with my student Violet, 1918 with the circus performer Lucinda, and now 1923."

"With our film," I said.

"If this attempt fails, he might be able to make one attempt in 1928," she replied. "After that, he'll need to wait for another eighty-five years. And a grandson to carry out his wishes."

"Why those dates?"

"Comets. A pair of twin comets, Camilla and Cassilda. Tiny little things, barely visible to the better telescopes. Predicted in 1801 by a French astronomer who had been left behind in Egypt and based on some texts that he discovered in a temple. Texts later stolen by Saturnin Fitzmaurice. It wasn't until 1828 that somebody actually spotted both comets and confirmed their existence. Then they disappeared for eighty-five years, reappearing in 1913. And every five years since."

Rituals, comets, magic. I shook my head. It made horrible sense and it was complete nonsense. "It's all like a fairy tale or a bad Haggard novel."

"Never doubt that there's fact behind fiction," said the professor. "Poets and other writers often use the metaphor of nightmares quite effectively to explain phenomena that scientists cannot. I don't know how or why these comets appear in such a strange pattern. One of my... odder... colleagues here has suggested that they come and go from our universe."

"I'm sorry?"

"Nobody ever said that Neely Chambers made sense, but he's been teaching at Miskatonic since the 1890s. He was a friend of Sydney's grandfather and tried more than once to liberate the Fitzmaurice manuscripts for his own collection. Neely, in his more lucid moments, has suggested that there are comets and other space phenomena that slide between two universes. He also claims that alien entities once colonized the South Pole." She looked a little embarrassed by the last statement. "Some days I think Neely should be writing for the pulps too."

"But what happens?" I said. "What will Sydney do?"

"I don't know," the professor admitted. She shuffled some papers on her desk, not looking directly at me. "I wasn't there when Violet disappeared. I should have been. I had enough doubts about the project. There was a fire. Everyone remembers that. The theater burned down and had to be rebuilt. The audience got out, mostly through sheer luck, as did the cast. But Violet was never found. I tried to push the police to investigate, but they claimed she ran off with Sydney. He took a train out of town that night."

"But that's not what happened?" I wasn't going to panic, I told myself. I was going to leave this closet and this crazy story, and I was going straight back to the house and make everyone leave. Everyone. Nobody was safe if Sydney believed he could open doors between universes with killing rituals.

"Nobody ever heard from Violet again. When Sydney reappeared as the ringmaster of a small Midwestern circus in spring of 1918, I read about it in the *Arkham Advertiser* and asked a friend to investigate."

"Mister Claude." Based on the conversation that I just had with him.

"An intelligent man. We met at an auction, both bidding on occult texts. I won," she smiled. "But we kept up a correspondence after that. He's visited a few times, to explore the stacks. Five years ago, I asked him to look into the circus and see if Sydney and Violet were a couple there."

"And no Violet?"

"No sign of her at all. But Violet had no family in Arkham. She was an orphan and at the University on a scholarship. So nobody cared." The professor straightened the pile of papers to her satisfaction and finally looked directly at me. "Julius made the same mistakes I did. He couldn't believe that Sydney would go so far. And there was so little real proof. Just a woman who disappeared. Strange talk about mirrors and doors. Then Lucinda disappeared, during the summer solstice performance. There was a fire, and confusion, and although nobody saw her get out, no body was found either."

"And no police investigation?"

"Julius tried. But he couldn't get anywhere. Carneys aren't particularly fond of the police. Nor do the police care for vagabonds." The professor tapped her desk. "So Lucinda vanished, and Sydney left the Midwest for the West Coast. That's as much as we knew when the articles started appearing about Fitzmaurice's terror films. His nightmares on the silver screen."

"He started making movies in November 1918," I said, wondering who the "we" was in her story. Florie, certainly, and Mister Claude, but could there be more people investigating the arcane events of Arkham? "At least that's when we met Sydney." However I didn't explain that my "we" meant my orphaned sister and I, either. "He'd married a woman in San Francisco. She gave him the money to start out as director. Then the studio recruited all of us."

"What happened to the wife?"

I shrugged. "Nothing much. A divorce. She wasn't interested in performing and she did have lots of family, wealthy family back in San Francisco."

"So, not the perfect victim," said the professor. "At least not the way that I think he picks his victims."

"No," I said. But Renee did fit that pattern. A woman alone, as far as Sydney knew, with no visible family. A woman who was grateful to him for her artistic career and passionate enough about making that career to overlook Sydney's more obvious flaws. And a sister who was going to save her, I kept telling myself, despite all the mistakes that we had made. "But our leading lady, Renee Love, she's much like the others that you describe."

"Julius said that there were two women playing the sisters."

"Lulu McIntyre. But Lulu has Eleanor, and Eleanor would kill Sydney before she would let anything happen to Lulu," I said. "Possibly with magic."

The professor raised her eyebrows. "Interesting."

"Except," I said, thinking back over our conversations at the house, "Sydney wanted them here. He recruited Lulu, for her scream, and Eleanor, for her witch ancestors. At least, that's the gossip. Eleanor might even know more about Sydney's manuscript. He keeps giving her quotes from it for her scenarios."

"Having a woman of magic translating his work into his current art form," the professor nodded. "That might be the key. Things have never quite aligned for the Fitzmaurice men. Saturnin had the comets and his priestess. But he failed."

"How?" I said, because this was important. I needed to know how to stop Sydney.

"Arkham has its protections. In the first case, Saturnin Fitzmaurice was opposed by a woman of magic, a maid in the house who got the children out. But she kept the terror in."

"That ancestor of Florie and Humbert?" This town, with its secrets and its families, we didn't need to be in such a town, I thought. We needed to be heading home to California, where everyone could reinvent themselves and become what they wanted to be. Not where they were caught up in family stories more than century old.

The professor nodded again. "A useful woman. Also, Saturnin lacked a mask. At least according to what Neely learned from Sydney's grandfather. For that old man, the explanation was the ritual had gone wrong because the priestess was improperly presented. She needed to be masked in silver, according to his notes. But Sydney's grandfather found a mask somewhere."

I didn't tell her that I'd found that mask. That it was sitting on a table in my bedroom, waiting for Sydney to find it and use it.

"But not just the mask, it can't be that simple," I said. I was arguing mystic rituals in a broom closet with a woman who taught poetry and collected occult texts. How had I gotten to this place? And what could I do to save Renee?

"No," said the professor. "We're sure that there is more to it than that. Every time, Sydney has tried this and failed, because he was missing some element. Every time was an experiment in magic, an experiment in opening a door for the Hooded Man. If he fails again, he'll have another chance in 1928, then the comets will be gone. Stop him now, and save your friends."

"But why me?" I said out loud, finally, the cry that was echoing through my head.

"Because you can," said the professor. "You can enter the house. You can pull the others out, like Rebecca Baker."

"But why can't you help me?" I said. "Come to the house. Explain to the others."

She shook her head. "Sydney dislikes me intensely. So the house will keep me out. It barely lets Ashcan Pete and Duke walk across the lawn, and you were with them, an invited guest. Julius made it onto the grounds, again as an invited guest, but he said that he could feel the house pushing him away the entire time. And as for poor Darrell, I understand it bruised his leg. I've tried three times to go up that drive and once through the woods. Neither path would open for me. Turned me right around and left me somewhere that I didn't want to be."

A house that pushed people away. A house that was waiting to devour us. I believed her but I couldn't say why.

I stood up. "I'll go back now," I said. "I still have time to get rid of the mask and get Renee out of the house. All of them." Fred, Betsy, Max, Eleanor, and Lulu. None of them should be hurt because of Sydney's strange obsession. But how was I going to make them believe me?

When I barely believed it myself.

As I walked back to the car, I tried different arguments in my head. None of my arguments convinced me. It all sounded like one of Eleanor's scenarios. Only more overwrought and underthought, as Renee had said once about a film that we'd both wanted to like more than we did.

But the mask. The mask was still up in my room. The mask and my paper copy. I could destroy the paper one easily. I could get rid of the other. Bury it, drown it, blow it up with Fred's flash powder. That might make Sydney pause. That could give me time to get the others out of the house.

During the ride back to the Fitzmaurice house, Fred kept talking about the microphone and recording device that he'd borrowed from the University. As well as the size of the Miskatonic laboratory that he'd seen. Apparently the engineering students and their professors had impressed him. Or at least given him ideas.

"Sound as a weapon," he said. "That's one of their ideas. Imagine, a shout that breaks a piece of glass and, if amplified, could crack a battleship."

"I think we don't need any more weapons in the world," I said. "Certainly no more noise."

"Well, just a scream or two," said Fred. "Luckily the professors were interested in what Sydney was trying to do. They want a copy of the recording and the film. One of them has an idea for synching film and sound. And then broadcasting it like radio."

"That sounds…" I was going to say "impossible." But was anything impossible in Arkham?

"It's a big leap," said Fred. "But there's others talking about it. Electric telescopes. But nothing like films. Just a simple image. But somebody will figure it out. There's an invention a minute, big stuff, little stuff."

"Maybe it will be you," I said.

Fred grinned. "Wouldn't it be great? To show films all around the world anywhere you want to watch them? The studio would love that. I can see Max totaling up the dollars."

"Except, how do you sell tickets? Wouldn't you need it to be in a theater?" I said. Because making money, that's all the studio cared about. At least, that's what Max usually said.

"Subscriptions. Like a magazine," Fred said. "Pay so much and get so many movies broadcast to your box. Max would figure something out. He likes money."

Max was smart with money. Max was smart. Fred was right when he suggested earlier that I go to Max. The studio had hired Max to control Sydney. So all I needed to do was to go to Max.

"How did your meeting go?" asked Fred, finally coming down from the clouds of contemplating all the ways that sound and pictures could be broadcast.

"She's an interesting woman," I said. "And Florie was right. The professor is worried about people getting hurt on the set. She said one of Sydney's plays started a fire at a theater here. And there was another at a circus where Sydney worked."

"He's careless," said Fred. "Sydney's always thinking about how something's going to look to the audience. He forgets that there are people on the set. Like his exploding mirrors. But was there really a murder?"

"Nobody knows," I hedged. I wanted to talk to Max before I tried to get Fred to believe in magic. Fred was just too practical for talk of rituals and other worlds. Max probably wouldn't believe it either, but he'd be worried about how such stories would impact the studio. This was much more serious than Sydney's known dabbling with the occult. "They never found any bodies, but two women did disappear."

Fred looked troubled as he turned the wheel and started to drive past the Fitzmaurice gates up to the house. "Maybe you're right, Jeany," he said. "Maybe this is the last film that we should make with Sydney. Hal shouldn't have been hurt like that. Paul had the right idea."

"So you think Paul went to California?"

Fred stopped the car in front of the house. He walked around it to open my door. "Where else could he have gone? But I'll look in the attic. After we record Lulu. If his trunk is there, we can investigate further."

"I'll go look in the attic," I said. After all, I had to pick up the mask in my room. Destroy it, hide it, do something with it. The solstice was almost on us.

As soon as we entered the house, Max and Sydney came popping out of the library. Soon all three men were in a deep discussion about the placement of the camera, the placement of the microphone, the recording equipment, the cords needed, and the sequence of events. Fred thought it best to record Lulu first, that would take the longest to do, then shut off the microphone and film the scene.

Lulu and Eleanor heard the talk and came out of the parlor to investigate. Neither Betsy nor Renee were downstairs. I ran upstairs looking for them, determined to talk to Max later, when I could get him away from the rest. If he listened, we could stop the filming today and all be on the train to California tomorrow.

Renee was in her room, looking much more rested than she had for days. She was looking at a magazine and eating strawberries. When she saw me, she waved me toward the bowl.

"They're delicious. Mrs Mayhew brought them from her garden. Wasn't that kind?"

I nodded, thought about discussing what I learned from the professor, and then remembered all Renee's objections the night before. Better talk to Max first, I decided. I grabbed a strawberry from the bowl, kissed her cheek, and told her that I had things to do.

"Helping Fred record Lulu's screams?" Renee said.

"Something like that," I said. "Looking for Betsy."

"She's out. She's packed a bag for Pola, who is staying near the hospital. Betsy said that she'd take it to her. She called for a taxi an hour or so ago."

"I'm sorry we didn't know," I said. "Fred and I could have taken her."

"Pola rang after you left. Hal's sitting up and talking a little."

"That's a relief."

Renee nodded. She kept looking down at the papers in her lap. What I'd taken for a magazine at first glance was a colored folder containing a few loose sheets of paper, densely written in Sydney's flamboyant handwriting.

"What's that?" I said.

"Camilla's ritual," said Renee. I started, but my sister didn't notice. "It's lovely. All about welcoming the hooded stranger into the world. To make the world anew. It's lovely." She murmured in a lower voice. "To open the way is simple – and the Hooded Man will stride the world in a moment of light."

The mirror behind her was full of shadows, shadows of women lost in smoke and fire, and I almost cried out. I wanted to spin her around on her chair and tell her to look at what Sydney was doing. But she was the elder, and I was the younger, and when had Renee ever done what I had asked? I needed help.

So I ran out of the room and down the hall. In my room, I pulled the mask off my desk and thought about how I could destroy it. But then I stopped. Sydney wanted the mask. He had made that clear. Maybe I could bargain with him. Give Sydney the mask, take Renee and the rest out of Arkham. He could try again in 1928. That's what the professor had said.

It was a terrible, cowardly thought. I was ashamed as soon as that idea came to mind. But I couldn't destroy the mask. The more I looked at it, that simple silver mask, the heavier the air became. It was as if the house was pressing down on me, stopping me from moving, preventing me from doing anything.

"No!" I said and lunged under my bed for my suitcase. I threw it open and tossed the mask into it. I slammed down the lid then I shoved the suitcase back under the bed.

Then the screams began, horrible, terrible shrieks, that rang through the house. Startled, I went out the hallway. What were they doing? We weren't supposed to film Lulu's screaming until tomorrow. Her cries continued. Screams that could break glass, sink a battleship, that could tear your heart from your breast. Lulu was screaming. And she wasn't stopping.

CHAPTER TWENTY-ONE

At the top of the stairs, looking down the long hallway, I saw the mirrors. I saw the mirrors more clearly than I should. They reflected a hallway twice as long as it really was. The mirrors reflected images that shouldn't be there. Not when I could see where people were standing. But, as usual, the mirrors caught and bent and reflected around corners all that was happening in that long hallway.

The reflections showed Eleanor, struggling in Max's arms, as he held her back from Lulu. Fred crouched over a recording machine, a statue of a man, responding to nothing but the whirling gadget before him. Sydney was to one side, watching, just watching.

Then I spotted Jim playing the hooded man. At least it should have been Jim. A tall gaunt figure in a hooded cloak, standing in the doorway, opposite Lulu. But the door was at an impossible, wrong angle to the hallway. The reflected hooded man in the doorway was too tall, too thin, elongated and stretched beyond ordinary human size. Everything was wrong, crooked, and out of true alignment. Everything that I saw was a trick of those mirrors and a deception of the reflections.

In the depths of the mirrors, another house stood, with hallways that opened onto rooms with windows full of alien landscapes. Burning suns and lavender skies, twisted trees and birds with impossible razor beaks, dog men scrambling over the window sills and loping down the hallways, closer and closer, to a hooded man who raised a fist to hammer on the mirror glass.

I froze. Terror held me still. Then I forced myself to take another step down the stairs. The world slid back to a wooden hallway filled with cables and a shiny metal microphone. The tall figure in the hood, the real man standing in the hallway, turned with an uncertain step. It was just Jim, a baffled looking Jim.

"Sydney," said Jim, pushing the hood off his face. "What now? Do we need to keep rehearsing?"

Sydney didn't respond. He seemed fascinated by something outside of our view, something reflected in the mirrors.

Lulu's scream dropped to a whisper as she shredded her voice in terror. Then she crumpled to the ground. Eleanor, with one last vicious kick at Max, broke free and ran to her, sobbing. I hurried down the stairs as Eleanor shook Lulu, trying to wake her.

"What's wrong with her?" Eleanor said. "I never wrote this. I never wanted this."

I turned to Fred, yelling at him, "What are you doing? Help us."

Fred shook himself free of the recording equipment.

Blinking like a man who had just woken up, he ran to us. "What is it? Did she shock herself on the mike?"

Eleanor said, "She fainted."

"What happened?" I asked Fred.

"We started recording. Then silence."

"Silence? She screamed forever."

Fred shook his head at me. "I couldn't hear anything."

"What were you doing?" I said. "You weren't filming this scene until tomorrow."

"Max wanted to test the equipment. So no more accidents," said Fred, who still seemed uncertain, almost as if he was sleepwalking through his responses. "This was just a test."

"I could hear Lulu all through the house," I snapped at him. "Eleanor, Eleanor, let go." I pulled at her hands, worried at how tightly she was clutching Lulu. "Let's move her into the parlor and onto the couch."

Lulu's eyelids fluttered and then she opened her eyes. She started to speak, but the only sound that she could produce was a reptilian croaking that clearly frightened her as much as it disturbed the rest of us.

Fred fetched Mrs Mayhew from the kitchen, who listened to our sputtered explanations.

"Hot water, lemon, black pepper, and mustard," she said. "Best cure for a strained voice."

The revolting beverage produced, Lulu sipped it with grimaces. Eleanor watched her with a forced smiled and reassuring comments.

Jim pulled off the hooded robe with a look of near loathing, announcing that he would be smoking in the garden. He pulled a hip flask out of his pocket as he exited through the kitchen.

I dragged Fred back into the hallway. The mirrors, when I glanced at them, were quiet, reflecting only ordinary things. Reflecting us standing there with a silver microphone between us.

"Now," I said again, wanting to understand what had happened. The professor, Julius, everyone seemed certain that we had until the summer solstice to stop Sydney. "What went wrong?"

"Nothing," said Fred. "Lulu started to scream, in fact she kind of played it up, like she does. Showing off. The microphone and recorder worked. But..."

"But what?"

He started moving down the hallway, unplugging cords and winding them neatly over his arm. Deliberate slow moves, like he did when he was worried, and then Fred said, "I couldn't hear anything. Not Lulu, not anyone else. Not you, not until you started shouting my name. It was as if..."

He stopped again and slowly packed the cords back into their box. He dismantled the microphone and put it away.

"As if what?" I said. I'd never known Fred so hesitant to speak, so slow to say what he was thinking. Usually he had a hundred ideas about why, and what, and how something happened, especially when it came to the gadgets in his clever hands.

Fred turned to me, his ordinary pleasant face screwed up into a grimace of remembered pain. "In the War, back when

I was driving a truck full of supplies to the boys at the front,
I got hit by a bomb."

"Fred!"

"Well, I got missed by a bomb. It exploded right in front
of us. And I was deaf for hours. Jeany, it was like that. Like
an explosion, and all of a sudden, I couldn't hear."

"But what did you see?" I asked, thinking of the strange
reflections in the mirrors, the alien landscape that I thought
I glimpsed.

"Nothing," said Fred. "I couldn't hear and… and… no,
it's like a dream. When you wake up and you're sure that
you remember everything, but nothing is there."

I knew exactly what he was describing. I felt the same.
The shadows in the mirrors, already the images were fading.
I struggled to hold onto those pictures in my mind. To hold
onto other ideas as well. Warnings from the professor, from
Julius, from Florie, and Pete. It was if the house knew how
much I hated it and was trying to make me forget. Make us
all forget how much danger that we were in.

A car honked outside and a door slammed. Quick
footsteps tapped across the porch, and Betsy opened the
door. "Do you have a dollar for a cab?" she said. "I spent
my money on chocolates for Hal and forgot to put extra in
my purse."

Eleanor came out of the parlor. "Do you have a cab? Tell
him to wait," she said. Turning to us, she added, "I'm taking
Lulu to the hospital. Somebody needs to look at her throat.
She can't talk."

"Are you coming back tonight?"

Eleanor paused, and seemed to recover a little of the

elegant poise that marked her when she first came to the Fitzmaurice house, but then she said, "We may send someone for the car and our things. I want to be out of here now. I never meant this to happen, but I don't dare write another word for Sydney. Here, you take this, I don't want it. I don't want anything to do with movies."

She thrust a piece of paper into my hand and went back into the parlor to fetch Lulu. The pair hurried outside to Betsy's cab. With a crunch of gravel, the taxi left.

"What did she give you?" Betsy asked.

It was a piece of paper covered with Eleanor's neat typing. Two scenes were laid out in two brief, pithy paragraphs. The ending of our film.

The first said, "The Hooded Stranger arrives. The younger sister recognizes that her doom is on her. Cassilda screams, a haunting sound that can never be forgotten, and then she is silenced forever. Her voice is gone."

That was the scene that they had just finished rehearsing. The scene that had destroyed Lulu's voice. But it was the second paragraph that terrified me. It was the second paragraph that described Renee's fate.

The second said, "Camilla dons the silver mask. She becomes a creature of the Hooded Stranger and opens the way, and herself is lost forever in the world of the Hooded Stranger. But the Hooded Stranger advances, stepping straight toward the audience and into our world. The power of the Hooded Stranger cannot be denied by any who watch."

CHAPTER TWENTY-TWO

The rest of the evening was my nightmares made real. Wherever I turned, whoever I talked to, it was if there was a wall of glass between us. As if they could hear nothing that I said. As if I was speaking to reflections in a mirror.

I went to Renee first, with Eleanor's horrible script folded in my pants pocket. My sister barely lifted her eyes from her dressing table mirror to acknowledge my presence. No matter what I said, no matter how I pleaded, Renee only shook her head and said, "Nearly done. Then we go home."

Betsy and Jim were just the same. Mumbling agreement but then retreating to their rooms. Locking their doors against me, even as I knocked, and cried, and in one angry moment, kicked the panels of Betsy's door so hard that it shook.

Fred retreated to the barn to blow up mirrors. Despite all he had seen and heard, he seemed determined to finish the film. Talking to him, shouting at him, I felt as if I was yelling at an imitation Fred, one who kept nodding at what I said but forgot it as soon as he turned away from me.

So I searched the house for Max, hoping to find him and get him to stop everything. To call the studio and tell them. Tell them something, but I found myself forgetting exactly what the professor said and so tired that I couldn't keep searching, so tired that I had to retreat to my room. I forced myself to drag open my sketchbook and began to draw. A young woman consumed by fire; two young women, one flying above the other, a college student and a circus aerialist – two women whose stories had been forgotten except by a few. Two women whose names were slipping away from me as well, the longer I stayed in that horrible house.

By morning, Eleanor and Lulu had not returned. Renee remained in bed, mumbling and rolling away from me when I tried to shake her awake. Everyone else was unnaturally silent at the breakfast table. I could barely hold my eyes open. I certainly felt as if I was being gagged, being smothered, by the atmosphere. We all were like wan ghosts of our normal selves.

Except for Sydney and Max; Max splendidly dressed for the final day of filming, chatting with an unbearably jolly Sydney. The pair spent the entire meal talking about box office expectations and predicting great profits for the studio. It was so horribly ordinary, but I couldn't seem to say anything there, inside the house, even now that I had Max in front of me.

After breakfast I fled to the porch, gulping the fresh air, glad to be out of the house, terrified to go back in, trying to think where to go next. Betsy and Fred followed me, and seemed more alert outside the house. But when I proposed that we pack our bags and leave, they turned shocked stares to me.

"But I'm going to play Cassilda," said Betsy. "Max says with Lulu gone, I can be the younger sister in this scene." Her eyes glittered unnaturally and her voice was brittle. An imitation Betsy, with none of her usual good-humored sparkle. I shook my head at that mad idea. This was one of my best friends, of course I could convince her of the danger.

"I'll wear the white dress and stand in the back, with a veil over my head, the second priestess, Max says. Max will tell the studio what a trouper I was, helping out when Lulu left, and that should help with getting bigger parts." Betsy spoke like a wind-up doll, the words sensible but the tone of her voice flat and almost drugged. How many times had she played the victim of a mesmerist, a vampire, a creature that sapped her will? How had she suddenly become the characters that she played in real life?

"Oh, Max says that," I said with some sarcasm, hoping to provoke a reaction. "And why do you want to stay, Fred? I thought you cared about us. That you wanted to prevent these accidents."

Fred sounded as compliant as Betsy. "I have prevented the accidents. Everyone is safe because of me. You are safe, Jeany." He spoke in a monotone, pointing at a stack of crates on the porch. "It's all in the can. And packed up for shipping back to the studio." He meant the film canisters neatly crated for shipping. "We'll all work together when we get back to California."

"It will all be wonderful, the best picture ever. Max said so," Betsy repeated.

"Max said so." I parroted her intonation from earlier. "But aren't you tired of waiting around for Max? Going to get on with your career?" It was as if she'd forgotten all that had happened in the last twenty-four hours. As if she'd forgotten everything that she'd said to me just yesterday.

"Max says everything will be wonderful," Betsy told me so earnestly.

"Max says the studio is very happy," added Fred. "I need to explode those mirrors. We need that to finish the picture. I have a job to do," He picked up 242. He even patted it on the side as he walked down to the barn.

Betsy grabbed the tripod and hurried after him, obviously not wanting to stay and argue with me.

And, as stunned as I was by their sudden change in attitude, I never thought once about the strangest part of the conversation. Neither mentioned Sydney. Both acted as if Max was in charge.

As the sound of shattering glass and probable bad luck filled the air, I paced the porch. No matter what I said, nobody seemed inclined to leave. We'd been loyal to Sydney for years, putting up with his fits and starts, but this was something different. This was a danger to Renee.

But nothing could happen without the mask, I thought. The mask was well hidden in my room. But was it? The more I thought about it, simply being in a suitcase under my bed wasn't enough.

I entered the house, determined to hide or destroy the mask totally. That would delay the filming. Once past the solstice, the professor had claimed that it would be another five years before Sydney could try again.

Peeking into Renee's room, I saw that she was still a dreaming beauty, lost amid the pile of lace-edged pillows. I closed the door softly and hurried to my room.

Pulling my suitcase out from under the bed, I flipped open the top. It was near bursting with my sketchbooks, each page filled with drawings of strange monstrous women, twisted pale spires rising above a mist-enfolded city, trees that dripped poison, dog-headed men, and the distant figure of the Hooded Stranger. All the records of my dreams during that long strange month in Arkham. And under and over and around the edges of every picture was sketch after sketch of the silver mask.

But as I lifted out the sketchbooks and stacked them on the floor, I realized that the bottom of my suitcase was completely empty. The metal mask and its paper twin were gone.

"Sydney," I gasped. Who else would take the masks? No wonder he had been so pleased at breakfast. He had everything now. Eleanor's scenario, the masks, the recording of Lulu's scream, all the elements that he needed for tonight's ritual, including my beautiful sister as his sacrifice. Suddenly my head was clearer than it had been for hours, anger at Sydney and his manipulations burning away the horrible fog that I had struggled in.

Now I would force Max to listen to me. I would tell him about the women who disappeared. I would make him realize that continuing this film could bring unprecedented scandal to the studio. That he should stop or at least delay Sydney past this year's summer solstice.

I heard the men's voices outside my bedroom window.

Looking out, I saw Max and Sydney walking across the back lawn towards the woods. Sydney carried a shotgun in the crook of his arm. Hunting for crows, I thought. As if he hadn't caused enough trouble the last time.

I ran out of the room and down the little hidden stair at the back, exiting through the pantry. The kitchen was eerily empty, all the breakfast dishes neatly washed and stacked beside the sink, but no sign of Mrs Mayhew or the cook. Their hats and coats were missing from their usual hooks beside the door. As if they too had vanished into a mirror.

But it was Friday, I thought, and Mrs Mayhew did her shopping on Friday for the weekend. No doubt Ethel had gone with her.

I crossed the lawn to the gate that led into the woods. I saw nothing of Sydney or Max. From the barn came the sound of more exploding glass. I hoped Fred's barrier of hay bales was protecting Betsy and him from the mayhem. Then I opened the gate and ran down the path toward the pond, determined to catch up with Max and get him away from Sydney long enough to talk. To stop the filming of the final scene.

The woods were worse than I remembered. Sticky hot under the trees and the buzzing of insects more shrill than ever before. As I ran, I heard a horrid panting sound amid the rustling of the bushes. I didn't slow, I didn't look, I just kept running, determined to catch up to the men. Even Sydney, carrying his shotgun, would be preferable to whatever stalked through the trees behind me.

I reached the pond. The murky waters smelled worse than before, a stench of decay, as if a thousand fish had died here. I circled the pond. There was no sign of the men. I kept to the path that we'd followed earlier. My panting shadow kept pace with me but never so close that I could catch a glimpse of it.

But after the pond I could find nothing familiar. Once or twice I thought I heard Sydney's big laugh or a shout from Max. But when I shouted back, nothing answered. Nothing but the buzzing of insects and the huffing bark of my shadow pursuer.

Every turn of the path took me deeper into the trees. The long, pallid trunks stretching above me, the branches bare of all but the most withered leaves, none of it looked like the summer woods that we'd filmed in. Nowhere could I find the foundations of the little burned house or the tree with the black coat swinging from its branches.

Instead I stumbled through my nightmare forest, endless shadowed paths twisting me around and around, until I nearly dropped to the ground, so tired, so hopeless, that I wanted to curl up in the muddy leaves and let whatever pursued me in the shadows finally win our strange race.

Somewhere, somewhere too close, a barking laugh of triumph mocked my despair. I knew I had lost. Renee was lost. I could not save anyone.

Then the crows attacked. With harsh cries they flew in my face, claws tangling in my hair, wings buffeting me. I flung my arms to the side, trying to beat them off, screaming in fear and frustration, as I'd wanted to scream all night. The crows swooped and dived unrelentingly, until I turned in my tracks. Under a rain of black tormentors, I ran through the woods as fast I could.

Every time I stumbled, every time I paused, the crows dived down again and drove me along the path with terrible shrieks and caws. The smell of the pond overwhelmed me. I wanted to stop, to vomit, to give up, but the crows wouldn't let me. I stumbled on.

At last I reached the gate to the lawn. With trembling hands, I wrenched it open and fell forward onto the newly mown grass. With long graceful swoops, the crows flew past me, whirling through the sky to settle on the roof.

As I watched the birds fly away from me, I saw that the sun had moved much further in the sky than I expected. Long evening shadows, the house's shadow the longest and crookedest of them all, stretched across the lawn. I'd lost the entire solstice day in those terrible woods.

I veered toward the barn, determined to find Fred and recruit his help. But the barn was empty except for the shattered remains of a dozen mirrors, the glass winking red reflections in the light of the setting sun.

Tired beyond anything that I had ever known, I turned back to the house. This time, I decided that nothing would stop me. I would find Max. I would keep Sydney from filming on the solstice. I would take Renee out of this cursed house and away from Sydney. Not even those terrible crows would keep hold me back.

I circled round the house to the front door. The crates for the studio were still stacked neatly at the end of the porch, ready to be sent to the train station, ready for the studio to take possession.

The sun was nearly down. Looking through the half-open front door, I could see that Sydney had lined the hallway with candles, the flames flickering brighter than I expected, reflected in every mirror. At one end of the hallway, furthest away from me, Fred was busy cranking old 242. Nearer to the door was Jim, dressed in the robes of the Hooded Stranger. Betsy was arranged beside him in a long veil that covered her hair and face completely. Between them and the camera, Renee stood perfectly still in the long white dress that I had made for her original performance as the murderous siren. But this time, she held in her hand the silver mask. As I watched, she slowly raised the mask to her face. I screamed at her to stop, but nobody moved, nobody looked at me. Once again, just like in my nightmares, I was on the wrong side of the mirror.

Somewhere further down the shadowed hallway, I heard Sydney's voice, not shouting directions, but intoning some sibilant syllables. Nonsense words, but the more he spoke, the greater my feeling of terror grew.

"Stop," I shouted. "Max, you have to stop them."

As I went across the porch, Max stepped into the doorway.

"Max," I sobbed in relief. Finally somebody who looked straight at me. Finally somebody who would listen to me. "You have to stop him. Something terrible is going to happen."

Max looked at me, as mild as ever, pushing his notebook into the breast pocket of his finely tailored suit. "Yes," he said. "That's what the studio is paying for."

"No, no," I cried. "Max, you don't understand. This time the magic is real."

CHAPTER TWENTY-THREE

I quickly realized that bruising my hands upon the door would do nothing to help Fred and Betsy, to save my sister. So I started around the house, determined to enter through the kitchen door. Max had obviously thought of that too. It was locked. No matter how hard I shook it or kicked it, the door would not budge.

All the windows were locked too. Every door barred. All the time, I could feel that horrible, terrible house pushing against me. I remembered what the professor had said. That the house could keep out those that it did not want. That it was part of the terrible Fitzmaurice magic.

I circled back to the porch and then I spotted it. A long heavy hammer sitting on top of one of the boxes on the porch. Humbert must have left it there after nailing the wooden crates shut. It was just what I needed.

I picked up the hammer. It felt solid and so right in my hand. I walked up to the parlor window. Through the glass I could see the smirking smile of that Fitzmaurice portrait, the one that Sydney's ancestor felt was more important than saving his children or his wife. I grinned back at Saturnin Fitzmaurice and swung the hammer hard against the window glass.

It took three strikes, but the windows shattered under my blows. I reached inside, careless of the broken glass, and unlocked the window. I shoved up the sash and crawled in, still clutching the hammer in my hand. Blood dripped from my hands, but I ignored the cuts as I crossed the room. After the crows, after Max's betrayal, nothing stung as much as my anger.

The parlor door, like all the rest, was locked. I used the claw head of the hammer to pry open the lock with a satisfying splintering of wood and screaming metal.

As I stepped into the hallway, I stepped into the hell of my worst nightmares.

Flames lit all the mirrors. But the flames were inside the glass, not outside, an impossibility that belonged to dreams. The smoke flowed out of the mirrors, overwhelming the vague light of the candles as the nebulous figures moved in it, some human, some not.

I did not care. I plunged into the smoke, crying out for Renee, screaming for my sister. I brushed against a long veil and the figure of a woman. It was Betsy. I tore the veil and my second paper mask off her face. She stared blankly at me until I grabbed her and squeezed her hand so hard that my nails dug into her skin and drew her blood to mingle with my own.

With a gasp, Betsy blinked and stared around her. "What is it?" she said.

"Fire," I yelled back, barely able to speak with the smoke

choking me. "Hold on to me. We need to get out."

Betsy grabbed my shoulder and we stumbled forward in the smoke. The click, click of the camera turning led me to Fred, bent over the viewfinder, oblivious to the smoke that billowed through a hallway now ten times longer than it ever was before.

I smacked the back of his head and knocked his silly cap forward on his nose. Fred straightened up with a cry. "Jeany?" he said, looking around him with puzzled eyes.

"Fire!" I yelled. "Hold on to Betsy. We need to get out."

Fred fumbled for his camera and hissed. He pulled his hand away from the metal body of 242 with blistered fingers.

"How? What?" he said. "How can that be burning?"

"Get away!" I said, pulling again on his arm.

Fred grabbed Betsy's arm with his unburned hand, and we went forward.

A hooded figure stood before us.

"Jim!" we all shouted, but the figure that turned toward us wasn't Jim. It wasn't like anything that I'd ever seen before. It might have been a man, but a man so impossibly beautiful that he seemed alien, with pallid skin and looking-glass eyes that reflected the flames now springing out of the mirrors. I froze, caught between awe and terror, and then my anger surged up again. This was the figure that had haunted my dreams. This was the creature that was trying to steal my sister.

With a shout, I flung the hammer at him. I swear that the Hooded Man didn't move but a mirror shattered behind him. Then the glass of the mirror ran in liquid drops, melting together until the mirror reformed on the wall.

We stumbled backward, an ungainly trio of three very ordinary humans trying to find their way and not lose their grip on each other.

And we smacked into Sydney. He stood entranced by his own spell, a burning manuscript in his hands. His skin was beginning to smoke, but he showed no sign of pain. He took no notice of the flames at all. But he looked directly at me when I tried to swat the burning paper out of his hands.

"What are you doing?" he cried.

"Leaving," I said. And then, because Renee had loved him, still loved him for all that I knew, "Hold on to us. Help us."

But Sydney turned away into the smoke, walking toward the stranger reflected in the mirrors. "My king, my king, I have found your way into the world. We will capture men's minds and control their simplest thoughts." Sydney's clothes smoked and began to burn, cloaking him in flame.

Horrified, I pushed the others away from Sydney, lost in his delusion, his final scenario, the end of his terror picture.

"Hold on to me," I said to Fred and Betsy. In the mirrors, a masked woman stood behind the Hooded Man. I turned away from the reflection and walked into the center of the smoke.

Renee stood like a glistening pillar of ice, a woman all in white, masked and crowned in silver, not in the costume that I had made but in the one that I had dreamed, the one that I had drawn on page after page of my sketchbook. An extraterrestrial garment summoned by dreams and magic to clothe this goddess, a stranger herself…

Until I reached out and grabbed her hand. I gripped her

fingers hard, the way that a little sister will when she wants to lead her big sister to safety.

At first her hand lay cold and lifeless in mine. Then she stirred, and clasped my hand as she always had, a squeeze of comfort, an intertwining of our fingers, that universal language that Sydney sought, the language of love.

I looked into the mask of silver and saw nothing but a reflection of myself. So that I was mirrored and twinned and paired in the smoke and darkness. Dark hair, dark eyes, half Chinese, half Swedish, all American, two sisters lost in a world that called them names and knocked them down. Two women who dared to overcome that. Two sisters who loved each other even when they forgot to say it.

"Renee," I called out, using the name that she gave herself on a train hurtling toward a future that she made happen by sheer force of will, my brave, my beautiful, my wonderful big sister.

"Jeany," she said in so soft a whisper that I could barely hear it over the crackle of flames burning in the mirrors. Then louder, and in the language of our mother, the musical and well-remembered words for "little sister."

I pulled her toward the door, or at least where I thought the door should be. We walked forward through the smoke. My sister holding my hand, my friends with their hands on my shoulders, moving together past the nightmares.

Then, just as we reached the door, there was Max. Still immaculately turned out, still looking more like a bookkeeper than a villain. Not at all what I expected to find in the final reel of a Sydney Fitzmaurice film.

"What are you doing?" he echoed Sydney.

"Getting out," I said, reaching around him for the door.

"You can't," he shouted, pulling at me, trying to shove Renee away from me. "We need this picture. This is for the studio." He cried it as Sydney had cried for his king. "I'll be rich. They've promised me so much money. The Hooded Man filmed for real. Pictures around the world to make his commands into our commands. I will never be poor again."

"Let me go, Max," I said, struggling to get by him. "We have to get out." The house was actually burning now. The smoke was bitter and real and stinging in my throat. The flames hissed, eating through the walls and the floor. This time nobody would try to save the mirrors and a portrait. Because there were more important people to save.

Max grabbed me, shoving me hard against the others, fighting to keep us from leaving.

"Get away from her," said my sister, my defender, who had always knocked down the bullies who challenged us. My Renee, suddenly speaking with all the strength she contained. She lifted her free hand and tore the mask from her face.

Max looked at her and screamed. I looked back over my shoulder and shuddered. For the mask had heated, burning part of her face, creating an unnatural scar of silver dripping from forehead to chin. She looked like a monster. But she also looked like my sister.

"We are done," I said, and pulled past Max. I felt the doorknob under my hand and the metal was still blessedly cool. I turned the knob and pushed with all my remaining strength. The door swung open. We staggered out of the smoke and onto the porch, all of us together.

Except for Max. Betsy tried to grab him as she passed. He reached out for her as if to draw her back into that inferno. Then the Hooded Man appeared directly behind Max, placing a pallid hand on Max's shoulder. Max gave a shout. With one great push he shoved Betsy through the door, sending her flying after us onto the porch.

The door slammed shut. I don't know if it was Max again or the house itself that locked us out.

But we *were* out.

Smoke poured from all the windows. The crackle of flames was louder than our harsh breathing. We ran together down the long drive to the gate, only to be met by a clamor of bells. A firetruck went swinging by, followed by Doctor Wills' rattletrap car and Mrs Mayhew's old farm truck. The professor climbed out of the doctor's car. Then Florie slid from the passenger side of Mrs Mayhew's truck.

I collapsed into my sister's arms, trying to hug her, Betsy, Fred, everyone all at once, unable to breathe for the happiest of reasons as I gathered them to me. We were alive.

Doctor Wills took us to the hospital to be treated for what she called smoke inhalation.

When I tried to explain what truly happened, she shook her head. "Only so much I can note on a chart," she said. "Smoke inhalation works better than saying that you were poisoned by the atmosphere of an alien world. A world that collided briefly with ours through ambition, greed, and magic stolen out of a lost temple."

After looking at the silver scar that ran down my sister's face, Doctor Wills recorded that as the result of burns, burning film to be precise. I stopped protesting to the doctor. Later, Florie, who had followed us to the hospital, leaned over to me and said, "Those who need to know will know. We'll do our best to keep everyone safe."

After the doctor bandaged Renee's face and the nurses gave her something to make her sleep, I sat on the edge of her bed, still holding tight to her hand.

Florie eventually gave way to the professor that night. The two paced outside our room like sentinels, guarding us from who knows what, and rotating in and out of the room to check on us. The professor gripped my shoulder tightly for a moment. "You did well," she said. "You got them out."

"Not everyone," I said. Although I could not mourn Sydney, I saw Betsy's tears when she realized that Max was lost. Nobody could remember seeing Jim at the start of the fire, but he was supposed to have been in the scene. If he was, then I feared that he had joined Paul elsewhere.

"You did your best," said the professor. "Sometimes that is all we can do."

EPILOGUE
Santa Monica, 1926

The wind blows through this little house by the ocean, cleansing it with the smell of salt sea air. The sun shines in every corner. There are no shadows. There are no mirrors to reflect ghosts or strangers. This house is as different as possible from Sydney's strange home in Arkham. It's also as different as possible from Renee's Alhambra apartments. There were, we found, too many reminders of Sydney in those rooms. Gifts that he had given Renee, the flower vases that used to be filled with roses, and even the coffee table Max piled high with newspapers so Sydney could read the reviews out loud. How Sydney would have loved all the press after his death, all the speculation on what had actually happened.

After the fire was put out, the Arkham firemen found Sydney's body. Unlike his ancestor, it was intact. A few months later, the studio claimed to have found a will in their files. It appeared to be signed by Sydney and left everything to Renee, as the muse of his heart. Did he write that? Or did the studio think that if they gave her an inheritance and a love story, she would ask fewer questions and let the verdict stand? I vacillated between the two explanations until Fred said, "What does it matter?"

The studio needn't have worried about Renee. She had no wish to reveal what had happened in those final days before Sydney's death. In fact, she stopped talking about him after we left Arkham. I was more than willing to let Sydney Fitzmaurice fade into a Hollywood legend. But I mourned Max, despite his equal villainy. For at the end, at the very end, I am sure that he pushed Betsy out the door to save her.

"The studio killed Max," I said. "Making him work for Sydney, exposing him to that evil."

"Is he dead?" Betsy asked me again and again. "They never found his body."

We disappeared for a time, so Renee could heal, but her silver scars never faded. Despite my suggestions for makeup and costumes, she shook her head and claimed that she was done. She had no wish to act.

Then Sydney's wife brought the lawsuit. The reporters hunted us down at our apartment, and newspaper stories started about the final, unfinished film and all the accidents surrounding it. The articles confused Renee with her characters, filling their pages with a woman who was more siren, more vampire, than ordinary mortal. Only the *Arkham Advertiser* printed other stories, all illustrated with photos taken by Darrell, about the beautiful Renee Love and her tender relationship with Sydney Fitzmaurice. Darrell's influence, clearly, and Renee sent him a long letter of thanks with an autographed photo from her unscarred days.

Some of the press dealt with the disappearances of those final moments, about the people never found: Max, Jim, and Paul. But Arkham's police refused to investigate, suggesting that Paul had gone back to California for another job, Jim had followed him, and Max had left town with some of the studio's money. I suspect it was someone at the studio that named Max an embezzler because they didn't want to explain why they had given him the money in the first place. Their plan, however outlandish and improbable, to control the world through films created with magic – that might be hard to explain to their shareholders or to a Congress that increasingly liked to hold hearings on the morality of the film industry.

"Movie people," the police and the press finally said, as if this explained the sudden and total disappearances, and left the mysteries at that.

In the end, the court ruled that as Sydney was legally divorced, the first Mrs Fitzmaurice had no more claim on his estate. They gave everything to Renee, including what was left of the Fitzmaurice house in Arkham.

Renee ordered the burnt and ruined house boarded up. A year later, we bought this little house here on the Pacific Ocean, not too far from where Fred lives. It's a short walk to the Pleasure Pier. Some nights Fred and I go dancing at the La Monica Ballroom.

Fred is working more and more on inventions. He has ideas, wonderful ideas, and there's always someone in Hollywood who wants to do the next thing bigger and better than the way it was done before. But Fred cannot run a camera anymore. His beloved 242 was destroyed in the fire and the burns on his right hand made his fingers stiff. Besides, Fred's hands tremble. Not too much, not so most people would notice, but I notice. When his hands start to quiver, I hold them between mine and wait for the shaking to stop. But we both know that he will never crank a camera as smoothly as before. So, being Fred, he is working on a motor and a way to turn the film without using his hands. I draw the plans and help with patent applications. It is one small way that we battle the curse that Sydney brought upon us. It is a battle that we will win.

Eleanor and Lulu write frequently. Ashcan Pete and Duke found Pumpkin wandering by the river the day after the fire. Eleanor wanted to give Pete a reward, but he refused.

After Arkham, Eleanor and Lulu discovered that New York was too much for them. Eleanor found it impossible to write plays. Even with the return of her voice, Lulu disliked the darkness of backstage in their theater. They've gone to Seattle to teach drama at a college there. It's all very Bohemian, says Eleanor in her latest letter, with dancers, musicians, and artists mingling in the classrooms. There's hours of debate about the meaning of art, but nobody thinks they can change the world. At least not the way that Sydney and Max planned to do it. Inspired by Renee, Lulu has bought a cabin on a beach and they motor out to it every weekend. Pumpkin, says Eleanor, would be positively sleek except that the founder of the college, a woman with a pug of her own, insists on feeding pancakes to all small dogs.

I write back as often as possible. I tell Eleanor and Lulu

about Hal and Pola and their chicken farm in Anaheim, as well as all our other news.

Betsy is in pictures again and doing very well. Sennett cast her in some comedies. Then she became the "flapper detective" in a popular series. Betsy now leaps from galloping horses or runaway cars. She flashes a silverplated gun in the shadows as she takes down the villain. All her stunts she does herself, seeking out people to train her on more and more difficult tasks.

Fred and I take her dancing and keep introducing her to other young men. Betsy speaks less and less of Max to us, but she keeps up a correspondence with the professor after meeting her at the Arkham hospital. She talks of going back. More and more after last winter, when Jim was found wandering down a road near Kingsport. He's in an asylum now, mostly because he never sleeps, just sits looking in mirrors or other reflective surfaces.

I hear from those we met in Arkham. Mister Claude mails me tickets for when he's playing a theater near Los Angeles. The professor sends me packages of pulp magazines and challenges me to find her stories in their pages. Florie writes the most. Her letters are funny cheerful scribbles, all about the gossip served with pie and coffee at Velma's. She sends clippings from the *Arkham Advertiser*, so I know what Darrell is doing.

Her feet hurt more and more, says Florie, and she's almost ready to give up the tips in return for a long sit someplace warm. Suzie has left Velma's for the brighter lights of Boston, says Florie. There's a new waitress, Agnes, who is a good gal, says Florie again.

If Betsy returns to Arkham, I think she should look up this Agnes. I read between the lines and know Florie means that this Agnes understands that not all doors and paths in Arkham lead to the places that we know. That some ways twist oddly and lead you out of this world. If Betsy does decide to go back, I will tell her to stop at Velma's first, before she tries to open the Fitzmaurice house. To talk to Darrell, whose newspaper stories hint at things unseen except by those who know how to look. To seek out Ashcan Pete and his faithful hound Duke. There are heroes in Arkham, and she will need them.

Renee's typewriter begins its daily clatter. She prefers to write outdoors, sitting at a little table on the deck that overlooks the ocean. Her face healed but the scars will never disappear. Eleanor put her in the way of script work. She'd been doing the work but found it tedious. Renee loves it. She always had a flair for a scene and now is writing whole scenarios, adapting other writers' stories and even creating a few from scratch. She receives requests from many directors who knew her during the early part of her career. All of her work now appears under R. Lin, rather than Renee Love.

I gather up my sketchbook, my pencils, and my fabric swatches. I have costumes to design, meetings to attend later in the day, and Fred will be coming over for dinner.

As I walk through the house, I hear Renee call. "Any letters today?"

There are. Letters from Eleanor, Betsy, and Pola. We will read them together over breakfast on the deck. As I sort through the mail, I find one envelope from the studio. I stuff the others in my sketchbook to share with Renee. This one I slit open and read by myself. The neatly typed letter is the same as all the others. A request for any information that we might have on Sydney's final film, any footage that might have survived the fire, any copies of the script, particularly Sydney's original manuscript. The last part is underlined.

I treat it as I treated all the rest of the studio's correspondence. I rip the letter into tiny shreds and throw the pieces off the edge of the deck. Let the wind take those words. Let the ocean drown them. I will never help the studio that encouraged Sydney and Max in their madness.

I will never tell them about the trunk filled with all those things, including the smoke-stained silver mask that Renee tore from her face. Humbert helped me empty the crates that had been marked for the studio and transfer everything into a sturdy steamer trunk. A trunk now locked and buried under old hay in the barn behind the Fitzmaurice house. Humbert checks on the barn, the house, and the trunk. He has instructions on what to do if somebody comes to Arkham with my key and a letter from me. He will show them the trunk, he will introduce them to the others. Humbert will let the crows know that there is somebody else to protect if they become lost in the woods.

I just hope that it is not Betsy. She wants to find Max. I would want the same if it was Fred. But still I fear for her. Despite her laughter and her courage, Arkham might destroy her. I feel in my pocket for the trunk key. It's there. It is always there. I never go anywhere without it.

The key is a reminder, like the letters, that I led my sister and my friends safely out of the hall of mirrors and flame. I hope that nobody who I love will ever return to Arkham. But if they do, I will help them as much as I can. And I am comforted by the thought that the professor, Pete, Darrell, and the others are still there. The ones who protect those who wander lost in Arkham's shifting ways.

Renee calls again. I answer and stride out into the California sunshine, to begin a new day with my sister.

ACKNOWLEDGMENTS

There is not enough room to list all the people who contribute to the making of a single book. For all of you, especially the many librarians and booksellers who helped me find information about early Hollywood and the lives of Chinese-Americans in 1920s California, please know that your suggestions from idea to finish were greatly appreciated. The mistakes are my own.

I do want to say a special thank you to Dawn, who sent a website link, Lottie, who answered an email with a tweet, and Phoebe, who asked "how many words today?" Without these ladies, there would be no book at all.

While the characters in this novel are fictional, a number of 1920s historical figures are mentioned in passing. I hope you have the time to learn more about Tye Leung Schulze, Anna May Wong, James Wong Howe, and others. Their histories deserve to be better known.

This story would not be possible without the many researchers, preservationists, and historians who documented the vast international silent movie industry, saved what footage they could, and worked hard to present the diversity of the industry. I greatly enjoyed seeing your contributions at film festivals and theaters in Seattle. I look forward to meeting again in the dark to watch the silver shadows.

Best wishes to all the readers who shared this journey and thank you.

ABOUT THE AUTHOR

ROSEMARY JONES is an ardent collector of children's books, and a fan of talkies and silent movies. She is the author of bestselling novels in *Dungeons & Dragons' Forgotten Realms* setting, numerous novellas, short stories, and collaborations. She lives in Seattle, Washington.

rosemaryjones.com
twitter.com/rosemaryjones

Defend the World from Eldritch Terrors in Arkham Horror

An international thief of esoteric artifacts stumbles onto a nightmarish cult in 1920s New England in this chilling tale of cosmic dread.

A mad surrealist's art threatens to rip open the fabric of reality, in this twisted tale of eldritch horror and conspiracy.

Dark incantations expose the minds of Miskatonic University students to supernatural horrors, in this chilling mystery novel.

Venture into a land of duty and warfare, with Legend of the Five Rings

Discovering a mythical city amid blizzard-swept peaks offers heroes an opportunity to prove their honor, but risks exposing the empire to demonic invasion.

A charming slacker aristocrat discovers a talent for detection and a web of conspiracies in the Emerald Empire.

Horrifying creatures run riot through an isolated village, unleashing havoc and death, but it will take more than one clan to resolve this lethal supernatural mystery.

WORLD EXPANDING FICTION

A brave starship crew is drawn into the schemes of interplanetary powers competing for galactic domination, in this epic space opera from the best-selling strategic boardgame, TWILIGHT IMPERIUM.

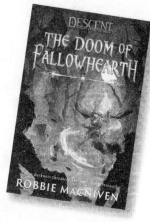

Legendary heroes battle the undead and dark sorcery, in the first of a rip-roaring new series for the fan-favorite epic fantasy game, DESCENT.

Take a whirlwind tour to the incredible planet of a million fantasy races, the Crucible, in this wild science fantasy anthology from the hit new game, KEYFORGE.